LADY JANE

Norma Lee Clark

FAWCETT CREST • NEW YORK

That leap of joy she'd felt through every vein, at her first sight of Jaspar emerging from the house, only confirmed what she had known inside to be true but had refused to acknowledge.

She had fallen in love with Jaspar Montmorency, in spite of her fear of him. That fear had slowly dissipated under the influence of his presence. It had been replaced by a conviction that he had not recognized her after all.

As Aunt Stanier had said, she had changed a great deal in the past six years. The fourteen-year-old serving girl had become an elegant young woman of twenty. He had no doubt forgotten all about the little maid in his sister's rose-pink dressing gown—and nothing else, she thought, turning over to bury her burning face in her hands.

And there, in the darkness, she remembered again, as she had more often than was good for her peace of mind, the day when he looked at her so meaningfully and spoke of "laughter lighting up her sherry-brown eyes."

For
Connie Clausen

"And the song, from beginning to end,
I found again, in the heart of a friend."

Longfellow
The Arrow and the Song

1

Jane Coombs set the heavy basket of wood down on the narrow step and held it in place with her knee as she stood panting on the steep, dark backstairs. She rubbed her shoulder, wondering if it would be pulled from its socket before she got the basket to the top, then, remembering Miss Wright's sharp tongue, lifted the basket with her other hand and struggled upward.

She paused only an instant at the top to catch her breath before hurrying on down the hall to the front bedroom, where she tapped on the door and was bidden to "Come."

"Took your time, Coombes, as usual," snapped Miss Wright.

And hello to you, too, thought Jane resentfully, setting the basket down with a thump and kneeling before the hearth to build up the fire.

Miss Wright gave Jane a blighting look and turned back to the guinea-gold locks she was artfully arranging on the head of her mistress, Lady Sarah Montmorency, who was so enraptured by her own countenance facing her in the glass that she seemed unaware of Jane's entrance.

Miss Wright finished and stood back triumphantly to await commendation. Lady Sarah turned this way and that to inspect her abigail's work.

"One of your better efforts, Wright," drawled Lady Sarah, as she rose from her mirror. "Now fetch my gloves and stop dawdling. Mama must have been waiting this hour."

Jane hid her grin, delighted to be present when the supercilious Miss Wright got her comeuppance. Miss Wright sniffed audibly and moved to the bureau to do as she was bid. Jane peeked from under her lashes at m'lady, standing in the middle of her blue and gold bedroom, dressed for a party. Gawd help us, Jane thought, to be goin' out in company like that. Might's well go nekked for all the coverin' *that* gown provides.

Lady Sarah, on the other hand, surveyed herself with great

satisfaction in the full-length mirror. The gown, of golden yellow gauze, matched her hair exactly, and was the first crack of fashion, being so sheer as to reveal her figure in its entirety. Lady Sarah felt that it was a figure that could afford to be revealed, unlike *some* she could mention, which their owners would have been better advised to drape more discreetly. Her own long, shapely legs were a matter for congratulation, she thought, and her bosom showed to advantage also, and she blessed the French *Merveilleuses* who had introduced this fashion that made it possible for her to thus display them.

Jane silently agreed with her as to the legs, but my bosom's better, she thought, and would show to better advantage nor hers, could I ever own such a low-cut gown. Also me face, for if ever I saw a colder eye than m'lady's I disremember it.

Lady Sarah, however, viewed her face with complacency as she smoothed the white kid gloves over her fingers. Her long green eyes, the cameolike perfection of her profile, and the smooth, matte complexion seemed to her all that could be desired. The habitual haughtiness of the set of her head, and the coldness of the brilliant blue eyes were not apparent to her.

Miss Wright placed a long chinchilla cloak over her mistress's shoulders and handed her her reticule. Lady Sarah sailed out of the room without a word to her abigail, leaving behind only a waft of delicious scent to remind them of her presence.

Wright moved about the room, putting away discarded clothing, turning down her mistress's bed, and laying out her robe across the foot of it.

"Hurry up then, Coombes. I'm going down for my dinner now. Do you sweep up that hearth good and get out of here. And don't touch anything, mind."

The door closed behind her, and Jane, in a spirit of defiance unlike her usual meek exterior, stood up abruptly and moved to the dressing table.

She stared at her reflection, lit by the candles, and was not completely dissatisfied with what she saw. The nose had an unfortunate tilt, unlike Lady Sarah's straight patrician one, but was not ugly for all that. The rest was better, she felt, inspecting her large, slanting sherry-brown eyes, and the full red mouth. She smiled at herself to show her approval and her small, white teeth. Unlike most of the maids, Jane's teeth, due to the mysteries of inheritance she neither knew of nor understood, were still intact and in good condition.

She turned to look at the door speculatively, and then, with a shrug, turned back to the mirror and pulled off her white mob-cap. She felt there was little cause to fear interruption for at least an hour, with the family gone out for the evening and old Wright only starting her dinner, and her a fierce trencherman, she thought, giggling.

She pulled out the pins holding her hair in a tight knot on top of her head, and it tumbled down almost to her waist. She ran Lady Sarah's comb through it, then switching it forward over one shoulder, she took Lady Sarah's brush and sensuously ran it again and again through the long, silky strands. She cleaned the brush and comb scrupulously, returned them to the table-top, and spread her long hair about her shoulders. It shimmered and waved about her like a dark cloud.

Hardly aware of what she was doing, her hands came up and began upbuttoning the high necked gray gown she wore, the uniform of all the Montmorency maids. The dress fell to her feet, and after it the shift and the cotton drawers and the stockings.

She eyed the round globes of her breasts with pride. I was right, she thought, much better'n *hers,* I'll be bound, and 'twould display a treat in a low-cut gown.

Dissatisfied with the limited view in the dressing table mirror, she crossed to the full-length glass by the wardrobe. On her way, she passed the robe laid out for Lady Sarah's return, and her hand caressed the silken folds for an instant, then drew it on. She shivered with delight as the cool silk touched her skin.

In front of the mirror, she held out the deep pink fabric to frame her body. It was the first time she had ever actually seen herself without clothing, and she inspected her figure critically, her hands running down the narrow waist and rounded hips. Me mam's right, she thought dispassionately, I'll do, though me legs are not so long as *hers,* they be just as nice in shape. She watched in amazement as her small, rosy nipples, reacting to the movement of her hands down her body, stiffened and stood erect. Crikey, would yer look at that, she thought, smiling at the phenomenon, there's summat me mam never told me about.

Then she emitted a soft scream and stood frozen as the door opened behind her and the mirror showed her the image of Lord Jaspar, Lady Sarah's brother.

He stood rooted for a second, a slow smile lifting one corner of his mouth. He turned to close the door behind him and then sauntered across the carpet to her. She watched him advance, unable to move or speak, until he was directly behind her.

He stood smiling over her shoulder at her wide-eyed reflection in the mirror.

"Well, well," he said appreciatively.

She could feel the roughness of his coat and the cold buttons of his waistcoat through the thin silk against her back, and she watched in disbelief as his arm came around her and his hand cupped one full upthrust breast. She quivered. Now the other hand, encouraged by the success of its twin, came around to capture the other trembling breast.

Jane felt completely detached, watching these movements in the mirror as though they were happening to someone else. But however far away her mind might feel from the two figures in the mirror, her body, of its own volition and without applying to her mind for permission, reacted. Her breasts seemed to swell, her nipples to thrust themselves against the warmth of the caressing palms, and various other parts of her body, including her fingertips, began to tingle most pleasantly. Her body relaxed back against his, her skin enjoying the rough texture of his coat through the silk robe, her head tilting accommodatingly for his lips in the hollow of her shoulder and throat.

With a moan, he turned her around, and crushing her against himself he reached to kiss the soft, red mouth.

And abruptly the spell she had been under was broken. Now it was not two figures in a dream she watched, but the reality of her own nakedness being explored by the clutching hands of Lord Jaspar. She twisted her face away from his mouth, and brought her hands up to push against his chest, but he held her fast, and only laughed exultantly as she struggled. She finally got one hand free and delivered a ringing blow to his ear, painful enough to cause him to loosen his hold. She whirled away, but he caught at the robe by the back of the neck, and there was the hiss of rending silk as it parted in a long tear down the back. She checked in dismay at the sound, and he caught her arm and spun her back into his embrace.

He clamped one hand on the back of her head and his mouth came down on hers, and struggle as she might, he had her fast.

Gawd, I'm for it now, she thought desperately, whatever happens, for if old Wright doesn't come back in a minute and catch us, she'll know for sure 'twas me to blame for the torn robe.

Well, go down fightin', as me mam says, and with this came another piece of advice her mam had given her. She brought her knee up briskly, and Lord Jaspar doubled over and sat down

4

abruptly with a moan so heartrending that she paused. But only for an instant. Panting, she ripped the robe off as she ran across the room, stepped into her gown, and buttoned it with trembling fingers. Then she snatched up the rest of her garments and sped to the door.

She opened it and peeked out, then turned back to the figure rolling in agony on the floor.

"Beg pardon, sir, for having to hurt you, but you'd no right to—to—well, o'course I don't say I'd no responsibility," she said, honesty compelling her to admit she hadn't exactly discouraged him, "but it was only the serprize, you see. But I ain't so easy as all that, nor I won't be forced neither." Then, irrespressibly, she dimpled at him, "I'll make me goodbyes to you now, sir, since tomorrow, I make no doubt, I'll find mesel' bein' shown the door. You'll feel better in a day or two, have no fear."

And with that she slipped out the door and sped up the back stairs to the room in the attic she shared with Sophy, the parlour maid, now thankfully in the servants' dining room at her supper. Jane reassembled herself and wound her hair back into its usual knot.

Might's well go down and have me supper, she thought philosophically, since there's no knowin' where I'll get it tomorrow!

Jane Coombes, at fourteen, was an independent self-supporting woman, and had been for two years. She had started in the Montmorency household at the age of ten as the lowliest kitchen menial, set to scrubbing out kettles. But Jane hadn't felt humbled by her job. On the contrary, she had been proud to be a wage earner, able to turn her few pennies over to her mother, who had been forced to find a job for Jane when her own failing health made it impossible for Mrs. Coombes to work any longer.

Mrs. Coombes, herself in service, had heard of the job for Jane through an acquaintance employed by the Montmorencys, and had taken her daughter around to the servants' entrance and secured the position for the child.

Actually "Mrs." was a courtesy title only, for though a respectably raised country girl, Jane's mother had strayed from the path of virtue one evening when she made the acquaintance of a handsome sea captain. She gave him, wholeheartedly, the only thing she had to give, but she had only the one opportunity for giving. He went out of her life the next morning, and she never saw him again. She was left with a trumpery little gold ring and the knowledge, some months later, that she was pregnant. She put the ring on her finger and proudly called herself Mrs. Coombes thenceforth.

She'd been a fiercely protective mother, working hard to provide for her child, cautioning her always to be a good girl and keep herself clean, to work hard, and try to better herself. There were many other bits of advice, mostly to do with the habits of certain men, which Jane was to beware of, along with some useful hints on how to protect herself, one of which Jane had made use of in her encounter with Lord Jaspar.

This night had been the first time she had ever been in the same room with the young man, for she had never been in the front of the house in all her four years with the Montmorencys. After two years spent ten hours every day in the scullery, going home to the room she shared with her mother, to nurse her and to sleep, two momentous events had occurred. Her mother had died and Jane had been advanced to an upstairs maid, and it was her deepest regret that the advancement had happened just too late for her mother to share in the pride of it.

After that she was given a room in the attic of the mansion, two smart gray uniforms with white aprons and caps, a slight increase in her wages, and the honour of hauling fuel up to the bedroom fireplaces, which she had been doing for the past two years.

She had been confidently looking forward to graduating to the front of the house in the very near future, but she was in no doubt, after tonight's events, that she could say good-bye to that ambition and the Montmorencys altogether immediately after breakfast in the morning.

In spite of the fate looming over her, she went to bed and slept soundly, her youth and the hard day's work she'd had insuring her against a night of worry.

The next morning she put on her best brown merino gown, packed her few belongings in her box, and taking her bonnet and black pelisse, descended to the servants' dining room. She sat down in her usual place at the table and ate her bread and butter and drank her coffee under the tight-lipped glare of the housekeeper and the curious stares of the other servants.

When she had finished, the housekeeper spoke. "Mr. Leach is waiting to speak to you, Coombes."

Jane rose meekly and followed the broad back of the housekeeper down the hall to the butler's pantry, where Mr. Leach was counting out the silver for the breakfast trays. He glanced up, but continued his task with great deliberation, not speaking until he had finished and locked the cupboard. Jane stood, chin up proudly, while the housekeeper waited behind her grimly, her hands folded beneath her apron.

"Well, Coombes, what you been up to, eh?" asked Mr. Leach finally, turning to her.

" 'Twere an accident, sir."

"An accident? To tear m'lady's gown to shreds? I shouldn't half-ring a peal over your head, my girl, causing me to have to listen to that Friday-faced Wright spitting fire at me this morning, before I even had my breakfast! Well! Speak up, what have you got to say for yourself?"

"Nothin', sir."

"And nothing's what you'll get, my girl, for they'll not give you a character after this caper."

"But I give 'un four good years of service—"

"Makes no never mind, they'll not give you more than the wages due you and they want you out of the house immediately."

She stared at him blankly, trying to fight down her rising panic, for well she knew how impossible it would be to be taken on anywhere without references. In spite of her resolve to take her medicine bravely, the tears rose in her eyes.

Mr. Leach came toward her. He'd had his eye on Jane for the past year, only too aware of the ripening figure, which he had looked forward to exploring at his leisure at some time in the not too distant future, as he had done with many another maid of the household. For Mr. Leach was a powerful man, his authority supreme in the servants' quarters, and the young girls, more often than not, had been glad to acquiesce to his demands in order to remain in his favour. But he was always careful not to take them too young, and not to get them into trouble, for he prized his position, an enormously lucrative one for him, and he knew that any hint of pregnant serving girls would land him in the streets.

His eyes flickered hungrily over the ripe red mouth and the perfect breasts, and he wished there was some way to get that hawk-faced old besom Wright out of the room. He sighed regretfully, for he knew she'd never budge, and contented himself with patting Jane's fresh, rounded cheek in an avuncular fashion.

7

"Well, then, crying mends nothing. Here's your money. I'm sorry for you, girl."

She turned away, swallowing a sob, and stumbled to the door. She was taken by surprise at his kindness, for she'd never cared for Mr. Leach very much, though some of the girls thought him handsome. Jane had thought his eyes set too close together and hadn't cared for the look she sometimes saw in them when he eyed her. And his mouth, she thought, was that cruel lookin', so thin-lipped he was. He'd never even deigned to speak to her before, and she felt he thought too highly of himself. But perhaps she'd been mistaken in him.

Presently she found herself standing in the street, her box in her hand, and shivering slightly in her worn black pelisse. As she stood in the entryway to the servants' entrance, trying to decide which direction to turn, she heard the main door of the house opening and turned to see who was coming out.

"Tell my mama I won't be in for luncheon," said Lord Jaspar as he came down the steps and crossed the pavement to his phaeton, waiting at the curb.

Jane noticed with some satisfaction that he was walking somewhat awkwardly, and her lips twitched with glee. He glanced up at that moment and saw her, and saw, also, the smile. He flushed painfully, and ducked quickly into his carriage.

Hmpf! thought Jane, you're nought but a cowardly boy, for all your pretty face and grand airs. No fear you told your mother and sister just *how* that robe got tore, and you as much to blame as me that's payin' for it. Well—not quite so much, to be sure, for if I'd not taken me clothes off in the first place, he'd not of tried his games.

She saw the coachman jump down from his perch and go to the side, where a hand came out and dropped something into the servant's palm. The man looked around, saw Jane, and came to her.

"M'lord says to gie' 'ee this," he said, holding out his hand in which rested a gold coin.

She stared at it for an instant, then snatching it up, she marched around the man and up to the carriage.

She stared at Lord Jaspar disdainfully for a moment, then with a flick of her wrist, tossed the coin into his lap, where it landed squarely on that section of his anatomy he was still most painfully aware of this morning. He gasped. She drew herself up regally, threw up her chin, and sailed away down the street triumphantly.

2

A week later she thought with regret of that gold coin, and acknowledged that the pleasure of the grand gesture of throwing it back at him would have been better foregone.

She had spent that entire first day trudging from one agency to another and being summarily ejected when she confessed to having been let go without references. When it drew toward evening, she'd finally made her way, barely able to drag one foot after the other, deep into the stews of Cheapside, to the only person she knew outside the Montmorency household.

Mrs. Blodgett and Jane's mother had come up from their country village together as girls to go into service in London, and had kept in touch as much as possible over the years. Jane had not seen the woman since her mother's funeral, but felt sure Mrs. Blodgett would take her in until she could get a situation.

She had done so, but Jane had never been more unhappy in her life. The Blodgetts lived in one wretched room that opened directly into a narrow, cobbled street, running with filth dumped from night pails out of upper floor windows. The smell seeping in the front door was indescribable. Inside the small, fetid room were a kitchen table, two benches, and two beds. One bed was occupied by Mr. and Mrs. Blodgett, and their small son, whose continually dripping nose and filth-smeared face caused Jane to lose her appetite every time she sat down to share their meager supper.

The other bed Jane shared with the two daughters of the household, both near herself in age, and neither any better than she should be, Jane suspected.

Bedtime had become a nightmare for her in spite of her aching body and desperation for rest. The bed covers were a brownish-gray from dirt and, she realized with growing horror, were occupied by animal life other than herself and the Blodgett sisters. She couldn't repress a shudder every time she forced herself beneath them. In spite of her distaste, however, she jumped in fairly smartly, for across the room she could feel the avid eyes of Mr. Blodgett, who leered at her continuously when she was in the room. Jane could only pretend not to notice, and pray that Mrs. Blodgett wouldn't.

Jane had left very early every morning, and plodded up one street and down another, hour after hour, knocking at the servants' entrances of every mansion she came to, asking if help were needed. She'd found nothing.

She was aware that her appearance was beginning to tell against her. Since there were no facilities for washing at the Blodgetts, she knew she was none too clean looking. The terrible air in the room, the poor diet, and the inability to sleep properly while clinging to the edge of the crowded bed being poked awake again and again by sharp elbows and knees, had drained the fresh colour from her cheeks and printed dark shadows beneath her eyes. The looks of contempt, or worse, pity, that now greeted her requests for employment had so shaken her that her natural ebullience had disappeared. The pert, laughing eyes were dulled by a failure she had, so far in her young life, not experienced. She had begun to think her life too insupportable to be borne much longer, though she could think of nothing more to do than she was doing to change it. She couldn't even dredge up comforting words of her mother's from her memory any more.

In a mood of flat despair at the end of the seventh day of not finding work, she turned her sore and aching legs for the long walk back to Cheapside and the end-of-the-day routine that had become more difficult to face every day, with the prospect of lewd remarks and grabbing hands from the men who lounged in the dark doorways of the narrow, cobbled streets, and, when she finally passed that hurdle, the quarreling Blodgetts and the greedy eyes of Mr. Blodgett crawling over her body.

It took her some moments to realize that the gentleman staring into the shop window was Mr. Leach. She nearly called aloud when she realized who it was, so great was her pleasure to see a familiar face from that very recent past which, in retrospect, seemed ideal. She stopped herself from speaking, suddenly ashamed to have anyone from that household see her in her present condition. Before she could move away, however, Mr. Leach turned and came down the street toward her. It seemed for a moment that he would pass by without recogniz-

ing her at all in any case, but at the last moment he stopped sud
denly.

"Here—is that you, Jane Coombes?"

She threw up her chin and forced herself to smile gaily,
"Well, well, imagine runnin' into you, Mr. Leach! Don't tell
me—let me guess—you've come lookin' for me because the
household is fallin' round your ears without me!"

"Sauce!" he said laughing. "Well, how is it with you,
girl?"

"Not so bad as it could be, thank you Mr. Leach."

"Well, if you want the word with no bark on it, I'd say you
was being less than truthful with me, Janie girl. Come on
now—out with it. You've found no work, eh?"

"Not yet—but it's not been more nor a week. I'll find
somethin', never you fear," she replied proudly, staring him
straight in the eye defiantly, daring him to feel sorry for her.

"Well, I like your spirit, that I do. Here—you come along
with me. I'm just on my way to my little house and a grand
meal cooked by m'sister."

"You got an 'ouse of your own, Mr. Leach?" she asked in
surprise.

"That I have, and a pretty little piece of property it is too.
M'sister takes care of it for me and on my day off I go round for
a good meal."

"Oh—but—but—well, I don't think I better, though I thank
you for the askin'," she said uneasily, aware of the grubbiness
of her appearance. "I doubt your sister would thank you for
draggin' home someone off the streets—"

"She's nothing to say to it at all. 'Tis my house and what I
says goes. And she don't like it, out she goes and well she
knows it!" he declared vehemently, his eyes turning hard at the
thought of anyone daring to defy his wishes.

Seeing Jane wince away at the change in his tone, he became
all affability once more, declaring he'd not take no for an answer, and taking her arm, he pulled her along down the street
with him.

The gimlet-eyed woman who opened the door to them stared
impassively at Jane when Mr. Leach introduced them, sniffed,
and turned away without speaking. Mr. Leach called her back.

"Not so fast, Lizzie. You'll take Janie here for a good
wash-up before you set out the supper. Up to the spare room, if
you please."

She turned back to exchange a long look with him, which he

11

returned blandly with a slight lifting of his lip at one corner. She finally shrugged slightly.

"Come along then," she said as she started up the narrow stairs leading to the second floor.

During this exchange Jane had covertly examined what she could see of the house from the tiny front hall. Though the house was small and unimposing from the outside, and cramped from what she could see of the inside, still it was compact and well-furnished, and *clean.*

Lizzie led her into a tiny room furnished only with a cot and a straightbacked chair, and in one corner a table with a basin on it.

"Wait here, I'll bring water," Lizzie told her and then left.

Jane stood uncomfortably in the middle of the room, wishing she'd never allowed herself to be persuaded to come here, in spite of the comfort of a familiar face and the promise of a good meal. Miss Leach made it very clear that she was not welcome, and the prospect of sitting down to a meal with such a starchy, Friday-faced woman was repellent.

Lizzie Leach looked exactly like her brother, but had none of his ability to dissemble. She had had a grim life, and found nothing much to smile about. She worked hard, did her duty as she saw it, and went about the business of life with a total lack of interest in anything outside the four walls of her brother's house. She was grateful to him for making it possible for her to leave the service of other people and move into a home of her own with no one to give her orders. Except Leach, of course, but she didn't mind it from her brother. He never stinted her on money, though as she was a frugal housekeeper he had no cause to worry that she would waste it, and if, from time to time, he chose to bring home a woman, Lizzie turned a blind eye. It was all she could do, since he never asked her opinion, nor accepted any criticism.

She carried a pitcher of warm water up to the spare room and poured it into the basin. She put the towel and soap down beside it and turned to the door.

"Miss Leach—"

"Yes?" asked Lizzie, her hand on the latch.

"Thank you. It's most kind of you and your brother to have me here."

Lizzie nodded coldly and continued out the door, closing it firmly behind her. Jane shuddered involuntarily, then turned eagerly to the warm water and soap. After only a moment's hesitation, she stripped off her clothes and hurriedly began washing her whole body. Might's well take advantage while 'tis available, there bein' no way of knowin' when me next chance will come, she thought.

When she came down the stairs fifteen minutes later, she felt much more like her old self. Her spirits had lifted just with the knowledge that she was clean again. Mr. Leach, waiting at the bottom of the stairs, nodded approvingly and without ceremony led the way down the narrow dark hallway to the kitchen.

The meal that followed, though simple, was well-cooked and ample. Jane tried not to appear as starving as she actually was, but it was difficult to turn down second helpings after the slim rations she had been on for the past week. She finally sat back, full and happy. She looked sleepily at Lizzie and thanked her for the good food. Lizzie, as usual, made no comment.

"Well, now, young Jane, so you've had no luck finding a situation?"

"No. I've near walked me feet off, too. I was wonderin' if you'd heard of any place, Mr. Leach?"

"Can't say's I have. Where you living, then?"

"With me mum's old friend in Cheapside. But I can't stay there for long. They've no room for me really and—well—" She stopped, unable to admit the true squalor of the Blodgett household.

"Cheapside! Never tell me you'll go all the way back there in the dark! Why, we wouldn't hear of it, would we, Lizzie?"

Lizzie didn't even bother to look up. She had finished her meal long ago, and now waited, hands folded in her lap, for a nod from her brother to clear the table.

Jane, uncomfortable under this silence, laughed nervously.

"Oh, I'll be all right, no fear. I've learned how to handle me-sel' this past week."

"No, no. I wouldn't be responsible for sending a young girl out to such a place at this hour. You'll stay here. We've the extra room, and it'll be no bother."

Jane was overwhelmed by this thoughtfulness. Never had she suspected that Mr. Leach was such a kindhearted man. His sister might be cold as the grave, but Mr. Leach understood. She felt a lump in her throat so large that though she opened her mouth to express her gratitude, no words would come out.

Seeing her tears, Mr. Leach laughed good-humouredly and smoothly led the conversation into other channels. He nodded to his sister, who rose immediately. When Jane saw this she also rose, preparing to help, but he would not allow her to do so.

"Come, sit. You've been on your feet all day, and Lizzie doesn't like anyone to help her."

So while the close-faced woman went about her work silently, Mr. Leach leaned back in his chair, stretched his long legs to one side, and spoke pleasantly with his guest. Jane began to relax finally, and asked eager questions about all her friends in the Montmorency household below stairs, and about the doings of the Quality above.

When she was finally taken back to the tiny room upstairs by the dour Lizzie, Jane could hardly wait for the woman to leave the room so that she could climb into the cot. After the filthy bed she'd shared with the Blodgett sisters this past week, the small bed with the clean sheets and no other occupants looked like heaven. She thanked Lizzie for the nightgown she'd lent and for the candle and wished her goodnight.

Two minutes later she was between the sheets and stretching luxuriously. One minute later she was asleep.

Slowly she came awake. It could have been minutes later or hours later. It was like swimming slowly to the surface from the bottom of the ocean. She became aware of hands caressing and kneading her shoulders and breasts as consciousness returned and her eyes fluttered open. She stared witlessly up into the face of Mr. Leach, and it took her a long moment to realize why he looked so different. He was naked!

She shrieked and sat up suddenly, pushing his hands away at the same time and pulling her gown back up over her shoulders.

"Now, now, girlie. It's only me. No need for hollering your head off in that way. You'll wake Lizzie and she'll be angry with you."

"Get *out* of here! What do you think you're doin'?" she hissed at him.

"Why, I got lonely thinking about you, little girl, and thought, Well, there she is—just across the hall so I'll just step across and pay her a call," he replied with a grin.

"Well, you can just step back, for I'm not receivin' callers at this hour of night," she snapped indignantly.

"Mustn't be rude, Janie—that's not nice—and you got no call to treat me rudely, have you now?"

"I hope I'm grateful for your kindness, Mr. Leach, and you may be sure I'd every intention of thankin' you properly in the mornin' before I left."

"There's better ways I know of to say thank you," he said, taking her two hands in one of his and pulling them away from the neck of her gown. With his other hand he ripped the gown completely down the front and pulled it down again, slowly, first from one shoulder and then from the other, so that she was naked to the waist.

She tried to pull away, but he held her hands in such an iron grip that she was immobilized. She watched in horror as he sat for a long moment, staring hungrily at her breasts. Then he let go of her hands and taking a breast in each hand, he lifted them and bent down to begin sucking noisily at them. She grabbed him by the hair and attempted to push his head away, but could not move him. She began twisting and writhing, and finally with a great heave of her whole body, pushed him aside and slid out of the bed.

He jumped up and they stood glaring at each other across the bed. She realized even more fully his nakedness, for now he was fully aroused, in a way she could not mistake. She stared in horror for an instant and then, in spite of herself she began to giggle and clapped her hand over her mouth to try to hide it.

"Laugh at me, will you," he snarled, and drew back his arm and slapped her with the back of his hand across the face. She went reeling back against the wall and fell to the floor. He stepped around the cot and stood over her.

"Don't you touch me," she said fiercely, in spite of a whole galaxy of stars wheeling before her eyes, "I'll yell the house down."

"Yell away—there's none will care."

"Oh no—and what about Lizzie?"

"Ho! Lizzie is it? She'll not even turn over in her bed. She knows which side her bread's buttered, no fear. Now enough of this yammering."

He jerked her to her feet and threw her back across the bed and fell on top of her. She screamed and kicked and hit him. She was pinioned so effectively to the bed by his enormous bulk that it was difficult to strike him effectively, but she persisted, fighting with all her strength. Finally she dug her fingers into his throat and began to squeeze. He had ignored her ineffectual blows as though they were fleabites, too busy exploring her young body with his mouth and his hands to be bothered, but her fingers on his windpipe were a matter he could not ignore. With a roar of rage he raised himself, and snatching her hands away from his throat, slapped her again.

"Now, we'll have no more of this, you hear? You'll either be nice to me or else. Now—what's it to be?"

For answer she bent her knee and kicked him in the stomach with all her strength, moving so suddenly that she caught him unaware. He fell back onto the floor with a resounding thud. But only for a moment. He rose slowly, his eyes gone cold and hard as his sister's as he stared at her. She hitched herself backward across the bed, more terrified than she had ever been in her life as she watched him move toward her. She had thought she would have no trouble fending off his amorous advances, as she had always been able to do with other men. But she knew in that moment that Mr. Leach was not in any way like those others. She'd never seen such a look in a man's eyes.

He reached out and grabbed her feet in one hand and pulled her back. Then he put one large hand about her throat, and holding her in position he began slapping her across the face, first one side and then the other, slowly and deliberately. Her mouth began to bleed and then her nose, but he continued until she went limp in his grasp, then he dropped her back on the bed. He walked heavily out of the room and across the hall, and then came back, swinging a leather strap in his hand. He flipped her body over face down, and raising the strap brought it down with all his might on the backs of her legs. She came back to her senses with a scream of pain with that first blow, and her agonized screams rang out again and again as he continued to beat her. Her legs were striped with red welts that soon began to bleed as the skin broke, and the screams became moans and then stopped as she lost consciousness again.

His fury and the passion he had aroused in himself by his brutality caused him finally to toss aside the strap and hastily flip her over again. He threw himself on top of her and entered her instantly and viciously, thrusting himself against her virginity, and it broke before him just as his own pent-up climax exploded. He sagged limply on top of her, then rolled off, and without a backward glance, walked out of the room and closed the door.

The first time Jane regained consciousness, her most immediate sensation was one of great cold. She started to sit up instinctively to reach for covers, and then she became aware of other sensations; abruptly, shatteringly, with such overwhelming pain from every part of her body that she moaned and swooned away again. She woke several other times during the remainder of the night, but never succeeded in covering herself. By the time the first pale fingers of sunlight filtered through the window, she knew better than to attempt to sit up. Her eyelids fluttered slowly, reluctantly, open and she lay quite still for a moment, then carefully raised one hand to her face. One eye felt swollen, almost closed, her lips were puffed nearly twice their size and were crusted with dried blood, and the very skin of her cheeks was sore to the touch. She raised her head slightly off the pillow and looked down at her sprawled body. Though she could not see the backs of her legs, she could tell when she moved them slightly that they were stuck to the sheets with blood. But the worst pain was between her legs, and she could see blood there, too, in dark smears against her thighs, and knew what he had done while she was, mercifully, unconscious.

It seemed suddenly as though the room turned red, so great was the explosion of rage in her brain. She shook with it, and wished he would walk into the room at that moment. I'd kill 'im, I would, I'd kill the great dirty beast with me bare hands, could I but find 'im. She fell back onto the pillow weakly, her whole body trembling with frustration, for she knew that even if he walked in the door at that moment she would be unable to move. If he chose to violate her again she would be able to do nothing to stop him. Even the effort of lifting her head had caused her to feel faint again. But I'll pay him out, she thought grimly, he's not heard the last of me yet! I'll pay him out if it's the last thing I do in me life!

Below, in the kitchen, Mr. Leach sat calmly forking down a large beefsteak Lizzie had cooked for his breakfast.

She set the coffeepot down with a thump and stood looking down at him.

"Did you kill 'er, then?"

"Pour my coffee and mind your business." Her mouth set in a hard, straight line over the retort she was about to make and she poured the coffee. He continued, "Clean her up. I'll be back tonight."

"And if she leaves?"

"Leave? She'll not move this day for sure," he replied, his mouth twisting into a grin.

Lizzie turned her eyes away, so unpleasant was the look this produced on his face. She knew better than to utter one word of expostulation against his activities, even words of warning

17

about the trouble he could be in if one of his "conquests" chose to go to the authorities and lay charges against him. Lizzie herself thought his sexual needs beastly and disgusting, indeed as she thought all men's were, but that he required very young girls for the fullfillment of them was doubly revolting to her. She thought that if he *must* indulge his animal nature, the least he could do would be to find mature, and willing, women.

After her brother was gone, Lizzie heated water and carried it up the stairs. When she opened the door and saw the body on the bed, she stood there in shock for a moment, thinking that he had indeed killed the girl, for she lay so still. Then Lizzie felt horror as she took in the swollen face, turning purple with bruises, the sprawled bloody legs. She moved slowly across the room to the bedside, and the eyes below her came open and stared up at her with such cold hatred that Lizzie started and almost dropped the pitcher of water she still carried.

She moved away to fetch the basin and bring it back to the bed. She experienced no pity, for Lizzie had no experience with the gentler emotions. She'd given them up too many years ago to remember, and sealed them off for good. All she felt now was revulsion at what her dependency on her brother's goodwill required of her.

Though not motivated by gentleness, her touch was light, and she washed the girl expertly. She had to soak the sheets before she could peel them away from the lacerated legs. When she had helped Jane into a clean bed gown, she assisted her into the room's one chair and proceeded to strip the bed and remake it with fresh linen, then helped Jane back into it. Throughout all of this, she never spoke a word, nor did Jane. When she finished she bundled the soiled sheets together and put them out into the hallway, picked up the basin and towels, and left, still without speaking. She came back presently with a cup of coffee and a plate of bread and butter and went away again, closing the door behind her quietly.

Jane pulled herself up carefully and reached for the food. I'll need every bite of it, she thought grimly. She broke very small pieces of bread and dipped them into the coffee to enable her to chew them, for her jaws were so sore it hurt to move them. It took a long time to eat her breakfast, but she had nothing better to do. She was as aware as Mr. Leach was that she would not be able to move today by herself. She was also aware that she must face the possibility that he would visit her again tonight, and that if he did she would be unable to prevent him having his way with her again. But she didn't dwell on that too much, knowing there was nothing she could do about it. She had better things to occupy her mind—escape and revenge.

3

"Oh—er—Leach—one moment, if you please," called Lord Jaspar to the departing butler.

"Yes, m'lord?"

"I was just wondering—not important, really, but I should hate to think—well, the thing is—that maid my sister—er—"

"You would mean Jane, m'lord, Jane Coombes?" asked Leach smoothly, though he was somewhat startled by the young master's query.

"Oh, is that her name?" Lord Jaspar asked, sorting through his letters with a great show of interest in them and none at all in the subject. "I was only wondering, you know, if she'd found a situation. Seemed a pity to throw the girl out in the streets for the sake of a gown or something."

"I'm sure I couldn't say, m'lord, though of course I could find out if you should wish to know."

Now Mr. Leach was very much piqued with curiosity. Why should the young master be interesting himself in the welfare of a maid? A maid, so far as Leach was aware, the young man had never so much as spoken to. Or had he? Perhaps he had been pursuing the girl unbeknown to Leach. A brazen enough piece she was, to be sure, and pretty enough to have caught the young man's eye. Though if there *was* aught between them one thing Leach knew for sure: He'd not bedded the girl, for Leach was in a position to swear to the girl's virginity up until last night. He smothered a grin discreetly behind his hand. However, if the young master wanted Leach's castoffs, Leach would be more than happy to arrange something—for a fee, of course.

"Would you like me to make inquiries, m'lord?"

"Well, I could do with knowing she was all right—such a

19

young girl to be out on the streets. If you should have word, just let me know to ease my conscience.''

''Certainly, m'lord. Anything else, m'lord?''

''No, no. That'll do.'' Jaspar waved dismissively and turned back to his letters.

But when he had the dining room to himself again he fell into a reverie about the girl—Jane—Jane Coombes—well, Jane was enough. Coombes was such a—a—unromantic-sounding name.

To do Jaspar credit, he had worried about Jane. He was only eighteen himself, and still not enough of a polished beau to carry off such an encounter as he'd had with Jane without tweaks of conscience. He was fully aware of his own responsibility for her dismissal, but unable to make himself confess to his share of the blame. Not that it would make any difference to Sarah or his mother. They would only say the girl had no business putting on Sarah's robe in the first place.

The thought of Sarah's robe brought back the picture of Jane in it, and, as he'd done for hours at a time during the days that had passed since the encounter, he went through the whole erotic incident moment by moment. Opening the door of his sister's room and seeing the girl there, not only reflected in the mirror from the front, but clearly outlined through the thin, gauzy fabric, her skin glimmering enticingly. He allowed his mind to roam lovingly over that vision first, savouring again the sweetly rounded behind, before allowing himself to remember the figure in the mirror: the thrusting young breasts, the delicious curve of her waist, and the long, full thighs. Only when he had lingered unbearably long over each part of her did he allow himself to remember the delicious moments that followed; the dreamlike caresses, reflected back so tantalizingly from the mirror. He could remember every second of it so clearly, including his fully aroused passion, that he always succeeded in rousing that same need again, producing an ache that was not at all pleasant, as that other had been. For Jaspar had still some pain to remind him of the disastrous ending of their meeting.

He had succeeded in forgiving her for that dreadful blow. Indeed, he had come to admire her for it, thinking that it was a sign of spirit and courage for her to defend herself so. She had the right, surely, to defend herself, as anyone would do when attacked. She had also been honest enough to admit her own fault, and this also he could not help admiring. He had never met such a girl in his young life, nor had he ever given so much thought to one. Naturally, he had had some experience, but always with some little Barque of Frailty who had mastered the art of teaching young men how to conduct themselves in the bedchamber. But these experiences had been few so far, and as for the other kind of female, the young girls at balls and parties, he'd had none at all. Though he attended a great many affairs, he rarely asked any of the girls to stand up with him. He despised most of them for their silly, missish ways, and was terrified of being trapped into marriage, being well aware of his own softhearted foolishness where women were concerned. Stupid as he might think the girl to be, he could never bring himself to say or do anything to embarrass her or make her feel unhappy, for he was much to good-natured to be cruel.

There were many lures thrown out to him, but he'd managed to avoid them all. But now he spent many of his waking moments and most of his sleeping ones, thinking and dreaming of a maid in his mother's house! Why the girl probably couldn't even speak intelligibly! But it didn't seem to matter how much scorn he poured on her, the fact remained that he was obsessed by the memory of her. He wanted her as he'd never wanted anything in his life before.

When Jane heard the door open she didn't move. She had been waiting tensely for him to come, knowing full well that he would. He stood by the cot holding the candle over to inspect her.

"Well, you're a sight, you are. Young master wouldn't be so hot for you if he could see you now. Never mind, you'll heal up pretty as ever and then we'll see what we shall see. There's a pretty penny to be made from him, I make no doubt."

He set the candle down and lay down beside her, eyeing her body appreciatively, happy that he'd been careful not to beat her in such a way as to destroy the beauty of the body for himself. He ran his hands down over her flat stomach and into the soft, feathery hair over her pubic mound. Like a baby's almost, he gloated, never touched by none but me, still full and rosy. Ugh, how he hated women! Only very young girls held any interest for him at all. Young, untouched girls.

Through all of this, and everything that happened after, Jane forced herself to lie perfectly still, never moving so much as an eyelash, never making a sound, even when the pain as he entered her was almost more than she could bear. She bit down on her tongue until her mouth filled with blood, but she would not cry out.

When he had finished and left her, she forced herself off the bed and, shuffling like an old lady, managed to get across the room to the basin of water to wash herself. She inched her way the few feet back to the cot and lowered herself with almost as much difficulty as she'd had in getting up. Lizzie had left salve for her and she spread it over the weals on the backs of her legs and lay down on her stomach to sleep.

She remembered then what Mr. Leach had said when he first came in, that she'd been too terrified to attend to at the time. Somethin' about the young master and makin' money. What could he mean? He couldn't know anythin' about Lord Jaspar and hersel'. She was confident *he* would say nothing about it to anyone. Coward that he is, she thought scornfully. And there was no one else who knew of it. So what could Mr. Leach mean? Did he think that now that he had despoiled her he could sell her to other men? That must be it—he planned to make a whore of her and bring men here to enjoy her for a night. Oh my God! I must get out of here. Tomorrow! Yes, tomorrow I'll leave if I have to crawl.

She fell asleep, but when she woke, her first thought was that she must leave. She got out of bed slowly and began to walk up and down the room, each step an agony as she stretched the partially healed slashes on the backs of her legs. She was glad there was no mirror in the room, for from the feel of it, her face was still swollen and bruised beyond recognition, and she knew if she saw it she might never have the courage to go out into the streets. When she heard Lizzie coming up the stairs she hurried back to the bed and got under the covers.

Lizzie had made her a kind of porridge this morning and Jane was so grateful to see it she nearly thanked Lizzie for it. But she stopped herself in time. Never, she thought, never will I say a word of gratitude to anyone in this devil's house!

She ate the porridge with relish, and the bread and butter and coffee, and felt much strengthened by it. She rose determinedly and went to the chair where her clothes were folded and with great difficulty dressed herself. She wished desperately for a comb or brush to neaten her hair, but finally pushed as much of it as she could up under her bonnet, shuddering distastefully at the feel of the matted and tangled locks.

The trip down the narrow stairs seemed to take years, every bend of her knee bringing tears to her eyes, but she ignored them and forced herself on. When she reached the bottom she found Lizzie standing there watching her with cold eyes.

"You're not to leave."

"Try to stop me. I should *like* to see you try to stop me," Jane hissed through gritted teeth. "Now get out of me way."

Lizzie stared at her silently for a moment and then stepped aside. Jane pushed past her and opened the door, stepped out, and closed it behind her.

The trip back to Cheapside was a nightmare. She kept her head well down, but she was aware of the horrified glances of people in the street. Her halting progress was a torment to her under this scrutiny, but she could not move any faster, and occasionally could not move at all, but was forced to stop and rest.

It was during one of these stops, while she supported herself on the railings of a fence fronting an imposing mansion, that someone spoke to her.

"Here, girl, are you sick? Move along now."

"Get out of it! Mind your own business. I'll move off when I've a mind to."

"Here—is that—why, it is! Jane Coombes! Whatever's happened to yer face? You look a sight!"

She looked up wearily to find Crews, a man formerly employed as under butler in the Montmorency household, staring at her with his mouth open in shock.

"Thanks for them kind words, Crews—jest what I need—encouragement," she snapped tiredly.

"Look—you come along down to the kitchen. I'll give you a cup of tea or sumthin'," he suggested kindly.

"Oh, yes, I can see the housekeeper's face now when she gets a look at me."

"Never you mind about *her*. It's my word that goes now, Janie me girl. I've moved up in the world, I have, since you saw me last. I'm butler here," he said proudly, "So you just come along and mind your step."

"Oh, I'll do that, never fear," she said with a tiny laugh that was part a sob. As he took her arm and assisted her down the area steps to the back of the house, she wondered if she were crazy. Was she again to be seduced by a butler? But then she pooh-poohed such a notion. Even if Crews had such an idea, there'd be nothin' he could do about carryin' it out in the kitchen of a mansion such as this, no doubt swarmin' with servants. No, no, she thought, she was bein' foolish to think such a thing. Besides, she could not walk another step for a while in any case.

23

She was right about the staff. It was fully as large as the one at the Montmorency's, and they were positively goggling with curiosity at the sight of Crews bringing in this poor, battered-looking creature, seating her in a chair before the fire, and ordering someone to bring her some tea—and the rest to go about their business and sharp about it! They scuttled away, but Jane was aware of wide eyes peeping around the doors and many dawdling, and no doubt unnecessary, chores being absentmindedly performed. She was too exhausted to care. She drank up her tea while Crews bustled away. He came back presently leading a stout, cheerful-looking body who could only be the housekeeper.

"Jane, this 'ere is Mrs. Hawks, the housekeeper."

Jane tried painfully to rise for a curtsy, but the woman pressed her back into the chair.

"Sit still, girl, sit still. Here, you, Mary, take this cup and get back into the scullery and finish those pots and stop standing about gawping like a fish."

Mrs. Hawks pulled up a chair opposite Jane and lowered herself into it. "Now, girl, tell me about it. What's happened to you, eh?"

"I—I—lost me position at the Montmorencys a week ago—"

"For what reason?"

Jane looked her in the eye. " 'Twas me own fault, I'll not be lyin' to you on that."

The woman stared back at her for a moment and then nodded, as though satisfied. "Very well, go on."

"I went to live with me mum's old friend and started lookin'. But seems there's little to be found in the way of jobs these days, and I'd no character."

"Yes, that'd make it hard, to be sure."

"Yes, well then, night before last I was on me way home and met Mr. Leach. You remember him, Crews, from the Montmorency's?" Crews nodded. "Well, he could see I'd had no luck and he asked me to come home to supper with him and his sister. Can you believe it, Crews, he's got hissel' an 'ouse of his own? So I thought 'twas kindly meant, and with his sister and all—well, anyway I went along of him and had a good supper. Then he said as how it was too late for me to go all the way to Cheapside and I must stay there in their spare room, though his sister was none too pleased at his askin' me. I—I—thought 'twould be all right and so I stayed. But he—he—came in durin' the night and—and—I kicked him—and—he—he—beat me

24

and—and—" her voice trailed away in shame, and the tears flowed down her cheeks unheeded.

She could not go on, but she had no need to. Crews and Mrs. Hawks exchanged a look of horrified comprehension.

"How old are you, girl?" said Mrs. Hawks softly.

"F-f-fourteen, ma'am."

"My God!" exclaimed Mrs. Hawks simply.

Crews cleared his throat and turned away, busying himself with poking up the fire to hide his pity.

"Well, anyway," said Jane, recovering and raising her head proudly, "I got away from there as soon as I could walk this mornin'—I'll be all right again in a few days."

Mrs. Hawks studied her for a moment. Then she rose decisively. "Crews. Ask Jem to fetch that extra cot to my room from the attic, if you'll be so good."

He turned to her in surprise and then began to smile. "Yes. At once, Mrs. Hawks, bless you, at once."

He hurried away and Mrs. Hawks put her hand under Jane's arm to assist her from the chair.

"Come along, child. You'll stay with me for a few days, till you recover and then we'll see what we shall see."

"Oh—but—but how can I? Won't the mistress—"

"She'll know nothing of it, and if she did she'd approve. My mistress is Lady Stanier, and she's *real* Quality. Kindest woman you'd ever hope to meet."

While she talked at great length about all the sterling qualities of her mistress, she led Jane through the kitchen and down the hall to her room, a large, comfortably furnished apartment with a cheerful fire and a large upholstered chair before it. She put Jane into this and told her not to move till she was bid, and went to hold the door for two footmen who could be heard shuffling down the hall to Mrs. Hawks' room. The cot was set up in a corner, and a maid came in bearing a load of blankets and sheets and made up the bed under Mrs. Hawks' direction. When all was done and the room was quiet again, Mrs. Hawks told Jane to come along now and get into the bed.

"Oh, Mrs. Hawks—I don't feel I should put you to all this trouble—" Jane began.

"Let's have done with all that nonsense, if you please. Just come along over here and let me worry about all else. I've a daughter of my own about your age, so I know what's needed at a time like this."

"Does she live here with you, Mrs. Hawks?" Jane asked, beginning to fumble with the buttons of her gown.

Mrs. Hawks pushed Jane's hands away and continued the job herself. "Lord love you, no. She's safe in the country, with my old mum. No child of mine would live in this wicked town!" she declared, competently stripping Jane's clothes away. "Oh, my dear Lord," she breathed in disbelief as the full extent of Jane's injuries were revealed to her.

But she would not allow herself to say more. Her lips folded in a grim line, she set about washing the wounds and applying salve to them. She bandaged the legs lightly, then pulled a nightgown, large as a tent, over the girl's head and assisted her into the bed. She plumped up a pile of cushions behind Jane's head and pulled the quilt up under her chin, then sat down heavily on the edge of the bed.

"Now—you mustn't mind me asking, child—but he *did* have his way with you, did he?"

Jane nodded, looking away in shame, before she managed to whisper, "Twice."

"What! You mean in this condition he—well, never mind that—are your courses regular yet?"

"Not often."

"Well, we must hope there's enough confusion in that direction to prevent your becoming pregnant. I'll give you something to drink which might bring you on, but it's in God's hands as you know, and we must trust in Him to help you."

"I'm sure I'm sunk too low in His sight to—" Jane began, her throat tight with tears.

At this Mrs. Hawks put her arms about Jane and drew her tight against her capacious bosom. "Never think it, dearie, never for one moment. You've done no wrong, but was done to, and well He knows it. You must always remember that, child, if any should dare cast a stone."

With a convulsive sob, Jane threw her arms about the woman's neck, and let go all the pent up rage and pain and humiliation she felt. Her sobs became deep and hacking, shaking her whole body, and through it all Mrs. Hawks held her tightly, urging her to cry it out, all the while the tears ran unchecked down her own fat cheeks.

Jane followed the broad back of Mrs. Hawks down the hall and through the green baize door to the front of the house. Her knees trembled and her heart pounded, not from pain or fear now, but only from excitement.

Three days of Mrs. Hawks' ministrations had erased most of the terrible effects of Jane's experience with Mr. Leach. Mrs. Hawks had tended her devotedly and firmly, refusing to allow Jane to move for two days during which she bathed, fed, and doctored the girl lovingly. By the third day this care and Jane's own fourteen-year-old recuperative powers had restored some of the lost sparkle to her eyes and a faint glow of colour in her cheeks. Her swollen lips had regained their former contours and the slashes on her legs had begun to mend, though there was still a faint greenish tinge around the flesh of her right eye, and a soreness and bruising in her jaw as reminders of her ordeal. The real, unhealed, scar, however was in her mind. Sleep, those first two nights, had been disturbed over and over by the same nightmare from which she awoke gasping and struggling to find Mrs. Hawks sitting on the side of the bed trying to soothe her. Jane would explain, in broken sobs, that she dreamed she was being smothered by a huge faceless form which seemed to press the breath from her body. Her waking dreams were nearly as bad, for the terrible scenes played themselves over and over in her mind while she imagined other courses she could have taken, other ways she could have protected herself from his attacks. If only—if only—she saw herself dealing Mr. Leach the same treatment she had dealt Lord Jaspar, and ground her aching jaws in frustration that she had not done so. She repledged herself to vengeance on Mr. Leach again and again.

By the third day the resilience that is the blessing of youth allowed her to forget somewhat these darkling thoughts and respond to the friendliness exhibited by the staff, who came for orders to Mrs. Hawks' room, or to bring trays for the invalid. One and all smiled upon her encouragingly. She could not help but wonder to find so much kindness from an entire household. Mrs. Hawks said that such things started from the top.

"As master and mistress, so will be the staff. I've found it always to be so. If you have coldness and meanness at the top it will seep down belowstairs for sure. Here we've Lady Stanier, and a mean thought never entered that woman's mind, and not one of us who work for her would ever want to do anything she would disapprove of. Them as starts any of that squabbling or backbiting is got rid of at once."

Jane had been allowed to join the servants at table for supper on her third day in the Stanier household, and though there had been some covert glances, she could feel there was nothing sly nor condemnatory in them. There was a general warmth in the gathering and they included her in it so naturally, she lost her initial shyness after only a few moments, and was able to enter the conversation of a group of giggling young upstairs maids her own age. That night her sleep was interrupted only once by the recurring nightmare.

And this morning had come the heart-stopping announcement from Mrs. Hawks that she had spoken to the mistress and there might be a place for Jane with Lady Stanier's sister.

"But I must warn you it's a far piece from Lunnon. Way down in Kent it 'tis, not even in walking distance of a village. Very different from all you've known in your young life so far," Mrs. Hawks warned.

"Oh, please, Mrs. Hawks, I shan't mind that, I promise you. And I shall work very hard, tell m'lady, and I am very strong, really. Never sick a day in me life before this," Jane pleaded urgently.

"I know, child, I know. Now don't get yerself in a taking. Go neaten your hair. M'lady will send for us directly she's had her breakfast."

The summons had finally come, and now she was to meet Lady Stanier, who was found in her morning room, seated before a delicate, rosewood desk. She was a lady well into her middle years, but she was still slim and youthful looking, with an exceedingly gentle expression.

"Here's the young person, m'lady—Jane Coombes."

Lady Stanier turned and acknowledged Jane's curtsy with a warm smile.

"Mrs. Hawks tells me you'd be interested in going to my sister in Kent?"

"'Deed I would, m'lady."

"Have you ever lived in the country?"

"No, m'lady, I'm a Lunnoner, born and bred, but me mam was from Dorset and's told me about it, and I think I should like it fine."

"My sister, Lady Payton, lives very quietly and is situated a great distance from the nearest town. I have sent girls down to her before, but city girls seem to find the country frightening and lonely and leave after only a few weeks," said Lady Stanier warningly.

"M'lady, if they'll but gie' me a bed to mesel' I'll not mind nothin'," Jane replied fiercely.

"A bed to yourself!" exclaimed Lady Stanier in amused astonishment, "well, I can't imagine that would present a problem. Larkwoods contains at least thirty bedrooms, and there can't be more than five in use to my certain knowledge, since the family consists of my sister and her son, and a staff of three elderly retainers."

"Excuse me, m'lady, but would I have the cleanin' of all them rooms? I mean—" Jane, willing and eager as she was for the job, couldn't help experiencing some doubt about the desirability of the position after all.

"Oh good heavens, no!" laughed Lady Stanier. "My sister lives very quietly, you see, and most of the rooms have been closed off for years. Her son is—er—an invalid, so they don't go out or entertain."

"Ah—well then, if you think I'll suit, I'm of a mind to go for sure, m'lady, and grateful to you for the chance."

Lady Stanier studied the girl for a moment, wondering why she hesitated. Was it the girl's youth? Her prettiness? For even through the bruises (and here Lady Stanier paused in her thoughts to direct a most unladylike curse in Leach's direction) it was clear to see that the girl was uncommonly pretty. I wonder where she came by those bones? Lady Stanier mused, never from the mother if she was a country girl from Dorset. Probably the by-blow of some lusty young lord. Good God! she thought suddenly, I wonder *where* in Dorset? There's a branch of my father's family in Dorset. The child might even be related to me. She smiled at the drift of her thoughts, and tried to bring her mind back to order. I wonder if I should mention Sebastian? It would be only fair to warn the poor child. But then she

29

thought of her dear sister, so good, so sacrificing, and the problems she faced trying to keep that great house running and tend to poor Sebastian. No, she decided, I'll say nothing. The girl's young and strong, and will take no harm, after all, and if it proves too much for her she'll come scurrying back to London like all the rest, no doubt.

"Very well, Jane, I'll make the arrangements. How soon would you be able to leave?"

"For all of me, this minute, m'lady," Jane replied, with such a blinding smile that Lady Stanier was quite dazzled. She laughed in genuine pleasure at so much happiness. "We'll make it tomorrow, shall we? That will give me time to write my sister and warn her of your coming. You will want to collect your belongings from your lodgings, I make no doubt."

Jane's smile faded at the thought of going back to the Blodgett's, but she knew she must go, if not to collect her pitifully few belongings, at least to thank Mrs. Blodgett for her kindness. Terrible as the accommodations had been, they had been offered with no hesitation, and if they had not been, Jane would have been in the streets, for she had had no place to turn to besides these friends of her mother's.

"You will of course come back here directly to spend the night, child. I'll send a footman to buy you a seat on the Mail that leaves in the early morning and you can leave directly from here," offered Lady Stanier kindly, guessing the reason for the fading smile.

"Oh—oh—m'lady—" Jane whispered, unable to express her gratitude for this kindness.

"Yes—I see. Very well, off you go. Mrs. Hawks will see to you when you come back and see you safe on the Mail in the morning, so I'll say goodbye to you now and wish you luck."

"Thank you—thank you, m'lady," Jane said, giving her her most respectful curtsy.

She sped through the streets back to Cheapside, joy making it seem a short journey. I'll give the few shillings I have left to Mrs. Blodgett, she decided, for I'll not need them now. This reminded her that she had not asked about wages, nor any other practical question, come to that. But she didn't really care about such things. If only I can have a decent place to sleep and be able to keep mesel' clean, I shan't mind anythin', she thought. And besides I'll have good food there for sure, and all that clean air—oh, I shall like it fine and not miss Lunnon at all.

When she opened the door of the Blodgett's, she was dismayed to find Mr. Blodgett in sole possession of the premises. He sat stolidly at the kitchen table and glowered from under his brows at her, his only greeting a grunt.

"I've come for me things," Jane announced, nervously edging her way past him to the corner of the room where her box stood. "I've found a place and I'm to go straight back. Where's Mrs. Blodgett?"

"She gone off to see her auntie and not back yet, and me wantin' me dinner and waitin' near an hour," he grumbled, swinging about to watch her as she hastily stuffed her things into the box and strapped it closed.

When she turned she found him eyeing her speculatively. His eyes slid around to the door and then back. He grinned, revealing the rotten stumps of teeth long gone, and rose ponderously from the bench and approached her.

"No need to go rushin' back, now is there? Two 'o us could have oursel's a bit 'o fun, eh?" he wheezed insinuatingly, reaching for her.

She flinched back from his hands and from the wave of ale-soaked fumes he breathed over her.

"Don't try your tricks on me, Blodgett. You should be ashamed of yoursel' anyway, and me the same age as your own daughters!"

She pushed roughly past him and started for the door. His hand shot out to catch her wrist as she went by, and without a moment's hesitation she turned and swung her box around in the same movement and hit him with all the force of her residual anger and outrage at Leach, the leather box slamming against the side of Mr. Blodgett's head with a loud thunk and knocking him to the floor.

She turned quickly to the door to make her escape and found Mrs. Blodgett standing there, holding her son by the hand, her two daughters gawking curiously around her shoulders.

"Mrs. Blodgett—I wasn't—he—" she began breathlessly, but then realized the uselessness of any explanation. She fumbled in her reticule, found the few remaining coins there, and held them out to her mother's friend. "I've found a place and must be off back straight away. I only came for me things and to thank you for your kindness."

Mrs. Blodgett's hand came up automatically to accept the coins. She stared at Jane for a moment impassively.

"Well—then take care o'yoursel', young Jane," she finally rasped out gruffly, and stepped back from the doorway for Jane to pass, ruthlessly elbowing her snickering daughters back-ward.

Jane could summon up only a sketch of a smile. Her mind was still in shock, her whole body shaking with reaction.

She turned away and walked up the street without looking back, her breath coming in gasps as she tried to subdue the sobs she could feel rising in her throat.

I must stop this snivellin' all the time, she thought, for I've not all that much to be cryin' for now. After all, I have a situation now, and I've been treated with kindness by everyone for the past few days, and I came to no harm with old Blodgett. The dirty beast, I hope he's got the headache for a week! I wished I'd 'it 'im harder whilst I was about it!

This anger acted as a better restorative than her attempt to reason with herself, and her agitation abated and the colour be-gan to return to her cheeks. She reviewed the last few awful moments, and remembered the satisfying feel of the impact of her box against his head. Her head came up and her lips began to twitch. Ha! she thought, guess I gave as good as I got that time. Me mam would 'a been proud of me!

5

The novelty of actually riding in a carriage cancelled out the terrible discomfort during the first half of Jane's journey; after that the discomfort made itself more compellingly apparent.

Mrs. Hawks had seen to it that they were in the inn yard thirty minutes before the scheduled departure of the London Mail for Maidstone. But Jane hadn't minded. The stir and bus-tle of the busy yard, with coaches arriving and departing, pas-sengers milling about, hostlers unhitching teams and leading up fresh ones, provided her with more entertainment than she'd ever experienced. She ran a feminine but inexperienced eye over the various travelling costumes exhibited by the lady pas-sengers, and picked out two that she would like to have had. Her own shabby black pelisse was now covered with a handsome Paisley shawl presented to her by Lady Stanier. Jane had demurred, thinking it much too grand to accept, but Mrs. Hawks told her not to be such a wet goose.

"Mistress would not have give it had she not meant you to have it, and Lord knows she's well-supplied with shawls, so you'd not be depriving her in any way. Now you just wrap that about your shoulders and be grateful and think no more about it."

Jane did so, and *was* very grateful for its warmth when she stood waiting in the early morning chill, shivering as much with excitement as with cold, and feeling excessively grand in so fine a garment.

She was blissfully unaware of the glances cast in her direction, glances of curiosity and speculation on the part of the women, admiration from the men. The women, estimating the cost of the fine Paisley shawl to the last halfpence, wondering where she could have come by it, dressed as she was in a shabby black pelisse and a bonnet that had seen better days, and being such a young girl—and then there were those bruises on the face. The men saw only the sparkling brown eyes, the full red mouth half-open with excitement and curved up in a delicious smile, and the slim figure.

When the Maidstone carriage was announced, Mrs. Hawks elbowed everyone aside in order to put Jane first into the carriage. A stout lady who felt it her privilege to be the first to ascend snorted indignantly, but Mrs. Hawks ignored her completely. She seated Jane by a window and saw that she had all her possessions before standing aside to allow the other passengers enter. But she didn't leave. She stood beside the window admonishing Jane on how to conduct herself on the journey until the coachman came from the inn and prepared to mount the box. There were already six passengers inside and four on the top, and one of these being a young boy of about fifteen years, Mrs. Hawks began immediately instructing the coachman that he was not to allow himself to be persuaded to give the reins over to this boy under any circumstances.

"The young lady inside has not been well, and I'll not have any harum-scarum young scamp with more hair nor wit thinking he can drive fine as five pence and scaring the daylights out o' my girl, you hear me?"

Mrs. Hawks was well aware of the latest fad among young men of taking over the strings of the coach, after greasing the palm of the coachman, and driving full out to the accompaniment of terrified screams from the passengers. Since these young men had usually had very little experience in driving these heavy coaches there had been many an accident, and she was determined that it should not happen while Jane was aboard. Mrs. Hawks' heart had been wrung by her first sight of the battered young girl, and every motherly instinct had been roused, so that in spite of the shortness of their acquaintance, she now felt quite possessive about Jane, and treated her in the same way she treated her own daughter. Jane, responding to the first love she had received since the death of her mother, felt the tears begin to rise in her throat as the actual moment of separation came, in spite of the thrill of being in a coach.

When Mrs. Hawks turned back to her after admonishing the coachman, Jane leaned forward through the door and threw her arms about the thick neck and kissed Mrs. Hawks's cheek fervently. Mrs. Hawks held her close for a moment, then pushed her firmly back into her seat.

"There now," she said, dashing a rough, red hand across her eyes, "you'll have me bawling in a minute. You be a good girl and mind what's told you and you'll be fine. And if you've the time, mayhap you could send me a word or two on how you make out."

"All right—stand back there, missus," warned the hostler, putting up the step and slamming the carriage door shut. He waved up to the coachman, who flicked his whip expertly over the backs of the horses and the carriage began to move forward. Jane strained forward to wave to the retreating figure of Mrs. Hawks as long as she was in sight. For some moments she was so busy fighting back the tears she was unaware of anything else, but then the glamour of her situation overcame the sadness and she sat back and stared with fascination out the window. She was so grateful for Mrs. Hawks seeing to it that she had this seat and was determined not to give it up under any circumstances. Mrs. Hawks had warned her that the carriage would stop every ten miles or so to bait or to change the horses, at which time the passengers could climb down to stretch their legs and take refreshment, and Jane must make sure not to lose her seat. Jane had decided she wouldn't need anything to eat or drink before the coach arrived in Maidstone, and if she felt near perishing for want of something, she still would not get down when they stopped and take a chance that someone would beat her back to it and then refuse to give it up. She wanted to see everything there was to see, to experience the whole trip to its fullest. Food she would, she hoped, have every day for the rest of her life, but who knew when her next carriage ride might come along?

She watched eagerly now as the carriage made its way south out of London, revealing sections of the city she'd never seen before, and then finally, to more sparsely settled areas before reaching the open countryside. She was so rapt by all she was seeing out the window she paid no attention to the passengers, until she gradually became aware of a pressure against her leg. Glancing down she saw a thick male thigh, so tightly encased in nankeen pantaloons as to seem in danger of bursting the cloth, pressed firmly against her own.

She pulled her legs as far away as they would go and turned a look of open inquiry at the man next to her. His red face flushed even rosier, and he coughed, looked away, and withdrew his leg, glancing around the carriage covertly to see if this had been observed.

He met the cold, beady glare of the stout lady sitting opposite, who stared him down before transferring her gaze to Jane. Jane met her glance squarely, staring back until the woman sniffed and turned her head away.

Jane glanced at the other passengers now, but found them less interesting than the scenery.

There were four gentlemen, the gimlet-eyed lady, and herself. The perspiring young man with the stout and wandering thigh was the youngest of the men, the others being middle-aged to elderly, and none showed any tendency to friendliness to any of the others. It seemed strange to Jane for six people to be in such uncomfortable, even embarrassingly intimate, contact and yet remain so aloof. The seats were really only meant to hold two people, so there was little the three people squeezed into each one could do to avoid their fellow passengers. Aside from this, the state of some parts of the road caused an almost constant bouncing and jouncing.

When the first halt came, Jane, though she remained in her seat, managed to refresh herself just from the relief of the pressure of another body jolting against her own and from the cessation of all movement. They were in a small country town and the sweet early spring air flowed into the open door of the carriage, and she became aware of the unusual quiet around her. She sat in a trance for a moment listening to birds twittering and singing from the hedge.

Everywhere she looked there were trees, all wearing the earliest spring leaves like pale green lace waving in the light breeze and the pale lemony sunlight. The world seemed new-minted as of this very morning; a fresh beginning, to match her own new beginning. I'm startin' over, she thought, and the world is startin' with me, and now everythin' will be different. I shall be happy in the country, I know I shall, and safe! No relative of Lady Stanier could be bad or allow anyone bad to be in her household, so everyone will be kind as they were at Lady Stanier's, and I shall work very hard and be a great help to the lady and her poor, sick little boy.

While she was thinking these virtuous thoughts the passengers began to enter the carriage again and after a short wait, the coachman emerged from the taproom of the inn and with a great boisterous laugh, clapped the innkeeper on the shoulder and climbed back up to his perch and they were off again.

At the noon stop the stout young man climbed over her legs to step out last and then turned back.

"Forgive me, Miss—er—" he doffed his hat and waited expectantly, but Jane remained silent. "—well, I was only going to say that you really should step down and have a bit of luncheon and stretch your legs."

She stared at him suspiciously. After the incident of earlier in the journey she had no trust in him anyway, and now it seemed he was trying to lure her out of her window seat. No doubt he had been coveting it all along. Well, he'd find she was not such a pea goose to fall for such blandishment.

"I've no wish for anythin'," she replied coldly and looked away.

The young man was so taken aback by this rudeness that he stood for a full minute gaping at her before pulling himself together and turning away into the inn.

Jane was not aware of the rudeness. She was protecting herself. After all, the man had dared to be lewd with her in a public conveyance, something she was sure he'd never have tried if she'd been Quality. Since he didn't pay her wages and had not earned her courtesy by any of his own, she felt no qualms about treating him as an enemy.

In fact, she was beginning to feel that most men were her enemies. Oh, of course there were exceptions, like Mr. Crews, but for the most part her experience with men had been all of one kind: leering looks, grabbing hands, and outright attack. Jane had till now been proud of her precociously blossoming body, and romantic enough to hope that love would come her way someday, and with it the opportunity to explore the sensuality she felt in herself.

But now she felt differently. She envied Lilly, the fat lump of a girl who was a kitchen maid at the Montmorency's, and Rosey at the Stanier's who was so painfully thin and chinless. They would never have to suffer the humiliation that had been Jane's this past week. Of course, neither of them would have dared to try on the mistress's robe in the first place, but if they had, you could be sure m'lady's randy young brother wouldn't have bothered himself to tear it off them! So they would never have found themselves in the streets because of a well-formed figure, and prey to the likes of Leach. Well, she hoped she'd learned her lesson once for all. Any man she had to do with in the future would need to prove himself innocent of lust before he should be her friend.

She looked up from these stormy thoughts to find the young man standing at the steps holding a steaming cup of coffee and a small meat pie in a napkin.

"I took the liberty—er—I thought as you wouldn't—well, I brought something out to you as you wouldn't come in. You must have something, you know."

She looked into the earnest pale blue eyes and seemed to see there an apology, and her own warm heart relented. She smiled warmly and took the food from his hands.

"Very kind of you, I'm sure, sir. That looks tasty, I must say."

He mopped his round, perspiring face and grinned as he watched her bite eagerly into the pie.

"Tell me Miss—er—"

"Coombes."

"Miss Coombes—why will you not get out of the carriage?"

"Mrs. Hawks said as how it would be best to stay put, else I might lose my window seat."

This simple explanation caused him to smile. "I'll admit it has happened, but no one would be so ungallant as to take the seat a pretty girl expressed her preference for, I assure you."

"Oh," was all she said. She finished her pie and drank her coffee and handed the cup back to him with another 'thank you.'

She would like to have said more to him in a friendlier tone after his kindness and compliment, but was tongue-tied with confusion. She wondered if she'd ever understand folks. Here was this man behavin' so slylike with her, as he'd never have

37

done if she'd been a lady, then next moment goin' out of his way to do her a kindness and speakin' all polite.

Then young master at the Montmorency's who'd almost surprised her into acquiescence, then grabbed her so bold when she'd tried to escape, and ended by trying to give her a gold coin in a shame-faced sort of way. She thought again of his look when she'd thrown the coin back into his face.

Well, not exactly in his face, she thought with a stifled giggle. But immediately she felt ashamed of herself. Her mam had told her that such a blow as she'd dealt young master was the most painful one a man could have, and Jane had never deliberately hurt anyone before. And certain sure, though he'd deserved it, he was not to be blamed entirely. She could not forget her own voluptuous acceptance of his embrace for the first moments, as though she were hypnotized. He'd been so gentle, and oh! such a pretty lad he was it was little wonder she'd forgotten herself for the moment. She shivered slightly as she remembered the soft kisses on her throat, the hands so—so reverently cupping her breasts—

Pooh! I'm naught but a clunch to sit here moonin' over a handsome phizz—when he's no more nor a scarce breeched calfling with not enough gumption to stand up and take his medicine as I had to do, she thought self-righteously. I'll think no more of him.

During all these ponderings, the passengers had returned and the coach was under way again. She began to think that the journey might never end. She rested her head wearily against the side of the coach, and in spite of her resolve to miss nothing of this journey, dozed off.

She came awake with a start as the door was suddenly flung open, to realize they had arrived at yet another inn, and all the passengers were stirring about, ready to step down.

"Where are we now?" she asked, looking about in a daze.

"We're at Maidstone, Miss Coombes," replied the stout young man.

"Good heavens, so soon?"

"It only seems so because you slept so soundly."

"If you don't mind having this conversation elsewhere, young man, the rest of us would be glad to be able to get down now," snapped the elderly lady waspishly.

Muttering a confused apology, he hastily climbed down and turned to offer Jane his hand in assistance. She took it gratefully, for she still felt half-asleep.

"Are you being met, Miss Coombes?"

"In the mornin'. A room has been bespoke for me here," she said proudly, "so I'll bid you good-bye now, and thank you for all your kindness on the journey."

He lifted his hat and bowed politely, and she turned and made her way into the inn, much gratified by having everyone see him behaving to her in so courteous a way, as though she were Quality.

She was taken up to her room, and though it was very small, she was enchanted with it. It was the first time in her life she'd ever had a room—a whole room!—entirely to herself. She bolted the door to make it more definitely *hers*. The landlady had told her that her supper would be sent up to her on a tray as had been ordered, and Jane marvelled that so much care was being taken of her by strangers. Lady Stanier's sister was surely the same good soul as Lady Stanier. There needed no further proof that Jane would be happy at Larkwoods with Lady Payton and her little son and the three kindly old family retainers.

The old family retainer who called for her in the morning, however, could hardly have been described as kindly. He had not descended from his perch to help her into the carriage, nor acknowledged her cheerful greeting with more than a grunt.

Jane subsided onto the seat and placed her box beside her. Well, she thought, I'm sure it makes no difference to me if he wants to be grumpy. Maybe he disliked being sent all this way to fetch a maid. But then Lady Stanier said she'd sent down several girls to her sister, so I should think he'd be used to it by now. Still, I won't pay any attention. Nothin' will be bad now, on such a day as this! She looked about with satisfaction at the rolling Kentish countryside. I shall certainly live happily ever after in such a place as this, she thought, her heart swelling with gratitude.

6

The house, when it finally burst upon her view, caused her to gasp. The curving road after they'd entered the imposing gates, was tree-lined, but did not totally obscure the view of low rolling countryside, with artfully composed copses scattered about. There were several deer grazing quietly at one point, and later a herd of sheep. The road swept around a curve and there was the house! A palace, she thought at first, so large it seemed.

The huge three-storied main body of the house was further enlarged by two wings going back at each side. The stones of the facade were a warm honey colour in the sunshine, and the twinkling panes of glass in the windows seemed to smile a welcome.

No such welcome met her, however, when the carriage pulled up at a door at the end of one of the wings, and the taciturn coachman pointed wordlessly at the door, indicating her direction. She climbed down and reached for her box. The coachman drove off and she was alone. She straightened her shoulders and knocked firmly on the door. After a moment it opened to reveal a portly, red-cheeked old woman with white hair peeping from beneath her cap.

"You'll be Coombes, then?" she said abruptly.

"Yes, that's right, Jane Coombes, sent by Lady Stanier in Lunnon," Jane replied with an open, almost coaxing, smile.

But the woman seemed immune to charm. She stepped back and made a small, economical motion with her head to indicate that Jane should enter. She closed the door carefully, and moved past Jane to waddle ponderously up the hall. There was nothing for Jane to do but follow.

After knocking softly on a door, the woman opened it and announced, "Here's the girl, Mrs. Plummer."

She turned and motioned Jane to enter, and came in after her. Jane was confronted with another elderly lady seated before a fire mending linen. The woman finished setting a very small careful stitch before looking Jane up and down with her faded blue eyes. There was no hostility in her glance, but there was a certain guardedness in her expression, as though determined to give nothing away.

Jane came forward and bobbed her a polite curtsy, and again smiled.

"You're Mrs. Plummer? I'm Jane Coombes. You'll be the housekeeper?"

"Yes. And this is Mrs. McKirk, the cook. She'll show you to your room. It's just down the hall. We're all in this wing. Are you hungry?"

"Oh, yes, ma'am, very peckish, 'deed. Must be all the fresh air in these parts, but it seems hours since me breakfast."

"Very well. Mrs. McKirk will give you something and then you can go to your room and change before I take you to m'lady."

"Change? What should I change to, ma'am?"

"I've put out a gown and apron in your room from the last girl we had. You're of a size, I think, so it should fit you."

Mrs. Plummer turned back to her torn bed sheet dismissively, and Jane turned as she heard Mrs. McKirk opening the door. What was the matter with these folks, anyway, she wondered? They acted for all the world as though they grudged her a few words, not to speak of a smile or a friendly look. If I'm to be takin' all the work off their backs, seems like they should show a little more friendly than this, she thought resentfully.

But she couldn't quarrel with the generosity of the portion of cold sliced ham and bread and butter Mrs. McKirk set before her. Evidently they didn't begrudge food, so she wouldn't starve at any rate.

The room she was taken to when she'd polished off every last crumb of her meal was not in any way like the room she'd shared at the Montmorency's. It was fair-sized and had a large window through which the afternoon sun streamed cheerfully. The bed, when she bounced on it experimentally, promised comfort and the linen was clean.

She hung her gown and pelisse on pegs behind a curtain in the corner and put on the dark blue gown. It was somewhat tight across the bosom, but otherwise fit fairly well. There was a white cap and apron and when she had the costume on, she returned to the kitchen to await Mrs. Plummer's summons.

She heard a bell tinkle presently from the hall outside the kitchen and jumped up nervously, smoothing down her apron and checking her cap. This would be m'lady, no doubt. Will I suit? Will she be as kind as her sister?

She heard Mrs. Plummer's steps in the hallway and went eagerly to the door. When Mrs. Plummer saw her she motioned Jane to follow and turned to go up the hall to the front of the house.

But before they reached the doorway that obviously led to the front, Mrs. Plummer turned aside and went up the backstairs.

Above stairs, the broad, carpeted hallway was dim and silent, lined with closed doors. Jane half-expected to hear the sound of the little boy laughing, or even crying, but it was still and hushed as a cathedral.

Lady Payton's apartment was at the very front of the house overlooking the drive. When they were bid to enter, Jane gaped at the elegance of the room before her, all furnished in white and gold and blue silk.

Lady Payton lay on a chaise before the deep windows with a book in her hand, and as she looked up inquiringly, a small honey-coloured bundle of fur that had been nestled beside her erupted from the chaise and leaped down, barking ferociously.

Jane backed away in terror, but Mrs. Plummer only reached down, lifted the dog in her arms, and put her hand around its muzzle.

"Here's the young person, m'lady."

"Oh yes, Jane Coombes. Welcome to Larkwoods, child."

"Oh—thank you, m'lady," Jane said, giving her a deep curtsy and a large grin in return for the kindest words she'd heard since she'd arrived.

Lady Payton smiled back warmly, though her heart sank when she saw how pretty the girl was. This one won't last even as long as the others, she thought, with no young men around to flirt with. Such a girl would be used to a lot of attention.

"I'm afraid you'll find us very dull here after London," she said, resignation tinging her voice, for it would be nice, she thought, to have this pretty child to liven up the household.

"Oh, not to worry, m'lady, I shall find plenty to do. This is a very big house to have the cleanin' of, and then I can help with the poor little boy."

Lady Payton stared at her speechlessly for a moment, trying to cope with her bewilderment. She turned to Mrs. Plummer, but saw immediately that there was no enlightenment to be had from that quarter, for Mrs. Plummer looked as totally befuddled as Lady Payton felt.

"Coombes, I'm afraid dear Caroline did not explain to you your duties. You will not be required to clean. We have women come in every day from the village for that. What you will be doing is taking care of me."

"Oh, m'lady!" Jane gasped, "do you mean I'm to be your abigail?"

"Well, yes, though of course I go about very little, so I'm afraid it will be more in the nature of waiting on me."

Jane could only stare at her, eyes like saucers, speechless with happiness at this unexpected rise in status that was being handed to her. From backstairs maid to lady's maid in one step! Why, she'd be almost on a par with the housekeeper in the servants' hall. If only her mam were alive to know this glory.

The glow of self-importance combined with the determination to justify Lady Payton's trust in her, filled her mind to the exclusion of all else for the first few days. She was awake every morning long before it was necessary, and waiting in the kitchen for Lady Payton to ring for her morning chocolate. After that she helped her into a morning robe, brushed her hair and helped arrange it, and cleaned the room. Later she carried up m'lady's breakfast tray, for Lady Payton never left her room in the mornings. On some days, when she was not feeling well, for she suffered from heart spasms, she kept to her room all day. But when she felt well enough, she dressed and came down in the early afternoon to read, or play the pianoforte, or receive a visit from a friend who lived nearby, and seemed to be her only caller, Miss Angela Gilbert, daughter of the parson.

In the late afternoon Lady Payton went to her room to change for dinner, which she ate in solitary splendour, attended by Jane. Jane supposed the invalid son to be either away or too ill to leave his room. She could not bring herself to ask, for at any mention of him Lady Payton's eyes would become sad, and sometimes she would whisper "Poor Sebastian," in such heart-rending tones that Jane would feel the tears start in her own eyes.

Neither did she feel that she could ask Mrs. Plummer or Mrs. McKirk. They were still as unbending and cool to her as they had been on her first day, and Jane was too proud to push her friendship on them. She had tried to be nice, now they must come to her, she thought defiantly. It may be they're jealous that I'm young and strong and close to the mistress all the time. Well, let them be, they'll not have the satisfaction of seein' they bother me! She was not, however, rude or pert to them, feeling that such behaviour was not consummate with her new dignity. She maintained a cool courtesy at all times.

When Lady Payton retired for the night, Jane helped her to undress, brushed out her hair again, and helped her into bed. Then she took away the gown to clean and iron it, and the delicate undergarments to wash by hand.

Another duty that she took upon herself was to walk Lady Payton's spaniel. She had never been near a dog before in her life, but she found that she liked to play with it and fondle its soft, silky coat.

Lady Payton, accompanied by Jane, sometimes took the dog out herself when she felt equal to a walk and if the weather was good, but mostly it fell to Jane to do so. And Wellington, the spaniel, clearly preferred Jane's company, for she ran with him over the smooth green grass, or threw sticks for him.

This was her solitary chore today, and she romped over the grass with him breathlessly, both of them infected by the gaiety of the spring day. The wind playfully tossed the new young leaves on the trees and flirted with the crocuses and daffodils in the flower beds, as though trying to say, "Come on then, look alive—it's spring!"

It certainly said that to Jane, who was so filled with restless exuberance she couldn't stand still for a moment, and Wellington obviously felt something, for he galloped around her in circles, ears streaming straight back, positively grinning with happiness. Suddenly he veered out of his circle and went tearing off around the far corner of the house, tossing her a look of mischief over his shoulder before he disappeared, in a clear invitation to catch him if she could. She giggled delightedly and ran after him, only to stop short at the corner.

There, stretched before her, was the entire wing of the house heretofore unglimpsed. Lord Payton's rooms—forbidden territory. Gasping for breath after her wild exercise, she peered around the corner in time to see Wellington skitter out of sight beneath a trellised arbor of vines built out over what must be an entryway. The vines were still in very young leaf and sparse enough to allow her to see they covered a flagstone terrace, two shallow steps, and the darkness of an open doorway.

She stood debating furiously with herself. Should she just go and have a casual peek? Busy and happy in her new duties as she had been this first week, she had not given the little boy more than a passing thought from time to time, mostly just before she fell asleep at night. It had somehow become fixed in her mind that the child must be away from home, perhaps being treated somewhere, for it didn't seem possible he could be there and never be allowed to visit his mother in her room or come into the rest of the house, unless, of course, he were completely bedridden, in which case his mother would spend most of her time with him, which she did not. Therefore it must be true the boy was away from home. Therefore—there could be no harm in just taking a peek, the very tiniest peek, into that temptingly open doorway beneath the arbor.

She advanced slowly toward it, calling, "Wellington! Bad dog, come back 'ere!"

She saw his honey-coloured head nose out of the doorway in response and then immediately disappear again, so obviously playing a game with her that she laughed aloud and lost all her nervousness. She walked boldly up to the doorway and peered inside. After the bright sunlight the room seemed very dark and she could see little at first. The first thing to take shape before her eyes was a very large round object in a sort of ornately carved cradle and she was drawn to it without any conscious volition of her own. She stared at it, a blue ball covered with strange shapes in various colours, and reached out a fingertip to touch it tentatively. It moved, causing her to snatch back her finger, but then curiosity overcame caution and she pushed at it lightly. It turned slowly, revealing other odd shapes on its surface. A toy or game of some sort for young master, she thought wonderingly, and pushed it again, harder. It spun around and she giggled softly, before turning away to see what other strange amusements were provided for the children of the rich. She clucked disapprovingly at the wild disarray of papers and books strewn over a long table; not much fun there, she thought pityingly. Cruel, really, to plague the poor sick little fellow with lessons.

The room was thickly carpeted, the furniture covered in dark red, the walls paneled between shelves of books, everything dark and still, but with a strange air of expectancy, as though only momentarily empty of life. Her eyes were drawn back to the door, a French double door standing full open to the bright day without, framing an enchanting view of velvety grass, rosebeds beyond, and further away the low rolling hills.

Just to one side of the doorway was a strange long black pole atop three legs—another toy, she supposed. She walked around it curiously, stopping to look into the end pointed out the door, but there was nothing to be made of it—a bit of glass and darkness inside. She moved to the other end and applied her eye—and jumped back in alarm when she saw a life-sized, moving, picture of the old coachman who'd fetched her from Maidstone busily staking rosebushes. With infinite caution she peeked in again, and sure enough, he was there plain as day! She stood up and stared at the contraption with awe.

Then she heard a low, rippling masculine chuckle that caused her to leap around with a shriek. There, standing in the shadows of a doorway to another room, was the child.

"Oh, you naughty boy to come on me so sudden like! Nearly the death of me, you was, my heart jumped so!" she gasped.

He stared at her silently for a full minute, and she studied him nervously, wondering if he'd be angry at her trespass and report her to Lady Payton. He was a full head shorter than herself and seemed very slim, though she could see little of him in the deep gloom of that corner of the room, especially after looking out into the sunlight. His complexion seemed to glow a greeny-white out of the shadows, his eyes only two spots of glitter in dark hollows.

His silence unnerved her and she finally decided to take matters into her own hands. She bobbed a little curtsy and launched into an explanation of her presence. "I'm sure I beg your pardon for comin' in like this, m'lord. 'Twere Wellington, you see, the silly creature. He *would* run away and I came to fetch him. I'm mindin' him, see, for m'lady, she bein' poorly. Anyway, I—I hope I didn't disturb you."

He sketched a brief bow in acknowledgment of her apology, but still didn't speak. Uppity little devil, she thought, her temper flaring suddenly, and as quickly dying as she remembered he was an invalid. Besides, she admonished herself, I've to remember my position, and show I've some manners even if he hasn't. She pulled herself up and smiled condescendingly down at him. "I'll go along now, m'lord, if you'll excuse me, and leave you to your games." She raised her voice to call flutingly, "Wellington! Come along now."

Wellington chose to ignore this invitation and another long, embarrassing moment of silence ensued. She clearly saw, in spite of the darkness where he stood, Lord Payton's eyebrow quirk up derisively and felt angry colour warm her face. But before she could react further he snapped his fingers and Wellington appeared as if by magic from the deeper darkness of the room behind Lord Payton and trotted up to Jane. She swooped him up and turned to the door.

Then for the first time Lord Payton spoke, in a startlingly deep voice that caused her to turn quickly to see who was speaking.

"That was a telescope, an instrument for seeing things at a great distance. I take it you've never seen one before?"

She shook her head speechlessly. It *was* the boy speaking, she thought confusedly, for she could see his mouth moving and there was no one else there, but it was a disconcerting voice for a boy. Then he was moving slowly toward her, and as he came into the light from the doorway his face eerily transposed itself before her very eyes from a child's to a man's.

It was a harsh, strong face, the cheekbones jutting almost cruelly against the thin, taut skin, lines deeply etched into the forehead and from nose to mouth. His eyes glowed with a feverish brilliance from deep, shadowed hollows and his mouth was a grim line. However, it was not an unhandsome face, for all its evidence of suffering. The incongruity was in the size of the head, too large for the thin, childish neck and the slight, boy's body.

Jane, brought up among servants trained never to betray feelings, was able to look him squarely in the eye with a blank, noncommittal stare. Her mind, however, was a chaotic jumble of flashing thoughts and emotions, few of which had to do with his appearance. Rather, she was rapidly running through her mind all that she had said to him under the illusion she was addressing a child, and whether he would be angry enough at her for so addressing him as to ask his mother to get rid of her. Had she—dear God, *had* she—called him a naughty boy when he first came to the doorway? Perhaps he hadn't heard her. Nonsense, of course he must have. Should she apologise? No, better say nothin' more.

Jane, in common with most of her fellow creatures, was more concerned with events as they affected herself than with the effect they might be having on the other person. It was not that she was unaware of his unusual appearance, but the few seconds allowed for her to readjust her ideas did not leave her any time to feel horror or pity, or any of the other emotions usually inspired by the abnormal.

Before she could resolve on the course of action most beneficial to herself, he had reached the telescope and was pointing out the door. "There, on that hillside to the left, can you see

47

that cow, a sort of brown and white spot just past the very large tree?''

She nodded wordlessly. He swung the instrument around, peered through it, made an adjustment with a knob, and then moved back. ''Now, just bend down and look through there and you'll see it as clearly as though it were standing just outside there on the grass,'' he instructed her.

She did as she was told, gasped, raised her head to stare at the hillside unaided, and then bent to the glass again. Finally she turned to him, her eyes wide.

''That's—that's magic, that is—and here's me thinkin' it were but a toy!'' she exclaimed.

''Yes, I suppose you could say it's a toy,'' he replied bitterly.

She flushed with shame at what she'd revealed to him and dropped her eyes, but he shrugged and moved away. ''This 'toy' is a globe. Do you know what that is?'' She shook her head, unable to speak or look up. ''Well, come and learn, girl, come and learn,'' he ordered impatiently.

For the next fifteen minutes he explained the globe to her, and gradually she forgot her embarrassment as she became fascinated by this first glimpse of the world and began asking questions.

Wellington, patience at an end, wriggled to signal that he'd learned enough about the world and required to be put down, whereupon he ran straight out the door into the sunlight.

''Oh—Wellington—wait, wait! Sir, I must go after him—I—I thank you for tellin' me about—Asia and—and all that.'' She bobbed a quick curtsy, ''Good day to you, m'lord,'' she gasped and whisked out the door.

Wellington gave Jane another brisk run before he scampered back to the front door, ready for a nap on the chaise with his mistress.

Jane, even as she ran, was preoccupied with thoughts of Lord Payton. No longer was it possible to think of him as a child, for in spite of his small stature he was clearly a man, and not so very young a man at that. His emaciated face was lined like a man of—of forty! And those dark shadows like bruises beneath his eyes! What ever could the poor soul be suffering from to give him that look, to have kept the man in the body of a child?

Well, she thought resolutely, no doubt I'll learn if I'm meant to. Meantime I'd best face m'lady and make me confession before she learns the story from 'im. In her heart, however, she knew very well he would not go complaining to his mother of her maid's intrusion into his private domain. How she knew this she could not have said.

7

Jane came awake very slowly, aware of and enjoying each degree of returning consciousness, especially the brief, final moment of hushed expectancy—then—yes, now! Her eyelids fluttered open just in the instant of the sun's rim appearing over the distant hills, a moment of such happiness for her that her sleeping mind made sure she woke in time for it.

She threw back the covers and ran barefooted to the window, blinking sleepily. The vault of the sky, a tender, almost pearly green, slowly warmed to coral. The gray, dew-soaked-predawn countryside waited in hushed expectancy, then blushed as rosily as a young maiden at her first compliment. The birds, as at a signal, began their chirping, which built steadily into an ecstatic greeting to another fine day.

Jane's sleep-warm body shivered deliciously in the cool morning air as she leaned as far out the window as she could, fervently breathing in the scented freshness. Like food it is, this air, she thought. Oh, Mam, if only you could have had some of this. She wondered, not for the first time since she'd been here, how her mother, brought up in the country, had been able to bear her life in London, with its smothering, fetid air and never a glimpse of a sunrise. I'll never go back, she vowed, not if they'll keep me. I'll do anythin'—learn to cook and keep the house good, so when the old ones die, I can do everythin' for m'lady, and she'll never send me away. And I'll listen carefully and learn to speak refinedlike and learn Quality ways so she won't be ashamed of me. And I'll make them old 'uns belowstairs like me, she decided fiercely, this very day. I won't sit at supper with all them frozen faces another day.

Her earlier vow to make them come to her was losing its

sharp edge under the strain of having no one to talk to. Of course Lady Payton spoke to her and was invariably kind, but Jane was still far too shy to let her tongue have its usual, carefree way. As for Lord Payton, the nearest person to her in age at Larkwoods, her chances of seeing him again were very small—and the Lord knows he ain't exactly a chatterbox, she thought with a grin. Of course, he'd plenty to say about globes and such, but he might as well be talkin' to hissel', for all I could make of them long words, though, of course, it was good fun to listen to, and most polite of 'im to presume I'd know what he was goin' on about.

For a moment, as she stood there in the morning sun, she wished she could have those moments to live through again, only this time she'd have her wits about her and really take in everything he said, and learn something. It was only since those few moments with Lord Payton that she'd become aware of the bottomless pit of her ignorance.

How must it feel to know so much as he does, she wondered enviously? Would one's head feel heavy carryin' about so much? She pondered at the possible size of his brain, which lead her to the inevitable conclusion that her own must be no bigger than a pea. I wonder if he knows how lucky he is to have been given all that learnin', she mused.

Then, with a shock, she remembered the man. Full grown, practically middle-aged, and no more than four feet tall, not to speak of bad health and a great deal of pain if those hollow, shadowed eyes were anythin' to go by. Lucky was *not* how he'd feel, no fear, bless him. No, I don't envy 'im, she thought, her hands automatically running down her strong, healthy body, but I don't pity 'im either!

He's had all this to look at, and all them books and that, and never had to work till he dropped, and for all his size he's a man and never had to be knocked about and forced to have a great, hairy body on top of 'im, doin' dreadful—

She felt a sob catch in her throat and her eyes filled suddenly with tears as the searing memory of Leach caught her before she could push it back, as she had so far been able to do. Oh God, don't let me be carryin' his seed inside of me!

There it was. The nightmarish fear she'd been holding at bay, rising now in a silent shriek to heaven. She sank slowly to her knees and resting her head on the window ledge, let the tears have their way at last, unchecked, crying out her fear in great wrenching sobs.

Below her Lord Payton was just passing on his usual early morning walk around the house. This was his only exercise, taken before the rest of the household was awake, and before any possibility of a chance encounter with unexpected callers. He paused at the sound of crying coming from somewhere above his head. He didn't look up. There was no need to speculate on the source of the sound. It was a young girl crying, and there was only one young girl at Larkwoods. He walked softly away.

When Jane brought Lady Payton her morning chocolate, all traces of her early tears were erased and her usual sunny smile greeted Lady Payton. Wellington, his feathery tail waving ecstatically, jumped down from the foot of the bed to put his cold nose against her ankle in greeting, causing Jane to giggle.

What a blessing, thought Lady Payton, to be greeted by this cheerful, light-footed young creature first thing in the morning, rather than poor Mrs. Plummer, creaking painfully in with the tray trembling precariously in her rheumaticky clutch, her old creased face screwed up with the effort.

In spite of her son's distaste for having any new servants in the house, Lady Payton had been forced to search for a young maid who could take the stairs. They'd tried the village girls from nearby, but though willing enough, they were clumsy and forever breaking china and spilling things, and worst of all, making the evil eye sign every time they caught a glimpse of Sebastian as though he were a devil. Then Lady Payton had written to her sister in London who'd sent down several girls, whey-faced and shifty-eyed every one of them, who'd pilfered the silver and complained about being so far from any company or entertainment, and sneaked around trying to catch a look at Sebastian as though he were a freak. None had lasted more than a month before she'd had to pack them off back to London.

Coombes, however, was a very different matter. Lady Stanier had written of the dreadful ordeal the poor child had been through, and Lady Payton could not prevent herself from eyeing the girl's waistline every morning, even though she knew very well it was far too soon to show, even if the girl did turn out to be with child. Lady Payton prayed every night that this would not be so for the girl's sake, though she had decided that if Coombes would stay she'd keep her, illegitimate baby and all. She thought fleetingly of holding the baby and then firmly pushed the thought away before it led to the depression that always washed over her when she was forced to acknowledge there would be no more babies at Larkwoods, no more for her, not the possibility of fat little grandchildren to tumble about and be swooped up for kissing.

She forced herself to turn a smiling face to Coombes—bah! she thought—Coombes! I can't bear to call such a pretty child such a hard ungiving name as that.

"I've decided to call you Jane from now on. Such a pretty name. Will you allow me?" she said gaily.

"Oh—m'lady! I should be ever so glad. I don't care for bein' called Coombes, mesel'. So—so cold it sounds, all bare like that I've always thought. How happy you are this mornin', m'lady. It must be the beautiful mornin' as makes us all so lighthearted."

"Are you lighthearted today, Jane?"

"Today and every blessed day since I come here. Who could be unhappy in such a place as this?"

"Some of us manage it, I fear," said Lady Payton, her smile fading and her eyes clouding over.

"Ah now, m'lady, don't think on it this mornin'. Here, I've brought you a serprize. Mrs. Plummer give me a letter for you."

"A letter? Who—oh, it's from Sebastian," said Lady Payton, taking the note and eagerly breaking the seal.

Jane's eyes widened in surprise. He wrote his mother *letters*, and him only on the other side of the 'ouse, she thought wonderingly. How could a person ever understand the ways of Quality? Then suddenly her nerve ends all jumped as it occurred to her what he might be writing to Lady Payton *about*. Oh lor, *why* didn't I tell her about goin' into his room yesterday?

She had put off her confession, trying to gather nerve for the ordeal and trying to think of how best to explain the way of it. She had determined this morning that she'd make a clean breast of the whole thing today and *not* put the entire blame on Wellington as she'd been inclined to do. Her hand went down to Wellington to pull his long, silky ears and scratch his soft head in apology.

"Oh! My goodness," exclaimed Lady Payton, her voice fluttering excitedly, "my son will dine with me tonight. He must be feeling very much better. Oh, Jane, he has had such a bad turn these past few weeks. I've been quite frightened."

"There now, and he's all better and takin' his dinner with

you. We must look out your prettiest gown and see there's no wrinkles in it.''

"Yes, the mauve silk, I think, and you must do my hair very specially—he always notices things like that. And you must make sure your cap and apron are fresh and—oh dear—child, there is something I must—'' she faltered, a stricken look in her eyes.

"Oh, I'll do that for sure, m'lady," Jane interrupted hastily, well aware of Lady Payton's sudden realization that she must prepare her new maid for the shock of her first look at Lord Payton. Jane was also clever enough to grasp this opportunity to make her confession under the very best conditions. Lady Payton would be so relieved that the worst part was past, she would not be so angry, or think Jane nosy and untrustworthy.

Jane explained the circumstances of her meeting with Lord Payton and of his kindness in explaining to her about the globe and the telescope. "I could see he'd not been well—such dark shadows round his eyes, just like me mam when she was ailin' so bad and couldn't sleep proper at night. But now he's well enough to come to dinner! I had wondered about that, though I know 'tis no business of mine to be concernin' mesel' about such things. I thought he must be away havin' treatments and such. Course, I'd heard from Lady Stanier as he was sickly. I even—'' she stopped abruptly as she realized her tongue had been clacking away for a considerable length of time and that Lady Payton was smiling at her in a bemused sort of way. "I—beg pardon, m'lady. You must think I'm a great gawk. Sometimes I forget me place,'' she said, hanging her head in shame.

"Not at all, my dear. It's such a pleasure to hear someone talking without complaining for a change. All of us here seem to do such a lot of that. Mrs. McKirk because Sebastian and I eat so little of her good cooking, Mrs. Plummer because she can't take the stairs anymore and about the new maids and—''

"Me? Mrs. Plummer complains about me?'' Jane broke in rudely, her temper rising.

"Not you, Jane. But before you we had a number of unsatisfactory young women and the staff, eager to make it pleasant for them, went out of their way to be friendly. They found their efforts were wasted and have grown wary of repeating their mistake.''

"They shall be singin' my praises before long, m'lady,'' said Jane impulsively with a grin.

"They will?"

"Oh yes, I've decided on it," Jane replied firmly. "I can see they'er good folks, really, even though they're so cold and unfriendlylike, and when they see I'm not like all those others they'll treat me different."

"You truly think you will want to stay here, Jane?"

"You'll have to have me dragged away, kickin' and screamin', if you'll be rid of me, m'lady," Jane said simply. "Now, it's time you were up and out into that good sunshine. Wellington wants his walk and it'll do you good," she ordered bossily, removing the chocolate cup from her mistress's hand, and throwing back the covers.

Lady Payton meekly swung her feet to the floor and rose.

By the dinner hour they had both reached a fever pitch of excitement; Jane at the thought of serving dinner to this mysterious man who would undoubtedly be watching her every move with a coldly critical eye, and Lady Payton with the joyful anticipation of seeing this beloved son across the table from her, still alive!

When Jane had finished dressing Lady Payton and seen her off down the stairs to the drawing room, she hurried up to her own room, where she'd laid out a freshly ironed cap and apron. She washed her face and hands carefully, then brushed out her long brown hair and coiled it into a smooth knot on top of her head before donning the cap which covered her hair completely. The stiffly starched ruffle framed her face like flower petals and was monstrously becoming, but for some reason she eyed it with dissatisfaction. She tweaked forward some shorter strands to feather softly around her face. Better, she thought, smiling impishly at her reflection. She tied her apron strings in front into a perky bow and twitched it around to the back, blew out her candle, and rushed down the back stairs to the kitchen.

Sebastian watched covertly as the girl moved slowly around the table with a plate of soup for Lady Payton, her eyes riveted to the plate in her hands, the pink tip of her tongue showing her earnestness. She carefully placed the soup in front of her mistress and straightened up, flashing him an irrepressibly triumphant smile as she met his glance, before she caught herself and lowered her eyes demurely and turned away busily to the sideboard to fetch his serving.

As she bent to place the soup before him he stared frankly at the round rosy cheek with the wisp of dark curl against it, and was aware of the fresh, sunshiny scent of her. It was all he could do to keep from reaching a finger to touch the smoothness of that cheek, and the impulse startled him. The only woman he'd ever touched had been his mother, and that was many, many years ago. He remembered the sound of this girl crying in the early dawn and wondered what could possibly cause such a merry-looking creature so much sorrow. When she went away to fetch the next remove he felt himself impatient for her return.

"Well, Mama, you seem to have somewhat more promising material in this girl than has been your fortune heretofore," he said as he applied himself to his soup.

"Oh, Sebastian! A treasure! If only she will stay," breathed Lady Payton warmly.

"Already hinting of her young man left behind in London, I suppose," he said sourly, instantly assuming that here was the source of her unhappiness of the morning.

"No, no, I assure you, but—well, she suits me so well I'm afraid to trust it. She's so pretty and quick and seems so—so grateful to be here. It's very hard not to allow oneself to grow too fond of her too quickly."

"Surely one cannot dictate to oneself in such matters, Mama. 'The heart has its reason,' as Pascal says."

"Does he, dear? How clever he must be to put it so aptly," replied Lady Payton, quite ignorant of who Pascal might be.

Sebastian smiled but didn't bother to enlighten her. Jane reentered bearing a very large tray, and so there was no further chance to discuss her with his mother until the end of the meal. He contented himself with watching her as she served them, waiting for what he could not help praying would not happen. The memory of the last maid from London still caused him to flinch: pasty-faced, eyes like raisins as she'd avidly slid them around to him at every opportunity. He'd finally flung down his napkin and fled the dining room with a muttered, angry apology to his distressed mother. The girl had been sent away the next day, but the memory of her sly eyes still caused his skin to crawl. He didn't want to think about such a look from this girl.

Jane was much too engrossed in doing her job to the best of her ability to have time for curious stares, even had she been inclined so. Such an inclination, however, was not part of her nature. Her innate trustingness in her fellow creatures caused her to approach all with directness and openness. Only once had her trust been abused, and though it now caused her to flinch away from men, she did not feel this instinct with Lord Payton.

55

She was unaware that part of the reason for this was the very fact of his small stature, which gave her confidence in her ability to prevail if he should attempt anything. It was purely an unconscious knowledge; consciously she was only fearful of him as far as his reactions to her would govern whether she would be allowed to stay in this paradise or not.

When she'd removed the last dishes and put the wine bottle in front of Lord Payton, she dropped a perky sort of curtsy, smiled blindingly upon both of them, and withdrew. Lady Payton, as was her custom when her son dined with her, stayed on at the table with him and took a glass of wine in order not to lose a precious moment of his company.

"Your maid paid me a visit yesterday, Mama," he said noncommittally.

"She told me all about it, dear. I hope you were not upset. I assure you she would not—"

"Only surprised."

"I felt sure you could not mind. She's such a taking little thing, is she not? No harm in her at all, and very pretty-behaved for a girl of that class. I wonder who her people were?"

"Some lord's by-blow, no doubt," he replied cynically.

"Sebastian!" she said reprovingly.

"I beg your pardon, Mama. I only meant there's more than peasant blood there. Brains too, or at least curiosity and interest, to judge by the questions she asked me. I wonder if she can read and write?" he mused.

"I'm sure I don't know, my dear. But I should think probably not."

"I could give her some lessons if you'd like," he said casually.

"Oh—my dear, it would be too much trouble for you, and it might tire you—" she began to protest.

"Nonsense, Mama. I've nothing else to do. It would help fill up some hours."

"Why, of course," she cried enthusiastically, turning about in her opinion abruptly at the bitter sting of his words. No one knew better than she how lonely he must be, day after day with no one to speak to but that man of his, who the Lord knows could not be a stimulating companion, however well-meaning he was. "She shall come tomorrow if you wish it for as long as you like."

She leaned back in her chair and sipped her wine happily. Who would have imagined that Sebastian would make such an offer? Sebastian! who would not even speak to any of the other maids who'd come here, and who had refused to even leave his room when Angela Gilbert came to call since he was a young boy of ten or so and she had made the mistake of calling him "Poor, dear child," in his hearing.

Bless the girl, she thought, her eyes misting with tears of gratitude, bless the dear little soul for coming here. I'll have the dressmaker come and make her up a pretty dress, maybe several, for Mrs. Plummer says she has only the one she wore when she came, poor child. So rosy and innocent—but no—not innocent, she remembered with a shudder of horror at the story her sister had told her.

"Sebastian," she said slowly, "I think I should tell you something of the girl's story. It is just possible she will—well, the fact is, she's had a perfectly dreadful experience—"

He listened stonily to the sorry tale, never betraying by a flick of the eyelid that he was moved by it, but somewhere deep inside, in an area hitherto untouched, he felt the first lick of a flame that built steadily into a fire of rage against the man who had so used a young girl. It was a startling sensation for Sebastian, the first time in twenty years he'd felt himself emotionally concerned by someone else's misfortune.

Oh, from time to time he'd felt pity for his poor widowed mother, left alone with himself for an only child, but it was not a deep emotion. Nor was he given to self-pity, at least not since he was nine and had finally realized that his condition was not just a nightmare from which he'd surely wake and find himself restored to the healthy seven-year-old body that had been his before that beautiful spring morning when his horse had balked at a jump and young Lord Payton had been flung out of the saddle.

It had been a bitter, hard-won victory over a mind that thrashed about ceaselessly, asleep or awake, in its efforts to deny the truth of his condition. The winning of that battle had burned away with it all the natural softness in his nature. He was now only a shell, a small freakish shell, he acknowledged with pitiless candour, who had, if he was fortunate, only a short life to get through, and the best way to do so was by living through the minds and ideas of others. He'd immersed himself in books and studies, submitting himself stoically to the inescapable pain that intermittantly wracked him, or the illnesses that invaded his enfeebled body. His bleak hope was that each bout would cause further deterioration, thus shortening the time he must endure on Earth.

He yearned toward death as a welcome release, though he refused to allow himself to contemplate finding that release by any positive action of his own. He knew he could not deal his mother such a blow after all she'd suffered for his sake.

He watched her now, her soft, faded face lit by her happiness in being able to give him something to interest him, and her gratitude to him for his offer, and he was glad he'd done something to give his mother pleasure. Other than continuing to exist, he could not remember anything else he'd ever been able to do for her.

8

Miss Angela Gilbert took a minute sip of her wine and bent her head attentively to her hostess, who was reading the Court news aloud to her, but her eyes followed Jane avidly as Jane served Lady Payton with wine and returned to the tray for a plate of iced cakes to hand to Miss Gilbert.

Jane was very conscious of those eyes. In the past six months of her stay at Larkwoods she had found only the moments spent in Miss Gilbert's presence to be distasteful. The woman had never addressed a word to Jane during her weekly visits to Lady Payton, nevertheless Jane found she could not accustom herself to the woman's bold stare. Like boiled gooseberries, those eyes, Jane thought, pale green and cold and like to pop out of her head.

Miss Gilbert's eyes were indeed bulging, and so scantily furnished with lashes and brows as to look strangely fishlike. A jutting arc of nose and a distressing lack of chin furthered this piscine resemblance. Her large front teeth bucked out haphazardly over her lower lip, making it impossible for her to close her mouth without conscious effort. This unsightly face, with its mouse-brown hair skinned back into a hard little knot on the back of her head, was regrettably perched atop a long, scrawny neck as though for prominent display. Altogether, she was disastrously ill-favoured.

Daughter of the vicar, born and raised in the manse, she had dedicated herself to a relentless pursuit of "good works," and to her credit, was always first on the scene of any disaster or bereavement with assistance and advice. The villagers, however, rarely heeded and never welcomed her interference, and sniggered at her behind her back, referring to her as "The Old Haddock."

She was long past the age of any "expectations," and had declared, always with a delicate shudder, that indeed she had never had any intention of marrying in any case, since the only man she found in the least tolerable was her father.

The only break in her daily battle against the backsliding, sloth and outright indifference of her father's hapless parishioners was her weekly visit with Lady Payton, whose friendship was precious to her. She considered herself so far above the local gentry on the social ladder that her condescension and arrogance had alienated all of them. They didn't care if her mother *was* first cousin to the Earl of Everly, and they disliked being reminded of it at some point during every conversation with her.

So, not only was Lady Payton, in Miss Gilbert's estimation, the only lady in the vicinity of equal social status with herself, she was the only woman who still received Miss Gilbert with anything approximating a welcome.

For Sebastian's sake, Lady Payton had long ago given up receiving visitors at Larkwoods, but her attempts to discourage Miss Gilbert had failed. Miss Gilbert, impervious to snubs in her determination, had persisted and Lady Payton, aware of the pitiful state of Miss Gilbert's social life, had been too good-natured to hold out against her. The weekly visit had become an established ritual, performed by Lady Payton as her own "good work," for she felt very sorry for Angela Gilbert, knowing full well that Miss Gilbert's regrettable personality was a direct result of her physical appearance, as much a disability as dear Sebastian's.

But though her charity allowed the weekly visits, Lady Payton was not disposed to encourage Miss Gilbert's attempts to establish their relationship on a more intimate footing. During the first few visits, many years ago now, Miss Gilbert had tried to draw Lady Payton into a discussion of Sebastian and his "condition," as Miss Gilbert delicately referred to it. But Lady

Payton would not be drawn on this subject and firmly turned the conversation into other channels, just as she rebuffed invitations to discuss her own lonely life which Miss Gilbert urged with many little, caressing pats on Lady Payton's hands. Lady Payton had withdrawn herself from the contact with such a quelling look that Miss Gilbert had not been tempted to try it again.

Each Tuesday, however, she arrived at precisely eleven in the morning. She was shown into the drawing room where Lady Payton awaited her, and after greetings and being served with wine, they spoke of neighbourhood occurrences, or Lady Payton read aloud from the London newspapers.

The routine had not changed with the advent of Jane, but Miss Gilbert's attention was not always so politely fixed upon her hostess. Jane could not imagine how her dear, good lady could bear Miss Gilbert, who never took her eyes from Jane and always managed to brush her hand when the wine and cakes were passed, as she did now. Jane flushed and turned away sharply. Lady Payton looked up and misreading her nervousness, smiled indulgently.

"There, dear, I can see you're afraid to keep Sebastian waiting, so run along to your lessons now."

Jane smiled gratefully and made her escape. Miss Gilbert watched until the door closed and then turned to her hostess.

"Dear Lady Payton, you are positively saintly, but I very much fear too innocent for this world."

"Great heavens, Miss Gilbert—innocent—saintly? How very flattering, but I fear I must deny all halos."

"Ah, there, you see? You're not even aware of your own goodness in giving up the services of your maid for Sebastian's—er—amusement. I fear it cannot be wise, however."

"Not wise? Surely education cannot ever be termed unwise —nor amusement."

"In its proper place, Lady Payton, certainly not. However, I cannot approve of too much education for the lower classes. They get ideas above their station and lose all respect for their betters."

"I cannot feel that any amount of education would cause one to lose respect for those who are truly one's *betters*, Miss Gilbert," replied Lady Payton blandly.

Miss Gilbert was far too safe in her own feeling of superiority to read anything personal into this remark. Indeed, in pursuit of her real objective, she didn't hear it. "Not to speak of the danger of placing a young girl in constant company with a man—"

"My dear Miss Gilbert, I really must protest," Lady Payton interrupted sharply.

"Yes, yes, I know it is only poor, dear Sebastian," Miss Gilbert rushed on heedlessly, "but he is a man nonetheless, and men, whatever their physical condition, are bedeviled by," here her voice dropped to a horror-filled whisper, *"dreadful needs."*

In spite of her previous annoyance, a gleam of mischief replaced the angry light in Lady Payton's eyes. Unable to resist the impulse, she leaned forward artlessly.

"Why, Miss Gilbert, do you tell me so!"

"Animals, all of them!"

"How shocking!" breathed Lady Payton, "I had never realized, Miss Gilbert, that you had experienced—"

Miss Gilbert reared back, her eyes nearly starting from their sockets. "Naturally I do not speak from personal experience, Lady Payton!" she gasped.

"Oh," replied Lady Payton, allowing the word to convey disappointment, her lips twitching.

"But surely you cannot have thought—ah—I see—you are having your little joke with me." Miss Gilbert attempted a smile. "Very amusing—how I envy you your sense of humour, dear lady. However, if you had seen, as I have, the results of men's beastiality, you would find it difficult to see it as a matter for humour—young girls' reputations besmirched, illegitimate babies—" Miss Gilbert's face had flushed unbecomingly and she seemed to be having trouble with her breathing.

"But, Miss Gilbert, I really must protest! Surely you are not implying that Sebastian would take advantage of an innocent child?"

"Propinquity, Lady Payton! Propinquity! He is the soul of honour, of course, but two people of the opposite sex who are thrown into one another's company day after day in this way will naturally take advantage. Such a situation would be bound to rouse a man's baser instincts despite all his good intentions—that rosy young flesh, that full, red mouth—she would be bound to tempt—"

Miss Gilbert stopped abruptly, her glazed eyes refocusing to find Lady Payton staring at her with a look of fascinated revulsion. After only the briefest of pauses, however, she turned away and picked up the latest copy of *La Belle Assemblée.*

"Here is a biographical sketch of Lady Charlotte Duncombe, which I'm sure will interest you, Miss Gilbert. Your mother was acquainted with her father, the Earl of Dartmouth, was she not?"

Without waiting for a reply, Lady Payton began to read, careful to keep her voice bright and her eyes on the print before her, while Miss Gilbert sat as though turned to stone, the red slowly draining out of her face to leave it an unpleasant grayish-white.

"That old trout still with my mama?" growled Sebastian as Jane came dancing in from the September sunshine. She giggled explosively.

"Oh, you've hit it exactly, sir. That's exactly what she reminded me of!"

"The idea is not original with either of us, since everyone around here calls her 'The Old Haddock.' "

She laughed even harder and he watched her, the shining sherry-coloured eyes lit with merriment, the red lips against the white teeth, the round, flushed cheeks, the entire youthful glow of her holding him helplessly spellbound as it did each day when he first saw her. The feelings she stirred in him were feelings until now sternly repressed, at least during the daylight hours, since his realization as a very young man that for him such things were never to be. His dreams, as a result, were wildly erotic, but he had long ago given up all feelings of guilt about this, having learned from his reading that it was not a phenomenon peculiar to himself.

However, he had never in his life had his senses stirred by a real woman and found it required the most rigourous self-control to prevent her from occupying his every waking thought. During sleep, his imagination, slipping the chains consciousness and conscience imposed, rampaged through every possible sexual variation with her, though never, as in previous dream encounters with faceless females, reaching with her that fulfillment that had come so easily before. Added to this frustration was the guilt he had foresworn so long ago. He was ashamed to use Jane in this way, an innocent young child who had already suffered so much at a lecherous man's whim.

He wrenched his eyes away from her and called her to order. She meekly subsided and sat down to her book, already spread open to today's lesson on the desk he had had carried to his room for her use, and began to read aloud.

As he listened he was aware that there was really nothing so surprising about such rapid progress in a reasonably intelligent fifteen-year-old who possessed great eagerness to learn. Still he felt all the pride of a maestro discovering and nurturing a prodigy.

He had left her free of all learning by rote and followed along as her mind leaped from geography to poetry to philosophy, allowing her to explore each avenue that was opened up to her by a word or an idea. In the process, due to quiet but persistent correction on his part, she had lost most of her Cockney accent, along with her fear that if she displeased him he would ask his mother to send her back to London. Contrary to Miss Gilbert's belief, however, she never forgot her place with him, always addressing him as "sir," or "m'lord," and though she giggled at the things he said, never became overfamiliar with him.

The other part of Miss Gilbert's dire prediction had, of course, taken effect as far as Sebastian was concerned. Several hours a day in close contact with him had, for Jane, created an image of him in her mind that had very little to do with reality. As the fount of all the good things that had come to her he was beyond judgment; his stunted body so unimportant in the totality of her respect and admiration for him that the fact of his physical appearance no longer entered her thoughts as a separate idea. She had, like everyone else in the household, succumbed to his dominating personality. Jane, like his mother and all the servants, was now devoted to making his life bearable.

The servants had slowly become aware that she had joined forces with them and their attitudes toward her had changed accordingly. They competed with one another in their efforts to spoil her, and Lady Payton, grateful beyond measure to see a new lightness in her son's face, and to have had him free from illness for six months, went out of her way to treat Jane with warm consideration. For Jane's birthday in the first week of September she had given the child a new gown of claret merino and insisted that she put it on and come down to the drawing room after dinner and drink a glass of wine with herself and Lord Payton.

Though Lady Payton had firmly resolved to forget the unpleasant episode with Angela Gilbert, the woman's words had taken root without Lady Payton's awareness. It wasn't, however, until a few days ago that Lady Payton saw what she recognized immediately as the sign she had been covertly watching for all this time. It came at the end of a meal when Jane, having been out of the room for the past twenty minutes, was summoned to clear the table. As the girl's familiar footsteps neared the door, Lady Payton glanced at her son and saw his eyes fly to the door, his entire face a picture of eager anticipation. Lady Payton hastily averted her eyes, knowing she was privy to information her son would not knowingly have shared with her.

Although Lady Payton had devoted the past thirty-five years of her life to her son she had never attempted to force herself into his confidence. She had been wise enough never to oppress him by doting over him or making continuous futile inquiries about the state of his health or his feelings, allowing him to exist without the destructiveness of her pity. She had thus given to him the only part of his manhood left to him: independence and privacy.

She had never considered her own lonely life in the light of a sacrifice, and had even come to look upon her husband's death before Sebastian's accident as a blessing for all of them, for though she desperately missed his love and support, she shuddered to think what their life might have become. Lord Payton had been a hard-living, robust, sociable sort of man who had no patience with illness in others, never having experienced a day's bad health in his life.

The involuntary information she now possessed regarding the state of her son's feelings filled her with an aching pity as she pondered what it would be best to do. The thought of sending the girl away filled her own heart with heaviness, though of course she must do so if it could prevent Sebastian from experiencing the terrible unhappiness that must await him if the girl stayed. Or was she too late to prevent anything? Had Angela Gilbert been right after all? But no, the look she had seen in Sebastian's eyes had not even remotely resembled beastly lust, if she was any judge. It was more as though a flower had turned to the sun, and there had been no discernible change in Jane's manner, either to herself *or* Sebastian. She maintained the same cheerful respect she'd always shown to both of them. There could really be no credence given to Miss Gilbert's prediction that the girl would forget her place if given too much education. Lady Payton fretted over the problem for several days before she observed something else that turned her mind in a most un-expected direction.

She was standing in the drawing room window watching as Jane and Wellington frolicked on the front lawn, kicking up clouds of autumn leaves. Jane would throw the ball and then she and Wellington raced each other to retrieve it. Sebastian strolled out on the lawn and stood watching them. The thrown ball landed at his feet, and he bent to pick it up to toss back, right over the heads of the girl and the dog racing toward him. They both pulled up short in astonishment, looked from the ball sailing through the air in the other direction, then back at Sebastian, with similar expressions of bewilderment. Then with one accord turned and went galloping off after the ball. Sebastian threw back his head in a great shout of laughter.

Lady Payton drew in her breath, her mouth gaping in surprise. She could never remember hearing him laugh aloud since his accident! She expelled her pent-up breath and sat down rather suddenly on the blue brocade chair that, fortunately, stood beside the window, her eyes retaining the image of her son's face laughing as her ears retained the joyous sound of it. Slowly she turned her head back to the scene outdoors, as though to verify it to her disbelieving mind. Yes, it was true, he was still laughing, his cheeks faintly tinged with colour, his face lit with happiness.

The two causes of this unprecedented event had reached the ball, Jane scooping it up just an instant before Wellington's jaws closed on it. She turned and threw it back to Sebastian and the game began. She was laughing now too and an ecstatic Wellington tore back and forth between the two, his mouth stretched into what could only be a grin. Lady Payton thought she had never seen a picture of such perfect felicity between three living creatures.

It was at that moment that the idea presented itself, full-blown, to her mind. She did not even start with surprise at it, not did her eyes widen in shock. Quite simply her mind set about rearranging her ideas to accommodate the plan.

Sebastian was in love with the girl, that was first and fore-most in importance. Whether Jane returned his feelings was not clear, but what was without any doubt at all was that she did not react in any unnatural way with Sebastian, as though she found him physically repellent. These were the established facts.

Next was the fact that Jane was the kindest, best-natured person Lady Payton had ever met, as well as being as pretty as could be and obviously the inheritor of some good blood from somewhere in her ancestry, for she had good bones and was instinctively well bred.

To these advantages could be added the fact that the child had, to her knowledge, no one in the world to turn to if she should leave Larkwoods, and no other prospects besides a life in service, other than marriage. And if she were to marry—why not marry Sebastian!?

As Lady Payton she would have the use of sixty thousand pounds a year, Larkwoods, and the Payton town house, as well as all the gowns and carriages she could desire—and as the mother of the future Lord Payton! Ah, thought Lady Payton with a soft, gasping sigh, surely this was not so impossible a dream? Sebastian's poor legs might have refused to grow after the dreadful injury to his spine, but this did not mean he was incapable of—well—performing as a husband.

As for Jane, so healthy and vital, surely there could be no problems there. That she had not conceived, thank the good Lord, after the terrible attack in London, Lady Payton discounted. The girl had been but fourteen at the time and pregnancy problematical in any case.

Lady Payton sat back and surveyed all of these plusses with some complacency. She was not so far removed from reality as not to be able to recognize that other people would without a doubt be horrified by such a marriage, but Society's opinion held little weight in Lady Payton's mind, balanced against the chance for Sebastian to be happy. God knows how many years he has left, she thought with a little catch of pain in her heart, but it's certain he'll never make old bones. It's a miracle he's lived this long. So—

She rose and paced briskly up and down the room, praying for inspiration. For in spite of having settled upon the rightness of such a marriage in her own mind, one large hurdle remained to be cleared, or rather, one large and one small hurdle, for she thought Jane would turn out to be a small one, but Sebastian was different! How will I bring Sebastian up to scratch, she thought, smiling at the cant phrase slipping so easily into her mind.

She stopped before the window again and watched as Jane

stood before Sebastian, laughing and talking with great animation. Then, as easily as the first idea, it came to Lady Payton what she must do to convince Sebastian to consent to the plan.

9

Lady Payton negotiated the stairs as rapidly as possible, one hand holding tight to the banister, the other clutching a crumpled piece of paper pressed to her painfully fluttering heart. The hallway, when she reached it, seemed to stretch endlessly before her. She stood for a moment, breathing hard, then made her way determinedly across it to the door of her son's apartments and rapped urgently.

The door opened under her knuckles and Eldon, the old coachman who also served Sebastian, stood there.

"Quick, Eldon, fetch my son," she gasped.

Before the elderly man could move, Sebastian appeared.

"Good God, Mama!" Sebastian led her to a chair and pressed her down into it. "Bring brandy," he snapped over his shoulder. Lady Payton opened her mouth to speak, but he laid a finger over her lips. "Not a word, Mama, till you've recovered yourself. Just lean back and take deep breaths."

Eldon came shambling back with a glass and the brandy bottle, in what was, for him, the closest approximation to a dead run he could manage with his rheumaticky knees. Sebastian administered the brandy to his mother in small sips, and presently the faintest pink tinged her parchment-white cheeks and her hand relaxed its spasmodic clutch against her heart. The piece of paper fluttered to the floor.

"What is this?" asked Sebastian, stooping to retrieve it and holding it out to her.

"It is—it is—read it," she quavered.

He smoothed out its crumpled folds and read:

Dear Lady Payton:

After all your goodness to me, never did I think I could bring myself to deny you anythin', but I cannot do as you want. I know the Quality don't feel on these things the same as us, but I must do right by my own lights. Don't think hard of me for disobligin' you in this way. I will never forget you and Lord Payton. Please remember kindly,

Your servant,
Jane Coombes

He gave his mother a swift, puzzled glance before bending his head to read it through again.

Finally he looked up at her. "I don't quite—what *is* this all about, Mama?"

"Oh, my dear, I do assure you it is all the most dreadful misunderstanding—"

"Yes, yes, but what does it *mean?*"

"It means she's gone, but I didn't—"

"Gone," he repeated, his voice flat.

"Yes. She didn't come down to the kitchen this morning for my tray and Mrs. Plummer went up to her room and found this note on her pillow and brought it to me. I realized at once that she must have misunderstood me last night, but Sebastian I assure you I only—I didn't mean—" she wrung her hands together miserably.

Sebastian swallowed his impatience when he saw the stricken look in her eyes. He took one of her hands and patted it reassuringly.

"Just be calm, whatever has happened we will mend it. Just start at the beginning and tell me everything." He saw her glance stray over his shoulder to the hovering Eldon and turned. "Thank you, Eldon, that will be all for the moment." Eldon faded away. "Now, Mama."

"I'll try, my dearest, but I hope you will—I promise you I meant everything in the most honourable way," she cried, with a pleading look.

"Surely you know you need not give me reassurances on that score, Mama. Just tell me simply—and quickly!" he could not prevent himself from adding.

"Yes, yes, you are right, we must not waste any more time. The thing was I—I—oh dear—I was persuaded, you see, that you—that you were in love with the child and—oh, Sebastian!" She cried out pitiously as she saw his brows contract into a

68

frowning straight line. He forced himself to relax and pressed her hand.

"Go on, Mama," he urged as gently as possible.

"Well, dearest, you know how highly I regard the child, she's become almost like—like a daughter to me and I thought —I wanted—anyway, I thought if you loved her why should you not—not marry her and—and—last night when she was helping me to bed I thought I would just find out her own inclinations. I didn't mention marriage, naturally. How could I do so when I hadn't spoken to you? I only said—well—that we had both grown very fond of her and that I thought *your* feelings went even deeper than fondness and how would she feel about that?"

"And then—" he prompted, his heart giving a painful thump.

"She blushed. Heavens, such a blush!" She paused.

"But surely there is nothing in that to make her run away."

"Not in that, no, but then—oh, Sebastian, I saw that blush and I was sure—oh such glorious visions of happiness for all of us flashed through my mind and I started babbling about gowns and jewels and carriages and I don't know what all. She hushed me and said I was becoming overexcited and would not let me go on. She said we would speak of it tomorrow—today, that is, and went away to her bed. Oh, I was so filled with joy! I couldn't even close my eyes for hours! I planned what I would say to you to persuade you. I knew that would be the difficult part, but I thought if I could come to you with the reassurance that your suit would not be looked upon unfavourably you—but then the moment I read her note I realized I had left out—that she thought—thought—"

"That you were trying to buy her—services—for me," he said bitterly.

"Yes," she whispered painfully.

"Eldon," he raised his voice. Eldon appeared magically. "Have the carriage brought round."

Eldon and Lady Payton gasped in concert. Sebastian turned to his servant and raised one eyebrow at him. Eldon vanished.

"Excuse me, Mama," said Sebastian. He pressed her hand and left the room also. He was back in a moment with his hat and cape.

She stared at him disbelievingly. "You—you will go after her—yourself?"

"Yes," he replied succinctly.

"But—but—my darling—"

"You will call Mrs. Plummer to help you back to bed and you must remain there quite quietly until we return. This has all been very bad for your heart, and I shall have to ring a peal over Jane's head for subjecting you to it."

"Oh, Sebastian, do you think you will find her?" she cried with a little sob.

"Of course I shall. How far can she have gone on foot? The nearest stage is Maidstone and that's fifteen miles away. I suspect she left at daybreak and it is now half past nine. She cannot have covered even half that distance. Have no fear, Mama, I will find her," he said firmly.

He did find her, not seven miles from Larkwoods, sitting on a pile of straw, legs dangling from the back of a farm cart lumbering along at a walking pace. She had removed one shoe and was lovingly massaging her stockinged foot as she jolted along. The sight of the carriage careening along directly toward her caused her to drop her foot, her eyes widening in alarm. As the small figure in the driver's seat became recognizable her mouth opened into a perfect circle of surprise. He wondered, with a grim little smile, which surprised her most: his coming after her or his being able to drive a carriage?

He hauled on the reins, came to a halt, and shouted out to the farmer to pull up. The man looked around, his eyes nearly starting from his head when he saw the diminutive gentleman leaping down from the carriage. The farmer pulled to a stop without ever once turning his head or attention back to his horse.

Under the riveted stare of two pairs of eyes, Sebastian marched up to the back of the cart, planted his arms akimbo, and glared ferociously up at Jane. He held out his hand.

"Jump down," he ordered shortly.

She took the hand he offered, obeying him wordlessly. He left her standing there and moved around to the goggle-eyed farmer. He handed up a coin, made a dismissive gesture with his hand, and walked back to Jane. The farmer gave the horse a flick of the reins and trundled slowly away, his chin resting on his shoulder as he stared back at them, reluctant to miss one moment of the best entertainment he'd had for years.

Sebastian glared coldly at Jane as the wagon rattled away. She gazed back numbly.

She had been in this state of numbness since the previous evening's conversation with Lady Payton, when the revelation that Lord Payton cared for her had caused a complete suspension of her thinking process. Then slowly, certain words began to penetrate: "money," "gowns," "jewels," and all became horrifyingly clear. Hardly aware of what she was doing, she shushed Lady Payton, rushing blindly about the room picking up clothing, closing the drapes, poking up the fire, and whisking out the door after a hurried "goodnight, m'lady." She wished the ground would open and swallow her and her shame. That Lady Payton would try to buy her for her son! Jane did not attribute any of this shame to Lady Payton, for Lady Payton could not perform a shameful act. Therefore she, Jane, must be held to blame. Something in her own self must have provoked Lady Payton and her son to make such an offer; the guilt was hers. She shouldered it humbly, but a door closed on the whole thing in her mind; it was simply too painful to deal with yet. She had only one clear thought: She must leave Larkwoods.

In her room, she pulled her box down from a shelf and folded into it only the things she had brought with her from London. In passing, her hands caressed the merino gown lovingly, but moved on to her own old gown and pelisse, which she'd not worn even once since she came here. She removed her blue uniform and apron, folded them across the bed, and put on her own gown. Then taking her candle she crept down the stairs to Lady Payton's desk in her private sitting room, where she wrote a note to Lady Payton, and took it back to her room. She spent the rest of the night sitting beside her dying fire, numb to every thought but that she must leave the house at dawn before anyone was awake. She felt a great, cold void of loneliness, which stayed with her as she slipped out of the house in the chill fog of early morning and set off down the drive, and was still her only emotion as she sat on the back of the dray nursing her aching feet several hours later.

When she recognized Sebastian she was first shocked and then confused at his angry countenance. It was a look she had never seen directed toward her from him, and it was as palpable as a blow. Was this rage because she had refused his offer? Had he come to drag her back whether she would or no? She tightened her grip on her box and stood up straighter.

Finally he spoke, the words falling like icy pebbles between them. "You have behaved with incredible stupidity."

"Maybe," her voice came out in a whisper, but then she spoke up more firmly, "I'm sure others would be glad of such an offer, but I don't need gowns and jewels and that."

"Are you seriously accusing my mother of being a—a—procuress?"

She gazed at him uncomprehendingly. "I'm—I'm not just sure what that means, but I'd never accuse m'lady of anything bad."

"It means that you think my mother was making you an offer to become my paramour in return for money."

"Yes, but I know she didn't mean anything bad to her own way of thinking. Quality don't feel that sort of thing is bad, but me mam—"

"My mother," he corrected her automatically.

"—my mother would turn over in her grave if I—if I—did such a thing."

"If she were dead, so would my mother—and no thanks to you that she isn't, giving her such an upset by running away."

Jane started forward as though to run back to her lady's side, but stopped abruptly at the foolishness of such a notion. Her eyes filled, but she swallowed, refusing to give way to tears. "She had an attack?"

"Not yet, but she will if you persist in this idiocy," he said, aware that he was taking advantage of the girl's soft heart and obvious love for Lady Payton.

"Then I will go back to her," Jane said simply.

"Brush the straw off your skirt."

She obeyed, glad to have something to busy herself with while she said what she felt she must say. "But I cannot—I mean no disrespect to her or to you—but I cannot—"

"You were never asked to do anything dishonourable," he interrupted her, angry again.

"It may not seem so to you, but me—my mother warned me never—"

"How tiresome you are! Please stop this nonsense at once before I lose all patience. I thought you'd grown beyond this finicking servant's prudery!"

"'Tisn't prudery," she cried, stung by his scorn.

"Then it's a vivid, even salacious, imagination," he retorted furiously. "My mother would never dream of allowing a servant in her home to consort with her son, much less attempt to arrange such a thing herself. As for me, if I want—that—I'm perfectly capable of getting it for myself. It may not seem possible to you, but I assure you money can buy anything! Even if I had two heads! *Do you understand me?*"

72

She flinched away from the raw fury of his voice, involuntarily gasping out, "Oh no! I didn't mean—"

"It was marriage she was hinting at, you cabbage-headed, paper-skulled pea-goose!"

"Don't you dare call me—" she broke off abruptly, then, "—ma-ma-ma—" she stuttered helplessly, unable to form the word, "—but who—?"

His face reddened, but he looked her straight in the eye. "Me. But not with any contrivance on my part, I assure you."

"N-no, ce-certainly not," she said, stumbling over her words in her haste to disclaim any such thought on her own part, "how could you think of such a thing!"

He looked away, giving the hedge his undivided attention for several long, uncomfortable moments. Then he cleared his throat and said, "Well, actually, I *had* thought of it—a great deal."

They were married two weeks later by special license, the ceremony performed in the drawing room by a minister brought down from London by Lady Stanier, the only guest attending, besides the servants.

Sebastian was adamant in his refusal to entertain his neighbours with the spectacle of a church wedding performed by Mr. Gilbert, the vicar, nor would he allow his mother to even hint to Angela Gilbert of what was afoot.

"But dearest boy, she will find out later and—"

"Let her."

"But she'll insinuate dreadful things—"

"How you can bring yourself to receive a woman with such a mind I will never understand. However, you will oblige me by not mentioning me or anything to do with me to her."

Miss Gilbert came as usual for a weekly visit, but though she eyed Lady Payton's flushed, excited countenance curiously, her only comment was that she hoped Lady Payton was not sickening for something.

Lady Payton tried very hard to remain calm, for she did not want to become ill and spoil everything for "the children," as she now called the betrothed couple, but it was difficult with so much to be done.

She had written immediately to her sister of the problem regarding the vicar and Lady Stanier had dashed off a hasty reply by return post that she knew the very man and would bring him down herself the day before the wedding. Then Lady Payton had written to say that with her sister's agreement she would return to London for an extended visit with her after the wedding. Lady Payton felt that since the young people could not go away for a honeymoon, the least she could do would be to absent herself for at least three months while they settled down to married life together. She also asked her sister to be on the lookout for a nice, steady manservant to wait on the children, since poor Eldon was suffering so with his rheumatism he could hardly walk.

The dressmaker was sent for immediately, over Jane's protests that she *had* the claret merino, surely enough for the finest lady.

"Good God, child," Lady Payton protested between horror and amusement, "you cannot wear it every day! And then there are undergarments and bed gowns and—great heavens—where are my wits got to? I must have Mrs. Plummer fetch my wedding gown from the attic. I'm sure it will come very near fitting you perfectly—though perhaps it will need to be changed—it is very old-fashioned."

But when Jane saw it she would not hear of having it changed even though it was made to be worn over panniers. She lifted it reverently from its silver paper wrappings, speechless at its fairy-tale beauty. It was of white velvet, elaborately embroidered with tiny crystal beads all over the stiff, pointed bodice and down the front and around the edge of the wide, sweeping hem. When she put it on and it was draped over the oval whale bone hoops she felt like a princess. Her waist seemed impossibly tiny, her arms, emerging from the foams of blond lace at the elbows, unbelievably delicate. The square neckline revealed rather more bosom than she thought quite proper, but she held her tongue, unwilling for Lady Payton to ascribe "servant's prudery" to her as Sebastian had done.

In fact, Jane had spoken very little since Sebastian's proposal, moving around the house in a haze of disbelief at this turn her life had taken, afraid to speak for fear it would not be true after all. She continued to do all the things she had done before, except wait on the table at dinner. Lady Payton had adamantly refused to allow her to do so, insisting that from now on Jane must take her meals with them and they would be served by Mrs. Plummer.

The first morning, when Jane went as usual to the kitchen for Lady Payton's chocolate tray, was the only time when she allowed her real fears to show. She saw at once that Mrs. Plummer and Mrs. McKirk knew everything from the uncertainty of their manner toward her. She immediately reached out her hands to each of them.

"Oh, dear Mrs. Plummer—darling Mrs. McKirk, please tell me how I must go on! I count on you to help me, for I vow I'm frightened out of my wits and don't know if I'll be able to go through with it!"

They responded unhesitatingly to this appeal, all their mistrustful feelings about the situation and Jane flying out of their thoughts on the instant.

"Nonsense, my girl, you'll not only go through with it, you'll do so with your chin up and your shoulders back," declared Mrs. Plummer stoutly.

"You'll be standing for all of us, remember, and if you disgrace yourself you'll shame us all!" Mrs. McKirk chimed in. "Frightened, indeed! Of what, I'd like to know?"

"Of everything!" Jane wailed, suddenly letting go of all her terror. "Of being a wife, of being married so grand, of doing or saying the wrong thing and making them ashamed of me." She threw herself on Mrs. Plummer's capacious bosom and sobbed. They caressed her and soothed her and said she was their own Jane and would do just fine and they'd always stand by her.

"Our own Lady Jane, you shall be, and make us all proud," Mrs. McKirk declared, and so they called her from that day, though of course, only amongst themselves, for like most servants of the day they prided themselves on their knowledge of the proper use of titles, and Jane, as they were well aware, while entitled to be addressed as Lady Payton on her marriage, would have had to be at least the daughter of an earl to have the privilege of being called Lady Jane. Their awarding her therefore with this private nickname was an expression of the fellowship they felt for her as a former servant, and their pride that one of their own could rise to such heights. In a large household of servants where factions, ambitions and backbiting prevailed, this warmth of feeling could not have been so easily achieved. But here, where the few, elderly servants had given most of their lives to Sebastian's comfort, their unity of purpose had given them different priorities, and Jane was doubly dear to them, having caused them all to love her, and then making happiness possible for their dear Lord Sebastian.

10

The very new Lady Payton sat up against her pillows in the large tester bed, the coverlet pulled up to her shoulders, allowing only a glimpse of the foaming lace at the neck of her bed gown, and above that a tumble of dark brown curls and sherry-coloured eyes wide with an apprehension she was doing her best to fight down.

The Dowager Lady Payton and Lady Stanier had departed after the wedding luncheon to spend the night at Maidstone and start for London very early tomorrow. Before her departure she had put the finishing touches to this boudoir she had created for her new daughter within Sebastian's wing of the house. It was in startling contrast to the dark, muted colours preferred by Sebastian, being all white and gold and blue. It had three large windows draped in blue velvet over a film of embroidered lawn which matched the bed curtains. In each window embrasure there stood a pedestal holding an enormous bowl of white and yellow roses from the Larkwoods greenhouse.

Jane had not been allowed to see the room until after the wedding, when the elder Lady Payton conducted her to it. It was her special bridal gift to her dear Jane. Waiting there to greet Jane were Lady Stanier's gifts: Fred Crews and his new wife, Betty, who was to be abigail to Jane. Jane lost every shred of her new dignity when she saw Crews, the friend from London who had been instrumental in getting her to Larkwoods. Clasping his hand in both her own she burst into tears. Crews sustained this display of emotion with as much dignity as possible, though his own eyes were moist as he turned awkwardly to introduce his new wife, who dropped the first curtsy Jane had ever received in her life. Still too new in her role to be aware of any solecism, Jane threw her arms around Betty and kissed her cheek.

Betty, round and plump as a robin, righted the situation with unruffled aplomb. "Thank you, m'lady, I'm sure. Fred and me want to wish you happy, and hope we'll suit."

The "m'lady" caused Jane to blush, but she pulled herself up and thanked her new maid with a shy smile.

Betty had been waiting for her when Jane came upstairs to prepare for bed, and had helped her out of her dress and into the new bed gown.

Jane watched the sweet, round face behind her in the mirror as Betty vigorously brushed out Jane's curls.

"I—I—hope you will not find it too lonely here, Betty," Jane said, unconsciously echoing old Lady Payton's words to herself when she had first arrived at Larkwoods.

"Never you worry yourself about that, m'lady. I've got Fred to keep me company, and I shall be too busy to need anymore. I'm to be trained to replace Mrs. Plummer," Betty replied with great satisfaction.

"Oh—I see. Oh, Betty," Jane burst out suddenly, "you can't know what a welcome sight you and Crews were to me, and how grateful I am to you for coming all the way down here to help us."

"Oh, Fred and me likes the country, m'lady, and Lord Payton's doubled Fred's wages," Betty answered complacently.

Finally Betty had tucked her mistress into the vast bed and bid her goodnight, and now, without her maid's calm, reassuring presence, all Jane's fears came flooding in on her. Besides the normal ones any young girl of Jane's class would experience on being projected into titled wealth in the space of two weeks, there was the great, overriding one of the sexual duties that would be required of her. Would she be able to go through with it without terror and revulsion of the whole business, which Sebastian would undoubtedly ascribe to himself and his physical deformity, the one thing she was determined not to allow him to think?

Her feelings for Sebastian were not those of a young girl who had fallen passionately in love. She loved him deeply, but her love was a compound of respect and admiration bordering on reverence. She had long ago decided that she would dedicate the rest of her life to taking care of him, though she had not envisaged herself in any other role than that of, eventually, his housekeeper.

Her gratitude for his proposal of marriage had deepened her devotion to him, for her need to be wanted and loved was almost as strong as her need to bestow her own bountiful affection, and he could not have given her stronger proof of love than to propose marriage.

Completely dazed by this knowledge and in a delightful state of confusion caused by all the preparations that had to be made in a very short time, she had had little time nor inclination for introspection. The building excitement had finally climaxed at eleven this morning in a simple ceremony attended only by Lady Payton, Lady Stanier, and the servants. A delightful luncheon party followed with the bridal couple, the two sisters, and the reverend gentleman from London. After this came the surprise of the boudoir and the Crewses, and the departure of Lady Payton and Lady Stanier. As the afternoon gently deaccelerated, certain emotions began to emerge which she had not experienced for many months. The nightmares which had plagued her sleep after Leach's vicious attack had ceased altogether after it became obvious that she was not pregnant, and then her contentment with her position at Larkwoods and her studies with Sebastian had so filled her mind she had no time to think of the past.

Now, however, the moment was approaching when she would be expected to experience again the horrible, suffocating weight—she gasped in terror as the memory flooded over her, and throwing back the coverlet, rose to her feet and stood there in trembling panic.

Then with a sigh she sank back onto the bed. How silly she was, she thought with a soft giggle of relief. Whatever else her husband was, he would *not* be a suffocating weight! This thought gave her so much relief she was able to lie back against her pillows and pull up the coverlet again. She sat staring straight before her with wide open eyes and valiantly tried to face what lay in store for her with a measure of equanimity.

Her husband, meanwhile, stood silently outside her door, one hand raised to tap. After several moments, he lowered his hand and turned to pace up and down the hallway, hands in the pockets of his brocade dressing gown, eyes on the pattern of the carpet.

How *can* I go in to her, he asked himself in despair? She will be horrified and unable to hide it and I will wish to die. How could I ever have imagined myself as husband to that delicious creature? How the world would laugh and sneer if they knew. I know, better than any of them, that she could not love me, though I know she honours me and will be kind. I thought I had resigned myself to asking nothing more of her. So why am I here?

The fact was, he had indeed decided that he would not rouse her disgust by forcing himself on her, but during the afternoon, spent romping on the lawn with her and Wellington followed by a long walk around the park with Jane decorously holding his arm, and later, during the dinner *à deux* before the fire in his study, he had begun to have other thoughts on the matter.

What if she *expected* him to perform his husbandly duties and would be hurt and bewildered if he stayed away from her? Or worse, thought he stayed away because he was incapable and too ashamed to admit it? Then she would pity him.

This thought caused him to determine that he would go to her, for he could not tolerate pity, particularly from her. He was not worried about his capability. After all, it was only his legs that had not grown, and though he might lack practical experience, his years of reading the literature of the world on the subject of satisfying women had given him a very good idea of how to set about it.

He was also aware that her terrible experience in London might have given her a dread of all men that she could not control no matter how eager she might be to accept him fully as a husband. That, however, could be overcome with patience and skill if he did not repulse her physically.

Well, I shall never resolve anything here in the hallway, he thought ruefully. The best thing is just to go in and say goodnight and leave if she seems frightened or revolted by the sight of me.

He marched resolutely back to her door and tapped firmly before he could lose his courage again. When he heard her hesitant "C-come in," he opened the door.

The sight of her, sitting up against her pillows, hair tumbling down over her shoulders, eyes wide, caused him to freeze in the doorway, heart pounding so riotously it was painful.

They stared wordlessly at one another for a full moment before her sense of humour prodded her into a tiny laugh.

"My goodness, we act as though this is the first time we've ever seen each other," she said.

He let go of his pent-up breath and smiled back. "Well, it *is* the first time I've seen your hair down—and it is very beautiful," he replied, stepping in and closing the door. He walked slowly over to the crackling fire and poked it unnecessarily with the tongs. "Do you find your room comfortable?" he asked without turning around.

"A little grand for the likes of me."

"Ah, but the likes of you are now Lady Payton, and such a room is not too grand for her."

"Not if she felt equal to the title," she said softly.

"You must not be fearful about that, Jane," he said, walking over to stand beside the bed, "you are equal to anything or anyone."

She blushed and dropped her eyes, unable to think of anything to say to such an overwhelming compliment. He reached out for her hand and felt her start with surprise. She did not withdraw it, however, and it lay trembling in his for a moment before he bent, kissed her fingers briefly, and restored it to her.

"You must be exhausted from this long day, so I will say goodnight, my dear. Sleep well." With that he turned and walked briskly away to the door before she could recover from the surprise of this abrupt withdrawal. Her hand reached out to him.

"No, no—I am not in the least—" she stopped, realizing that she was being tactless, for of course *he* was the one who must be exhausted.

"I beg your pardon?" he asked and turned to find her hand outstretched as though for help.

He rushed back to her side. "Jane, darling! What is it? You must not be frightened!"

"I'm not exactly frightened, m'lord, only—only—the room is so big and the b-bed is so big, and I feel—I feel—"

"Try to tell me," he urged.

"It's only that I seem—somehow—smaller—with so much space about me and—and—cold."

Made bold by her distress, he sat down on the side of the bed and took both her hands in his own to warm them. "Perfectly natural way for you to feel," he said reassuringly. "In a few days you will grow into your new space and it will all seem friendlier. I think you might begin to make it all seem—er—

friendlier, if you could bring yourself to call me Sebastian. M'lord is—distancing—for both of us.''

"Then I must try—Sebastian," she said with a shy smile.

They sat for a few moments, each wishing they could think of the right thing to say, and each experiencing the same two widely disparate urgings, though they were unaware of sharing them. The first was to be alone because the situation they were in was too emotionally charged to be at ease in. The other urge was to hold on to one another for the comfort each derived from the other's presence.

He longed to suggest that he spend the night with her but was afraid she would think it just an excuse to climb into her bed. She longed to ask him to stay and hold her but was afraid he would think she was being forward in asking for more than he might be willing or able to give after the long, tiring day.

The impasse was resolved when into the quivering silence came a loud snap from the burning log in the fireplace. She threw herself against him with a little shriek and his arms quickly folded around her and held her close.

"How foolish I am," she said with a shaky laugh, starting to pull away. But he held on to her and she subsided against his chest again. After another long moment he forced himself to take charge of the situation, feeling that as the man, it was required of him, even at the risk of a rebuff.

"Jane, my dear, would it please you to have my company for this first night?"

"Yes," she whispered simply.

He released her and rose to remove his robe. She moved over and he slipped into bed beside her.

"Now put your head on my shoulder and I will hold you and you needn't be frightened anymore."

She obediently slid down and put her head trustingly on his shoulder. He held her, one hand on her shoulder, the other across her waist against her back. It took every effort of his will to lie perfectly still. His hand on her shoulder longed to squeeze the firm, round flesh beneath his fingers, just as his other hand longed to explore the deep indentation of her spine. After awhile just thinking of this made it necessary for him to shift the lower part of his body away from her, carefully since her slow, regular breathing seemed to indicate that she had fallen asleep. But in case she were not asleep he did not want to frighten her by his very obvious arousal.

Jane had drifted into a delightful state between sleep and wakefulness in the warmth and safety of his arms. Without waking fully she instinctively followed the movement of his body when he withdrew its warmth. His hands could no longer be denied the pleasure they ached for and infinitely slowly they began caressing her. Feather-light, his fingers traced the delicious crease down her back and up again, each trip expanding their territory until he found little dimples just above each cheek of her round little bottom. He wished the delicate lawn bed gown were at this moment smouldering in the fireplace.

Jane was now more waking than sleeping and the caressing fingertips, so blissful at first in their slow travelling up and down her back, began to seem too agonizingly slow in their movement, too neglectful of other areas which began to long for touching also. She slowly turned her body so that the fingertips trailed over her ribs. He hesitated only an instant and then began the operation there, allowing his fingers to touch, as though unknowingly, the side of her breast. This became such exquisite torment that without even thinking of it she sat up, pulled the gown over her head, and tossed it away and lay back expectantly—on her back now, willing him to continue.

Sebastian froze in shock for a moment at her movement, then it seemed that every vein in his body was leaping and boiling with blood. He swiftly ripped off his own gown and lay down again, subduing his impulse to throw himself upon her, knowing instinctively that the wisest course was to continue what he had been doing with so much success until now.

He passed his hand over her breasts, experiencing a frisson of pleasure all the way to his toes when he found her nipples hard and taut with desire. Deliberately he moved his hand way, down over the delicious incurving of her waist, across the smoothness of her stomach and up the other side, exploring slowly, rhythmically, each time a little more of the silky skin, finally touching delicately the undersides of her full, young breasts. She gasped and then made a tiny sound of disappointment when his fingers moved away and down to the rounded satin of her thighs and the silky triangle that lay between them. He continued to tease her in this way while time lost all meaning. They had both floated off into a trance of pleasure, hypnotized by the slow movement of his hand, when of itself, it began to linger more and more over her breasts, finally to gently roll her nipples between his fingers. She moaned, arching her back until her breast seemed to swell into his hand. He eased his body gently onto her, took her breasts in both hands and lowered his mouth to them reverently, wonderingly. She abandoned herself completely to total sensation, her body quivering and melting with desire for more and more.

No coming together of a man and a woman for sexual pleasure could have happened more naturally, without any consciousness on either of their parts of his physical shortcomings or her fear, so patient had he been in his preparation of her to receive him, to finally insist upon the ultimate end. For it was at her urging that he slowly, as teasingly slow as his entire lovemaking had been, penetrated the warm pulsing center of her.

She gasped, locking her legs around him in an effort to force him to go farther and faster to relieve the exquisite ache within her. The long torture could not withstand any more and they each swiftly climaxed and lay gasping and shaken as their bodies pulsed together.

He raised himself finally until he could look into her face, and then he kissed her eyelids and her mouth lingeringly, gratefully. She took his head into her hands and held it there to her lips. Without releasing her he rolled to the side and they lay, still mouth to mouth, bodies still joined until they drifted into sleep.

11

The Dowager Lady Payton looked up eagerly at the sound of a soft tap on her door, which was followed at once by the entrance of her daughter-in-law bearing a cup of chocolate on a small silver tray. The older woman eyed the younger with appreciation, and indeed Jane was as beautiful as a picture in her high-waisted, sprigged dimity of yellow flowers on sheer white. Her riotous dark curls were loose on her shoulders, held back by a yellow satin riband, her amber eyes were sparkling and her cheeks and lips glowing with rich pink. Lady Payton held out her arms hungrily, eager to touch the healthy youth of this girl, as though to absorb some of her vigour into her own weak and aging body.

Jane put down the tray and flung her arms about her mother-in-law. She always looked forward to this morning greeting and would not relinquish the task of bringing the elder Lady Payton her morning chocolate even to Dorrie, the new young maid Lady Payton had brought back with her from London. The approval and acceptance implicit in this loving embrace were still as necessary as ever to Jane, in spite of fifteen months of marriage; months of such glorious happiness as she had never expected to be hers in life. I'm sure to wake from this dream sometime, she often thought.

Not that she lazed about on silken cushions and ate sweets all day. That had never been a dream of hers in any case. But being treated with respect as a human being had been, and she was given that here. Both Sebastian and his mother took it for granted that she was capable of intellectual accomplishment, and that, to Jane, showed real respect.

Sometimes even the long country days seemed too short to hold all the things she wanted to do. Sebastian had decreed two hours of study each morning and two each afternoon. And then, when the Dowager had returned from London, another hour was added for Jane to be coached in all the social niceties. She submitted without demur, although secretly convinced they would never be called into use, for she never intended to leave Sebastian's side and he would not receive visitors nor go into company. She was, however, determined never to behave in any way that would cause embarrassment to her mother-in-law, so she plunged into the study of how a lady conducts herself with the same seriousness with which she approached her other studies, even though with less interest.

Sebastian had evolved a method of teaching her whereby he simply let her read aloud to him, correcting her grammar and accent as they went along, and the books they read—poetry, religion, geography, history—were so fascinating that each paragraph or stanza seemed to provoke discussions of their contents, giving her an ever-expanding general education in the process.

She never ceased to wonder at all the things there were in the world she had never dreamed of, and at all the ideas that could be conceived of by the human mind. But most of all she was amazed at how many of her hopes and fears and dreams had been shared by people of genius all over the world and throughout the centuries. There was infinite comfort for her in the realization of the universality and timelessness of human emotions. She felt more in touch with the world around her and with the people in it.

Heretofore, she had had a basic mistrust of the rest of mankind, and had never confided fully in anyone besides her mother. With her mother's death she had felt that she stood alone in a world inhabited, for the most part, by enemies out to take advantage of her unless she kept her wits about her. She had become a wary, pugnacious young girl with a pert tongue, all senses alert in her own defense, intent on working her way into the rarified strata of upper servants. Her great ambition was to become some grand lady's dresser and be addressed by the other servants as "Miss Coombes" and take her dinner in the housekeeper's room in the exclusive company of the butler and the gentleman's valet of the household for which she worked.

Her life now was so far removed from that ambition it seemed impossible to believe it had ever been. Now her sole ambition was to make Sebastian happy and his mother proud of her, which was the only way she knew of to in some measure repay them for their patience and loving kindness to her. The giving, she felt, had all been on their part. The one gift she longed to give them had been denied so far. For the past month, however, she had begun to suspect that it might be possible to fulfill this dream after all—which made her breathless each time she thought of it.

The thought now caused her to squeeze Lady Payton hard and sit back with a radiant smile. "There now, the day can properly begin, dearest Mother Payton. Dorrie is lurking in the hallway, if you are ready to dress."

"In a moment, darling. I'll just have my chocolate, though I musn't dawdle, of course, or Caroline will catch me out. You remember she will be here today?"

"As though I could forget! Darling Aunt Stanier! You see, I'm wearing the gown I had made up from the dress length she sent me two months ago."

The substitution of the honorifics for the more intimate titles of "Mother" and "Aunt" had been one of the most difficult changes for Jane to learn, but were ineffably dear to her for the kinship thus conferred. That those two exalted ladies should request, even insist, that she address them so had seemed difficult to believe at first. Jane had wondered often how it was possible for them to accept a mere maid-servant so unreservedly into their family. But the answer, when she came to it, was quite simple really: They were truly good and loving women, and their sole object was to give Sebastian any measure of happiness within their power. That he should love and marry at all had been beyond their wildest imaginings. When this miracle had come about, the bride's social standing had no relevance for them at all. Naturally, if the girl had been sluttish or obviously motivated by a greed for money or title they would have felt bound to protest. But Sebastian's refined and delicate sensibilities would never have permitted him to make such a choice, so the problem did not arise.

Jane leaned forward to plant a kiss on Lady Payton's cheek and then rose. "I'll leave you in peace and send Dorrie in. Besides, Sebastian frets if I'm not at the breakfast table when he gets there."

She waved from the doorway, motioned the hovering Dorrie forward, and sped off down the stairs and across the hall to "their" side of the house. She checked abruptly at the door of their tiny dining room when she saw her husband sitting, arms folded, at the table.

He gave her a mock scowl. "Ah ha! Late again! Nattering away with my mama, I suppose, like two old hens and leaving your husband to starve for want of his breakfast. Well madam, speak up! What have you to say for yourself?''

''Forgive me, m'lord,'' she said, casting her eyes down demurely as she slid into her seat.

Crews, waiting at the sideboard, came forward to serve her buttered eggs and thin slices of York ham, her favourite breakfast, and then went away at once to leave them alone as they preferred to be. Sebastian watched approvingly as she attacked her meal, thinking it a fine thing for her to have such a good appetite, though he only took tea and toast in the mornings.

''I see a good night's sleep has made you monstrously sharp-set this morning,'' he teased.

''Oh no, sire, 'twas the exercise before sleep that caused it. I'm a great believer in exercise,'' she declared virtuously.

''Sauce!'' he replied severely.

She met his eye and instantly they both began to laugh at her naughtiness, delighted with one another. After fifteen months they felt entirely comfortable together, filling each day with studies and long walks, Wellington romping around them demanding that sticks be thrown for him, and their nights with lovemaking, which sometimes involved only cuddling and falling asleep in the special tangled position they had evolved for sleeping together.

On very rare occasions Sebastian came to her bed in a more urgent, demanding mood, never brutal or hurtful to her, but definitely with more roughness than was in his usual exquisitely slow and tender approach. Because she trusted him absolutely this didn't frighten her, not even the first time. On the contrary, she found, she was immensely aroused by this touch of savagery in him that seemed to demand complete submission. He would brusquely flip her over to bite what in more playful moments he termed her ''saucy backside,'' kneading her flesh as though his hands could not get their fill of it. Then, still without words, his face intent, he would flip her onto her back and starting with the tender flesh on the inside of her thighs would nip and kiss every inch of her body up to her breasts, where the pain was so deliciously exquisite she would feel her bones melting and cry out for him. At the sound he would plunge himself into her ruthlessly, causing her to climax almost instantly. Then he would go on tirelessly as she avidly demanded more and more, climaxing again and again until she was so spent she

87

could only lie there helplessly, unable to assist in her own pleasure but unwilling for him to stop producing it in her. When, at last, he allowed himself release it was a deliberate decision. He would pause for a moment as though to change the direction of his impulses from her to himself, then drive himself to an explosive finish that beat and throbbed so wildly inside of her that it produced a final burst of pleasure for herself.

These sessions were so shattering for both of them that they invariably fell asleep just as they were, he sprawled limply atop her body.

The next day they would continuously seek out each other's eyes, to exchange a little smile in acknowledgment of this rapturous secret between them, and it was to such a night that Jane had just referred.

"You are shameless and must work extra hard this morning to make up for it," he grinned.

"No, no, my love. Have you forgotten? Aunt Stanier comes today. In fact, she will be arriving any moment, so you must not distract me or—"

"—you will not get to finish every last bite of your breakfast," he finished for her.

"I must keep up my strength if I am to—er—be a good wife," she said primly, which set them both off again. They were still laughing when Crews entered to announce the arrival of Lady Stanier. Jane rose at once with a glad cry and rushed around the table.

"Do come quickly, Sebastian. I want you to see me meet her and tell me if I have done it properly," she urged, bending to drop a kiss on the top of his head as she passed. But he reached out and pulled her back to him. She stood looking down into his eyes for a moment, then they smiled their secret-sharing smile and she bent to kiss him lingeringly, and amazingly felt the sweet stir of desire again. Goodness, she thought, I am really insatiable! I wonder if that is wicked of me? I must ask Sebastian—tonight, she promised herself with a delicious little shiver of anticipation.

"Now sir, for shame to hold me here in this way when your dear aunt is being kept waiting," she scolded.

"I'm sure she won't mind if she knows why. Very understanding woman," he answered, but he rose to accompany her. When they reached the hall they found Lady Stanier and Lady Payton hand in hand, both of them talking excitedly, and at once. Lady Stanier as always was a picture of *à la modalité* in a loose Spanish-brown three-quarter length pelisse of sarcenet, wrists and edges trimmed with a narrow band of swansdown, worn over a round gown of French cambric in the palest coral. Her smart straw bonnet was tied beneath the chin with wide taffeta ribands of the same coral shade.

Jane forced herself to a stop, then walked sedately forward with a smooth gliding step, dropped an extremely pretty curtsy, and then rose to kiss the lady's cheek.

"Dearest Aunt Stanier, how kind of you to give us all so much pleasure by honouring us with a visit. We hope you plan to make a very long stay or we shall all be devastated."

This was delivered in her best "drawing-room drawl" as she termed it, and Lady Stanier was smiling appreciatively by the end of it. She flung her arms around Jane and hugged her warmly.

"Minx! You've got that perfectly, though I'm not sure you're not making fun of us!"

Sebastian came forward to kiss Lady Stanier's hand. "Well, Aunt, as always you are the picture of fashion. I vow, the *ton* must tear their hair with envy when you make an appearance."

"My dearest Sebastian, how good to see you! I shall take your comments as a compliment, though you didn't exactly say that *you* liked my costume."

"I like it excessively," he replied promptly, in a parrotlike way.

"When you were a boy you were sent to your room for such pertness," she replied tartly, but then, with a surprisingly youthful giggle, she added, "and that is no doubt exactly what you would like now."

"Not at all, dear Aunt, I am at your service for the length of your stay," he replied gallantly. "What is your pleasure?"

"Do you know, I should like to go for a ramble in the Park. I saw the dearest little wildflowers as I drove along, and though I longed to stop and pick them I was too eager to get here to take the time."

So, after changing her costume for a dress more suitable for a walk in the country, she was taken out and returned happily with a large basketful of pale pink wild roses, honeysuckles, and harbells which she handed over to Crews with instructions for them to be made into an arrangement and put beside her bed where she could enjoy their scent all night.

They were all very merry at the elaborate dinner prepared by Mrs. McKirk, which consisted of two full courses with at least

89

five removes in each, and it was late before they had reached the end of it. At last Lady Stanier pushed aside the *Gâteau Mellifleur*, declaring that not even to keep in Mrs. McKirk's good graces could she force in another bite.

"—and if you will all forgive me I think I must seek my bed almost at once, for I am faint with fatigue. No doubt I have only myself to blame for I *would* have that long walk."

"Oh, dearest Caro!" exclaimed Lady Payton contritely, "of course you must be exhausted after your long journey! You must come along at once and let me put you straight to bed."

The two ladies said their goodnights and went away and Jane and Sebastian made their way downstairs and back to their own quarters. When Sebastian entered his wife's boudoir a half an hour later he found her seated before her dressing table having her dark curls brushed out by Betty, who promptly laid down the brush and left the room.

Sebastian seated himself in the chair before the fire and Jane came to drop on her knees before him in a cloud of blossom tulle negligee. She rested her elbows on his knees and gazed up at him with luminous eyes, feeling her glorious secret bubbling up irrepressibly, trying to think of just the right words to tell him of it.

"Do you know something?" Sebastian said, studying her intently, "impossible as it seems, you are grown even more beautiful. If you go on like this you will be an impossibly gorgeous old lady."

"Will I make a gorgeous mother, do you think?" The words burst out unstoppably, though this was not how she planned to tell him.

He stared at her blankly for a full moment and then as the import of her words sank into his mind a look of dawning horror grew in his eyes. He sat up and grasped her shoulders fiercely.

"No! You mustn't—I don't want—"

"Sebastian! What on earth—what is it?" she gasped.

"I don't want this! Are you sure of it?" he shook her shoulders impatiently.

She looked up at him dumbly, her beautiful secret smashed into pieces and lying about her. Her eyes filled with tears which ran slowly, unheeded, down her cheeks.

"Answer me! Are you sure?"

She nodded mutely, not daring to trust her voice.

"Oh my God!" He let her go abruptly and fell back into his chair, his eyes closed. Jane sank into a huddled heap on the floor, more miserable than she'd even been in her life. Even her dreadful experience with Leach was as nothing compared to the pain of causing Sebastian to be unhappy and angry with her! The constriction in her throat rose into a convulsive sob and then she gave way completely and put her hands over her face to weep unrestrainedly.

Immediately she felt Sebastian's arms come around her and he pulled her up against his shoulder. "Darling! Darling! Forgive me. Oh, what a brute I am to make you cry," he said contritely.

"B-b-but—why—why d-did you?" she sobbed. "I—I—w-wanted to make you h-h-happy! I th-th-thought you would be gl-gl-glad."

"Oh my love, I never meant to make you cry! Listen to me—listen, my darling! I am afraid, you see. It is dangerous for you—I might lose you! I—I could not bear for anything to happen to you!"

"But nothing will—" she began, withdrawing a little to look into his face.

"But it might! And nothing—*nothing*—is worth taking that chance as far as I am concerned. I simply *could not* bear to lose you!"

"Oh—oh Sebastian!" Jane cried, throwing her arms about his neck with a little laughing sob of relief. "Is that all!"

"*All!* No, no, Jane, you must listen to me, I can't—" he pulled her arms away and held her again by the shoulders.

Jane put her fingers over his lips. "No, love. Now I will speak. I know men worry about these things, and of course bad things *can* happen. But you need not fear for me. My mother always said I was made from the same mould as herself '—and ye'll find birthing easy when yer time is cum, Jane lass.' " Jane fell easily into her mother's speech pattern for she could hear her mother saying it plain as day. "She was seventeen when she had me, as I shall be, and she said it was the easiest chore she ever had in her life," Jane giggled at the memory of the story, "and I shall be just the same and very careful besides

91

and do everything I'm supposed to do. Oh Sebastian, please, *please* don't worry about me. The last thing I could bear would be to know I was causing you worry. I've wanted this so much and I want you to want it too. Say you will be happy!''

He could not withstand those tear-shiny, earnestly pleading eyes, and with a sort of groan he gathered her in his arms again and held her tightly.

"Promise me you are happy, Sebastian," she begged, her lips moving against his neck, "and that you won't worry about me, and I promise you nothing will happen to me."

He wondered if it were possible to make such a promise, on either of their parts, but he could not deny her; it was quite literally the first thing she had ever asked of him since the day they met.

"I promise, darling Jane," he whispered.

12

"Stop that sniveling now, girl, and get along to the kitchen for a meat broth for your mistress. She's right as a trivet and so's the babe," ordered Dr. Clegg, briskly drying his hands on the towel Betty held out for him and rolling down his shirtsleeves.

"Lady Stanier went to fetch it while I cleaned the baby," Betty replied, dashing her sleeve across her eyes, "and I'm not sniveling! But I suppose there's nothing wrong with feeling pity for the poor little mite to lose his gammer afore she can even see him, and her counting the days, and now most like to be fatherless afore he's even opened his eyes."

"Not so loud—she'll hear you," warned Dr. Clegg, "and she needs the rest. I'll go along now and see his lordship. Keep that broth warm when it comes, and feed it to her when she wakes. I'll send Crews along if—" he bit his lip, glanced at the bed, and then abruptly left the room, the picture hazily seen through the filmy bed curtains of the beautiful, young mother sweetly asleep with her cheek against the small, downy head of her newborn son accompanying him down the hall. He swallowed a lump in his throat, silently apostrophized himself as "a damned old fool," and softly opened the door to Lord Payton's bedroom.

Crews turned, and on the other side of the bed Eldon looked up anxiously at the doctor's entrance. Dr. Clegg crossed the room and took Sebastian's wrist. Pulse thready, breathing shallow, heartbeat—hum—he put his ear to Sebastian's chest—very bad, poor devil, lucky to last out the night. Knew all along he might as well sign his own death certificate as sign a marriage certificate, but there, he's had at least two happy years in as wretched a life as could be wished on a man, and he leaves a son behind to carry on his name.

Dr. Clegg pulled the coverlet back up to Sebastian's chin. "Well, well, nothing to do but wait, I fear. If he wakes try to get a little brandy into him. I'll go for my supper now, but call me if—"

"Yes, sir. At once, sir, you may be sure," Crews interrupted, not wanting to hear the rest of the doctor's sentence.

Dr. Clegg went off to Sebastian's study, where his supper waited on a table before the fire. Mrs. McKirk had made him a meat pie and Dorrie was mulling wine over the fire in anticipation of his arrival. Dorrie still wore the bereft look she'd worn since old Lady Payton's death two weeks ago. She'd grown very fond of "her lady" in the few months she'd been with her, and besides, she was now expecting to be sent, jobless, back to London, and she'd no place to go when she got there and no prospects. A thought, however, occurred to her: maybe Nurse, who was due to arrive tomorrow, could use a nursery maid. A comedown to be sure, but better than nothing. Also it was possible that in the near future Betty Crews would be taking over from Mrs. Plummer and an abigail for the young ladyship would be required. She brightened considerably with this thought, and she carefully carried the wine to the doctor.

"We'm a new young master, I'm told, sir."

"That you have, that you have," agreed Dr. Clegg, tucking his napkin under his chin and taking a great draught of the warmed wine before attacking the meat pie.

"And Lady Jane is well?"

"Fine as five pence, no worry. Here, Dorrie, where's my bread and butter, eh?"

Dorrie gasped, cast a horrified look at the table, and hurried off to the kitchen. The doctor continued his meal, one ear cocked for footsteps coming from the other direction. He leaned back in his chair and sipped at his wine. Damned if he wasn't nearly run off his legs, he thought tiredly.

He had been summoned two weeks ago to attend old Lady Payton, who had suffered a massive heart attack which had taken her almost before he could reach her bedside. He'd been attending Sebastian constantly before that, watching helplessly as he grew weaker and weaker, succumbing to one bout of fever after another that drained life and strength from his diminutive frame. Lady Payton and Lady Jane hardly left his bedside for a moment and the result, a heart attack for one and a slightly premature birth for the other, could have been foreseen. Dr. Clegg had simply moved in after old Lady Payton succumbed, to support Sebastian through the obsequies, then through his inevitable collapse after the funeral, and now, tonight, to attend Lady Jane's lying-in.

Not that the last had given him the least difficulty, even if it had come two weeks before expected. Never seen an easier birth, he thought, though a rare plucked 'un she is for all that, with hardly a squeak out of her from beginning to end, no doubt for fear Sebastian would hear her and be upset. And come to think of it, it was probably a blessing that it had come prematurely, for now, at least, the father would have a chance to see it. Dorrie interrupted his thoughts by returning with his bread and butter.

"Missus McKirk 'as a damson pie for when you've finished," she announced, panting slightly.

"Ah ha! Nothing I like better than a bit of damson pie. Now, if you'll just pour me another sip of that—" he broke off as he heard running footsteps coming down the hall. He dropped his knife and fork with a clatter, pushed back his chair, and was nearly to the door before it burst open to reveal Crews' frightened face.

"Doctor—!"

"Yes, yes—" the doctor pushed past Crews, "fetch her ladyship," he flung over his shoulder as he hurried down the hall.

"But how—?"

"Carry her if you must, but fetch her. I promised him. Hurry, man."

When Dr. Clegg reached the bedside he found Sebastian

propped up by an extra pillow, accepting sips of brandy from Eldon. Despite this appearance of recovery, however, his skin had taken on an unearthly waxen pallor and the bones of his face were sharply defined through it.

When he turned his head to the doctor his eyes were clear and serene. He spoke only one word. "Jane?"

"Very well. I've sent Crews to bring her to you. She's given you a fine, healthy son with no trouble at all. You can be proud of her."

"Take care of her."

"Don't you fret yourself about that, my boy. I'll see she comes to no harm. Now, don't speak any more. Save yourself for your wife," advised Dr. Clegg hoarsely. He turned away to the fireplace and stood there looking into the flames, blinking rapidly to hold back tears.

The door opened to admit Crews with Jane in his arms, followed by Lady Stanier carrying the baby.

"Put me there, Crews, on the side of the bed," Jane ordered, her eyes fastened on her husband's face. Sebastian smiled up at her. When she was seated she turned to Lady Stanier who came forward and put the baby into Sebastian's arms.

"Here's your son, dearest boy, and a beautiful lad he is," she said, leaning forward to kiss her nephew's pale forehead, and then walking away to join the doctor by the fire. Crews and Eldon withdrew to the other side of the room.

"Do you like our son, Sebastian?" Jane asked softly.

"He's certainly a funny scrap of a thing, isn't he?" he replied, smiling down at his son. He held out a tentative finger to touch the tiny, frail hand which immediately clutched his finger tightly. "But a good strong grip for his size!" he laughed softly. The baby's eyes opened at that moment and he stared up, blinking his filmy blue eyes at his father. Then quite distinctly a corner of his mouth quirked up exactly as though he were returning his father's smile. This effort obviously exhausted him and he abruptly fell asleep.

"Willing to be friends, but finds us boring on the whole," commented Sebastian wryly. He reached a hand out to Jane, who took it in both her own, holding it tight as though she could keep him with her by force. "Was it dreadful for you, my darling?" he asked.

"Certainly not! I hope you have not been in here indulging crochets on my account. I am not so paltry a creature that I

95

could not withstand those tiny little tweaks of pain, I assure you!'' she replied with pretended indignation.

He laughed. ''Ah, what a girl it is! You are such a joy to me, my Jane. Every moment with you has been pure happiness. The only happiness I've ever known.''

''I hope you will still be saying that in twenty years when I've worn you down with my whims and complaints,'' she replied pertly, though her voice was tight with her efforts not to give way. She had no intention of forcing her husband to contend with her grief during his last moments. That these were his last moments it was impossible to deny.

''Complaints? You? Not possible! You are all—'' he stopped as though too tired to continue, but only for an instant, ''—sunshine, beloved girl.''

She forced herself to smile, ''Why sir, you are a blatant flatterer!'' She put her cheek against his and closed her eyes so that he wouldn't see the tears. ''But I forgive you, my darling, because I love you so much.'' She whispered the words against his lips and then kissed him. For a moment he returned the pressure of her lips and then she was aware that his lips were still and she knew he was gone from her. She raised her head and studied his face, closed now to her and the world.

''Oh, Sebastian—no,'' she said softly, and slid quietly to the floor into blessed unconsciousness.

Dr. Clegg and Lady Stanier hurried forward, the doctor motioning to Crews to come forward, while Lady Stanier bent to take the infant who still slept serenely within the crook of his father's arm. She stood for a moment looking down upon her nephew, then gently caressed his cheek in farewell and turned to follow Crews, Jane across his arms, back to Jane's boudoir.

Miss Gilbert stood on the doorstep, a determined light discernible in her eye. She had called to pay her condolences to Sebastian upon Lady Payton's death, but had been met by Lady Stanier who told her Lord Payton himself was too ill to receive visitors and young Lady Payton could not leave his bedside. Whereupon Miss Gilbert offered to relieve ''the poor child'' in the sickroom, explaining that she had had a great deal of experience with invalids. Lady Stanier had politely, but firmly, declined the offer, and within moments Miss Gilbert found herself being shown out. Undeterred, however, she called each morning to inquire about Lord Payton's health, but never managed to gain admittance again, for Crews, on Lady Stanier's instructions, informed her that visitors were not being received at this time.

Word had reached Miss Gilbert that Lady Stanier had been suddenly called away soon after Sebastian's death to the bedside of her own daughter who was soon to give birth, and she had arrived at Larkwoods this morning confident of achieving her goal. Crews' attempt to turn her away she ignored, walking past him into the front hall.

"I'll just step in for a word with Lady Payton, Crews. Since Lady Stanier had to leave so suddenly, I'm sure Lady Payton will require the support of a gentlewoman, and as I am the only one in the vicinity who had even made her acquaintance, it is clearly my duty, as my father agrees, to be at her side during this difficult time."

As she spoke she marched firmly across the hall, opened the door to Sebastian's quarters, and continued down the interior hall to Jane's boudoir, for all the world as though she'd made the trip many times, though it was, in fact, the first time she'd ever penetrated Lord Payton's side of the house in all the years she'd been visiting Larkwoods.

Crews was at something of a nonplus. Although he was aware that Lord Payton had never received Miss Gilbert, old Lady Payton *had*, and it was true Lady Jane was alone here except for the servants. Besides, Miss Gilbert *was* Quality and he could hardly use force to keep her out. Therefore he could only trail ineffectually after her, and she had reached Jane's door without any means of stopping her presenting themselves to Crews' mind. She boldly opened the door "without so much as a knock for politeness sake," as Crews related indignantly to the staff belowstairs.

Nurse Watkyn, thinking it was Dorrie, turned with an admonishing finger to her lips, enjoining silence. Her eyes widened in astonishment. She had never seen Miss Gilbert before and was at a loss to explain this unannounced visitor to m'lady's bedroom, especially now while the baby was being fed.

"It's quite all right, Nurse. I'm an old friend of Lady Payton's. Ah! The darling baby! How beautiful he is!"

Nurse Watkyn, though shocked at the woman's boldness and by the fact that she did not withdraw at once when she saw that Lady Payton was in a state of undress, still felt her animosity melting at this praise of her charge, and hesitated. Before she could quite make up her mind what to do about the situation, Miss Gilbert crossed the room, pulled up a small gilt and brocade chair to the bedside, and sat down beside Jane with a great air of cool confidence.

Jane, her trancelike gaze on her baby's face, didn't look up. Indeed, she seemed unaware of Miss Gilbert's presence altogether. Miss Gilbert slowly removed her gloves, her eyes fixed unblinkingly on Jane's full, white breast. Her hand went out to touch the arm so near her and when Jane didn't react, continued to caress it. Presently, the baby's mouth released its hold on the nipple and Nurse came to take him away to his crib. Miss Gilbert jerked her hand away, flushing darkly under Nurse's curious stare.

"Well, my dear, now we can talk. I didn't like to disturb you while the child was—er—. How well you are looking, and the dear babe blooming. We shall have to arrange some drives in the carriage soon. I'm sure you would benefit by some fresh air." She babbled on, eliciting no response whatsoever from Jane, who fastened up her gown, stared blankly at Miss Gilbert for a brief instant, and turned away to the window. "Well, my dear, I mustn't tire you. I'll call again tomorrow. Must keep my eye on you for my dear old departed friend, as I know she would expect of me."

She took her leave, nodding amiably to Nurse Watkyn. Crews, still hovering uncertainly in the hallway, showed her to the door, receiving an amiable nod in his turn.

From that day on she arrived promptly at eleven-thirty each morning, watched the baby being fed, caressed Jane's arm, spoke to her briefly, and took her leave. Nurse at first had hoped the visits might succeed in drawing m'lady out of her fit of melancholy and made no objection, though she could not like the woman coming always while the baby was being fed. This had not been the way of Quality in any of the great houses where she had been in charge of the nursery. After the first week, when it became obvious that m'lady got no good from the visits, Nurse became more and more uneasy about the situation.

Today the feeling was stronger. Miss Gilbert had come and gone, the baby had slept and wakened, crying sharply, demandingly, for attention.

"Well now, your little lordship, I can see what's troubling you, and if you'll stop crying and kicking I'll fix it for you. Oh dear, oh *dear!* Well, it'll all be better in a trice. There now—

how's that then? Oh, you like that do you? Like your blessed papa, you are. Just the same, he was, always liked to be clean and dry. Poor little mite, it's little enough else you get, but never you fear, Nurse is here now and will take care of you, even if there's others that won't.''

This breathy monologue, delivered sotto voce, was audible to Jane as she lay in her bed staring unseeingly out the window at the tangle of bare, black branches against the cold, gray of the December sky. The meaning of the words, however, did not penetrate her consciousness, any more than the presence of Miss Gilbert had. She existed, as she had in the weeks since Sebastian's death, in a state of apathy bordering on the catatonic. She only roused herself when the baby was put into her arms to be nursed. One of the few words she had spoken had been an emphatic "No" to the suggestion that a wet nurse be found. She would bare her milk-swollen breast and sit staring gravely down at the tiny face without movement or comment. Clinton Brede Atherton Payton, Seventh Baron Larkley, stared solemnly back, minute mouth working away industriously, tiny fist punching and kneading away at his mother's soft flesh. Finally his eyes would slowly close and the downy head would fall back on Jane's arm, the milky mouth slightly open. Nurse, hovering in the background, would come forward to take him and Jane would resume her contemplation of the window. Nurse would invariably "Tsk, tsk" to see it, but it had no more effect on Jane than her monologues.

Today, Nurse Watkyn made up her mind, something must be done. It was all very well to grieve. She herself had shed a great many tears when she'd heard of dear Master Sebastian's death, but there was the baby now who must have attention, and there was this odd, dried up old stick of a vicar's daughter, sitting there day after day staring at m'lady's bare bosom in that strange way. 'Twasn't proper, that wasn't, and she didn't care who heard her say it and something must be done to put a stop to it. Accordingly, when she had tucked the baby back into his crib, she said, "I must just step along to the kitchen for them clean napkins, your ladyship. Won't be but a minute. That Dorrie! I can't think where she's got herself to. I sent her for those napkins a quarter of an hour ago.''

She marched firmly away to the kitchen in search of Crews, where she found him taking his dinner with Mrs. Crews, elevated now to housekeeper since Mrs. Plummer's departure. The two deaths had taken the heart out of her, Mrs. Plummer had told Lady Stanier, and she would retire to spend her remaining years with her daughter. Lady Stanier had taken her up in her own carriage when she left for London, to drop her with the daughter in Barnet. Lady Stanier had felt quite sanguine about leaving with Betty Crews waiting to step into Mrs. Plummer's shoes, Nurse Watkyn installed with the baby, and Dorrie on hand to assist her.

Betty Crews smiled up at Nurse and cordially invited her to sit down and join them for a meal.

"I thank you, Mrs. Crews, but I'll take my dinner later. I've come about something serious. In my opinion something has got to be done about her ladyship. Just lying there staring out the winder and never saying a word. It ain't natural. And another thing ain't natural neither! That Gilbert woman coming into m'lady's boudoir every day and staring. Fair makes my flesh crawl, it does, and I won't have it. It's not a healthy atmosphere for a newborn babe."

"What would you have me do, Mrs. Watkyn? She just marches in as though she owns the place and—"

"You must write to Lady Stanier."

"But I can't do that!" Crews protested, aghast.

"You must. You must tell her she must come back as soon as may be and speak to her ladyship and stop that woman from coming into the bedroom. Lady Stanier's the only one who can attend to it proper."

"Well now, I don't know that I—" Crews began doubtfully.

"She's right, Fred," said Betty positively. "I've been that worrit myself, only I couldn't just think of what was best to be done."

"But I don't know that I've the right to—"

"Then you must talk to Lady Jane yourself," Betty declared.

"Me!?"

"You're her old friend and the one as should do it if you won't write to Lady Stanier."

Crews looked dismayed at such a choice. He had decided, when he'd made up his mind to come here, that Jane, whatever may have been her previous station in life, was now within the ranks of Quality and would always be treated as such by him. During this past year in her service he had succeeded in maintaining an attitude of deferential respect that had put them both at ease. To have it suggested that he now approach his mistress in the role of old friend outraged his sense of what was proper.

Not that he wouldn't do anything possible to help her, but this he felt was beyond him.

"Besides, I wouldn't know what to say to her. What if I said the wrong thing?" he finally managed to protest.

"Exactly! That's why it would be best to write to Lady Stanier," replied Betty calmly.

He was finally persuaded and the letter laboriously written and dispatched, and came at last to lie on top of the pile of post deposited on Lady Stanier's bed along with her morning chocolate. Lady Stanier, sleepily sipping her morning drink, ignored her mail, content to watch Ames, her dresser, as she moved quietly about the room, unpacking the boxes and portmanteaus and putting things away. She was happy to be back in her own bed at last, after weeks of jauntering about the countryside, attending deathbeds and birthing couches. But presently her eye was caught by the inelegancy of the unfamiliar handwriting on the top letter and she reached a reluctant hand for it, sensing that there would be something in it to distress her. She turned it over, and there, sure enough, was confirmation of her fear, for the seal was Sebastian's, which meant it was from a servant at Larkwoods. She broke it and read the letter and her hand finally dropped limply, resignedly, onto the coverlet.

"Ames," she said quietly, "pack them up."

Ames turned with a bright smile. "Bless you, m'lady, but I am unpacking."

"No. I said pack them up again."

Ames looked at her as though her mind had become unhinged. "Pack them, m'lady?"

"Yes, and order the carriage brought round in an hour," replied Lady Stanier decisively.

"But surely you can't mean—"

"I'm afraid I do, Ames. We must leave for Larkwoods at once."

13

Lady Stanier, having broken her journey in Maidstone, emerged from her elegant travelling carriage before the front entrance of Larkwoods shortly before midday, looking excessively fresh and smart in a stone-coloured pelisse with a chinchilla cape, a large chinchilla muff, and a most becoming Capote bonnet in dark gray velvet.

Crews goggled appreciatively for a moment before he could recover his dignity and bow profoundly. "M'Lady! I had not expected you so quickly. We are all most grateful to you for coming and I hope you will forgive me if I have been overforward in writing to you."

"If the situation is as bad as you intimated in your letter, Crews, then it is I who am in *your* debt. Has anything changed?"

"No, m'lady. Lady Jane is just as she has been since Lord Payton's death, and Miss Gilbert still comes each day. In fact—she is in there at this moment. She arrived only a few moments ago."

Lady Stanier's lips tightened. "Did she, indeed, Very well, Crews. Would you be good enough to remain here to—er—show her out. In approximately one moment!" Shoulders back, a distinctly militant gleam in her eye, she marched across the hall and disappeared. Crews grinned delightedly.

Lady Stanier quietly opened the door to Jane's boudoir and stood silently taking in the scene before her. Nurse Watkyn, her back to the door, was folding impossibly small clothing in one corner. Jane, in a shaft of pale, wintry sunshine, sat up against her pillows in the canopied bed, nursing her child. Angela Gilbert sat beside the bed. Lady Stanier drew back with distaste as she noted the hand sensuously caressing Jane's bare forearm, the bulging green eyes fastened shamelessly on Jane's bare breasts.

Lady Stanier advanced soundlessly across the pale blue and yellow Aubusson carpet. "Miss Gilbert!"

Miss Gilbert's head jerked up, she stared incomprehensibly at Lady Stanier for an instant, then rose so suddenly her chair toppled over, as the colour drained from her face. Nurse started around at the sound of Lady Stanier's voice, her eyes lighting up.

"L-l-lady Stanier!" stammered Miss Gilbert. "What—why —I mean—you have taken me so by surprise I—I—"

"Evidently," replied Lady Stanier succinctly, a wealth of meaning expressed in the one word.

"I was only—I felt it was my duty—" Miss Gilbert faltered, the colour rushing back into her face at Lady Stanier's tone.

"Very good of you, but we won't presume on you any further. Good day, Miss Gilbert."

There was so much finality in her words that even Miss Gilbert realised there was nothing further to be said. She gathered up the tatters of her dignity, bowed frostily, and left the room.

Throughout this encounter Jane remained seemingly oblivious of what was going forward, never lifting her eyes from her contemplation of Clinton's face. Nurse Watkyn however, hurried forward with the closing of the door to drop a respectful curtsy.

"M'lady! Never was I happier to see anyone in all my days! It were a rare treat to see you put that old stick to rout so neatlike."

Lady Stanier reached out to pat Nurse's shoulder. "That was the easy part, from the looks of things."

Nurse followed her significant glance at the bed. "Yes, madam, I take your meaning. There's deep doin's there, right enough, and I'm blessed if I know what to make of it. Hardly a word has she spoke these two weeks now. Fair makes my skin crawl to see it, it does."

Lady Stanier did not allow even a flicker of impatience to show as she waited through this loquaciousness, realizing that Nurse Watkyn was only relieving her long held-in anxiety, now hopeful that help was at hand. When she had finished, Lady Stanier patted her shoulder again and smiled. "Not to worry, Nurse, we'll all come about, you'll see."

They moved instinctively to the bedside. "Lord Payton has dined well from the looks of him," she said. They stood for a moment smiling down fondly at young Clinton, who, glutted at last, slept profoundly, a trickle of milk escaping from his greedy, half-open mouth, his dark lashes fanning across his fat, rosy little cheeks. Lady Stanier bent to pick him up, cuddling him in her arms happily for a moment before handing him over. "Perhaps you could put him down to sleep elsewhere for a while, Nurse."

"Certainly, m'lady, I'll take him down to the kitchen and Betty Crews will rock him by the fire while I have a bite to eat. She's that wild to get her hands on the babe."

When she was gone Lady Stanier removed her bonnet and gloves and sat down on the side of Jane's bed, taking the limp hands into her own.

"This will never do, child," she chided Jane gently. She waited, but there was no response. She put her hand to Jane's cheek and turned her face to look into her eyes. "Jane, my dear, won't you speak to your Aunt Stanier? Try to tell me what is wrong."

Jane's sherry-brown eyes gazed blankly back, registering no emotion whatsoever. Lady Stanier felt a cold chill of horror pass over her at the bleak impersonality of Jane's regard. "Dearest girl! What has happened to you?" she gasped. She shook Jane's face slightly with no result. "Jane! *Jane!*"

After a moment Lady Stanier rose and began to pace back and forth across the carpet, ending finally at the window where she paused for a few moments in thought. She swung around finally to study Jane's vacant face, then marched purposefully back to the bed, turned the unresisting face toward herself and without hesitation, for fear that she would lose her resolution, slapped Jane's cheek resoundingly. Jane cried out and threw herself back against her pillows, her eyes wide with shock, her hand flying to her cheek where the imprint of Lady Stanier's hand was coming up quite clearly in bright red. Then her face crumpled and she began to cry, the tears, childlike, spurting from her eyes. Lady Stanier, with a sympathetic little moan, sat down on the bed and pulled Jane into her arms. The sobs increased their intensity, racking the slim young body painfully. Lady Stanier's own eyes filled and she rocked Jane back and forth, crooning softly to her for quite fifteen minutes before there was any diminution in the flow of tears.

Then Lady Stanier held her away to look into her eyes. She smoothed the damp, tangled curls away from the tear-wet face and with her own handerkchief began to dry it. "Jane, my little love, look at me now," she commanded.

Jane raised her swimming eyes, but now in place of the blankness there appeared so much pain and despair that Lady Stanier cried out involuntarily, "Oh no, darling, you must not grieve so!"

"I cannot bear it," Jane said starkly.

"But of course you can. I know it seems impossible, but we must all learn to bear it when we lose those we love. I have known that pain myself, believe me."

"Did you also know the guilt?"

"Guilt?"

"Yes. It was me, you see. It was my fault they both died. I killed them."

"Nonsense, child, I can't think what on earth—"

"He would have lived years more if he had never met me. I took those years away from him. And his mother, also. His illness was too much for her weak heart. I killed them both," she reiterated flatly.

Lady Stanier stared at her before she spoke." How very god-like you are, Jane. You quite frighten me with such power. You give life and you take it away."

"Ah—don't laugh at me!"

"Laugh? I have never been less amused in my life! Astonished, even awed by your claim, would be a more accurate description of my feelings at this moment! Until now it has always been my belief that such powers as you profess to hold were to be found only in the hands of God!"

"But I caused them to die! You know—"

"I know nothing of the sort! You must be all about in your head, my girl. Let me set the record straight for you. My nephew, poor soul, lived entombed for twenty years on one side of this house, while dear Lelia endured the same sort of existence on the other. Neither of them seeing anyone or living the sort of life to which their fortune and station in life entitled them, not to speak of enjoying the simple pleasures that are given to make the most ordinary life endurable. Do you think, given the choice, either of them would have exchanged the past two years for five or even ten years more of—of—living death?'' Jane opened her mouth to protest, but Lady Stanier raised her hand. ''No! Let me go on now that I've the bit well between my teeth. Sebastian had with you the only happiness he has known as an adult, and there isn't the least doubt in my mind that God *meant* this marriage to be. He kept both of them alive beyond any expectation of mine until you could come into their lives—it was nothing less than miraculous! Now you may take the credit for giving them that happiness, as I certainly believe belongs solely to you, but always remember you were *His* instrument, as we all are. There now! I have had my say, and you may speak.''

Jane, however, sat unmoving and silent, her eyes cast down, for so long that Lady Stanier began to fear uneasily that she had accomplished nothing and that Jane had retreated into her mind once more. But presently, Jane sighed and spoke. ''It seemed so clear to me, you see. They gave me everything. I took all of it. And then they were gone, as though I had—had depleted them. I felt quite—deadly. It seemed that where I loved, I destroyed and it would be best for me not to be even tempted to do so again, especially with little Clinton, so tiny and fragile, so—'' she was unable to repress a little sob, ''inexpressibly dear to me. All that was left, you see, of my other dear ones. I thought if I loved him too much—or even at all—I might cause his death also. So I tried to cut myself off from everything, even thinking, so that I would not be tempted to love.''

''Also, I expect, it made the grief more bearable,'' said Lady Stanier shrewdly. ''But I fear there is no escape from that, my love. Sooner or later grief must have its way. Tears must be shed. Much the healthiest way to shed them at once.''

She tilted her head interrogatively at Jane, and in her eyes was a clear invitation. Jane didn't hesitate for a moment to accept it, but threw herself back into those comforting arms in a fresh outburst of tears, though these tears were as healing to the spirit as the rain to a parched field.

Before the day was over Lady Stanier had overseen the transformation of Sebastian's bedroom into a temporary nursery. She forebore to suggest that the child might perfectly well occupy the nursery in the other part of the house where generations of infant Paytons, including Sebastian himself, had spent their first years. She knew Jane could never be persuaded to remove to that part of the house herself to take up her proper place as mistress of Larkwoods in the state apartments. At least not for the present. She was even somewhat resistant to the idea of having her child removed from her own boudoir, but Lady Stanier managed to convince her that everyone would benefit by the separation, and finally Nurse was allowed to carry Clinton away.

Mrs. McKirk was consulted and a light dinner was ordered, after which Lady Stanier set out to entice Jane from her bed.

"Oh—I'm not sure I—" Jane looked quite frightened at the suggestion she might like to dress and come join Lady Stanier for dinner.

"I really must insist on your company, child. I dislike dining alone above all things, and it will do you good to leave that bed. You are not really ill, and lying in bed when one is in perfectly good health can be most debilitating, I assure you."

Lady Stanier's calm, good-natured, down-to-earth attitude did its work, and Betty was sent for to dress Jane and arrange the tumble of dark curls. After the long weeks of illness and mourning, the house assumed again the agreeable stir and bustle of activity it had known, alas all too briefly during the past years, and although it did not resemble in any way the rejoicing of those two years of Jane and Sebastian's marriage, at least the shroud of gloom was dispelled.

The table had been laid before the fire in Sebastian's study, where the couple had been accustomed to take their meals when the elder Lady Payton had not been in residence, and Jane felt a weak quaking when she entered the study and saw the familiar setting of so many happy hours. But Lady Stanier, sensing that she would feel so, came forward to lead her to a comfortable chair at the table, and without any appearance of strain, began to speak quite openly of Sebastian, telling her of some of his exploits as a small child, and then passing on quite naturally to speak of herself and Lady Payton when they were girls. Jane managed to eat a respectable portion of the simelles of carp, broiled fowl with mushrooms, and Savoy cake placed before her, and even to laugh aloud once at one of Lady Stanier's stories.

When Crews had removed their plates and withdrawn, they

remained comfortably relaxed in their chairs, sipping the last of their wine, a contented silence between them.

Lady Stanier was pondering the strange workings of Providence, which had brought this young girl into their lives less than two years ago. A frightened, bruised little Cockney girl, who yet managed to project spirit and courage in her eagerness to begin again in a place totally foreign to her. Now, still months short of her seventeenth birthday, the little backstairs maid had become a mother, a widow, an heiress to a staggering portion of the Payton fortune and the guardian of an even larger amount held in her son's name, and the bearer of the title of Baroness Larkley, one of the oldest and most prestigious in England.

A real-life fairy story, Lady Stanier mused, with Jane as Cinderella, or Beauty and the Beast, although, of course, Sebastian had not been beastly in any way. Actually quite good-looking except for his lack of inches, which most people tended to think of as freakish, and the dourness of his manner really overlaid the original sweetness of his nature. She well-remembered the loving, happy little boy he had been before that dreadful accident. It was that nature that had been allowed to surface again in the warmth of Jane's sunny disposition. They had all, in fact, basked in it and grown to love and depend on her so much that not only were they not shocked by the misalliance but eager to promote it. Honesty compelled Lady Stanier to admit that beauty and sunny nature notwithstanding, such a marriage could not have come about in the ordinary course of things, however that had nothing to say to anything since there had *been* nothing in the least ordinary in the course of things.

And circumstances were bound to become even more extraordinary, for Lady Stanier had determined that she would not go away and leave this child here, prey to depression and loneliness and Angela Gilbert. She would take her away with her to London, where, inevitably, she would come to the attention of Society, and a victim to its voracious appetite for gossip. Lady Stanier silently thanked the Lord for Sebastian's adamant refusal to have an announcement of the marriage sent to the papers. If Lady Stanier could slip very quietly into London with the new Lady Payton, allow the news to be disseminated to a select few, spread, and become an accepted fact before the child need face anyone, for actually nothing was demanded or even expected of her while she was in mourning, then she might be able to accomplish her acceptance without too outrageous an uproar. She and the old Lady Payton had settled it between them at the time of the marriage that they would let it be known, where they felt it necessary, that Miss Coombes was a young country girl of good family fallen on hard times and to deflect any further inquiries with enthusiastic descriptions of Jane's beauty and sweetness. It had worked, for the greater part, at the time.

Now, however, circumstances made the position even more difficult. For here was an excessively young widow, whose inheritance would draw every fortune hunter in England and whose beauty would have half the beaux of the *ton* dangling at her shoestrings. However, Lady Stanier turned decisively to Jane.

"My dear, I have been thinking of what to do, and I think, you know, that now, before the roads become impassable, you and the child had best come back to London with me."

Jane stared uncomprehendingly at her for a moment before the full import of the words reached her brain, and then her whole face expressed shocked protest. But before she could utter it, Lady Stanier held up a hand to halt her.

"Wait! I know what you are going to say: the baby is too young for such a journey, that you prefer to stay here because you feel safer here, that—oh—everything you are preparing to say to me. But let me tell you my reasons first. I cannot stay with you. I have obligations in London, and I cannot feel right about leaving you here—especially now when you are bound to feel especially alone and unhappy. And as for the journey—pooh, I make nothing of that. I daresay we would all be as comfortable in my carriage as we are here by this fireside, and certainly the child could take no harm."

Jane pictured Lady Stanier's elegant, well-sprung, extraordinarily warm and luxurious travelling coach and smiled faintly in acknowledgment of the truth of her statement. It was indeed possible to imagine a journey of any length in the coach equipped with braziers of hot coals, voluptuously soft, velvet-covered squabs, and a capacious food basket stowed under the seat.

"Dear Aunt Stanier, I'm sure all you say is true," she answered with a fond smile, "however, I could not take Clinton away from his home. He should grow up here, knowing it and feeling its influence. He—"

"Nonsense! Until the child is at least a year old the only influence he will respond to is yours and Nurse Watkyn's, and if you are depressed and unhappy *he* will feel it. Besides, I'm not speaking of taking him away forever. Naturally, you will come back when the weather improves and it is possible to take advantage of the outdoors. I'm speaking of these long dreary winter months ahead when you stand in need of your family about you—I speak of myself—as well as being occasionally in company—''

''Company? Oh no, I could not face—Society!''

''Who speaks of Society? I'm referring to taking a cup of tea with an old friend or two of my own from time to time, or attending a musical evening. Naturally I do not intend anything more myself while we are in mourning. As for not 'facing' people, I will not allow you to bury yourself down here forever. My sister had no choice. She felt she owed it to her son to remain here if he insisted upon doing so, just as you owe it to your son to do whatever is necessary to give him a healthy, happy childhood. And I don't believe staying here alone is conducive to either of those qualities.''

''But—but—the servants—I—''

''I've thought of that. We would take Nurse with us, of course, leaving the rest here, since you will be staying with me. It would be foolish to open up Larkley House for just a few months. However, next year you should come up early and open it for the Season and bring Mr. and Mrs. Crews with you, and Dorrie, of course. I'm sure Mrs. McKirk will be wanting to retire by then, and I doubt she'd ever go to London in any case.''

''Payton House?''

''The Payton town house. Surely Sebastian mentioned it to you.''

''We—never talked of such things—his possessions or money—and I never thought to ask. There were so many things to talk about always that I suppose we never thought of it. Of course I am not so hen-witted as not to know that there is a great deal of money left to Clinton, and Lady Payton told me just before she died that I need not ever worry about anything again, because they had seen to it that I needn't—but I wouldn't let her go on, she could hardly speak anyway and I couldn't bear to let her waste—well—'' she dashed a hand childishly across her swimming eyes, "anyway, about Payton House. I think I will go there," Jane said decidedly.

"But my dear child! It will not be suitable now. All the furniture in Holland covers, no staff—"

"Well, I will come to you for a few weeks while Fred and Betty Crews close up this place and come up to prepare it and hire some more servants. I don't like to go away and leave them here for months. They have all been so good to me, and I think we should all stay together."

If Lady Stanier had been prepared to expound upon the unnecessary trouble and expense such a plan would entail, she forgot it quickly at the firmness of this last declaration. Besides, she thought, refurbishing the house would distract Jane's mind from her grief and prevent the possibility of her becoming an unhealthily doting, overprotective mother, and Heaven knew the expense need not be a concern.

So it was settled between them that in a week's time they would travel, by easy stages, to London with little Clinton and Nurse Watkyn, to be followed a week after that by Mr. and Mrs. Crews and Dorrie, who was to come to Lady Stanier's to be trained as a proper abigail by Ames. They would make the journey in the Payton travelling chaise, which would then be available for Jane's use in the city. Mrs. McKirk, if she chose not to accompany them, would be given her very generous pension, plus what she had been left by the late Lady Payton in her will, and conveyed to her sister's house in Dorset in one of the smaller carriages.

It wasn't until Lady Stanier was in her bed that night that she began to wonder, enviously, what Jane and Sebastian had found to talk about so endlessly. Lord knows Percy had been an exemplary husband, and Lady Stanier had truly loved him and grieved dreadfully when he was taken from her, but she was forced to acknowledge that interesting conversation had *not* been his long suit.

14

As Jane and Lady Stanier mounted the curving, shallow staircase to Mrs. Medvers-Platt's drawing room, Jane's knees were trembling so badly she had some serious doubts about ever reaching to the top. This was her first venture into Society in the three years since Sebastian's death, in spite of Lady Stanier's repeated efforts to persuade her otherwise. True, she had been present in Lady Stanier's drawing room on several occasions when visitors had been announced, and had received Lady Stanier and various lady friends of hers at Payton House, but she had remained adamant about going out in the evenings long after the year of mourning had been observed. Lady Stanier had remarked, rather pithily, that such an attitude was "quite gothick" and she was sure Sebastian would have agreed with her, but Jane had only smiled and changed the subject. Not only had she no inclination for entertainment, she had not yet weaned the baby and became very uncomfortable when his mealtime approached and she was not near to relieve both him and herself. More important, she had not yet acquired the courage to do it.

She had seen the curiosity and speculation in the eyes of Lady Stanier's friends, hovering behind the kindliness and courtesy with which they had treated her, and polite inquiries such as "—would you be related to the Coombes in Yorkshire?" had reduced her to such a blind panic that she could only gape dumbly at her inquisitor and wait to be rescued by Lady Stanier.

She had, however, enjoyed refurbishing Payton House. At first she had been loath to allow anything at all to be changed, content to oversee the cleaning, waxing, and polishing, a prodigious enough task in itself. Lady Stanier had managed to convince her, however, that the draperies in the drawing room would fall apart if any attempt were made to clean them, since they had been hanging there when the former Lady Payton was a bride, and Jane had reluctantly agreed to accompany her to a silk warehouse in search of suitable fabric for replacements. After that the sad condition of the upholstery on several of the dining room chairs was pointed out, and one thing led to another until Jane was caught up in a swirl of redecoration. She steadfastly refused, however, to replace any of the furnishings themselves, saying she wanted the house to retain the character given it by all the Lady Paytons of the past, and that she much preferred its style to the present mode for console tables with crocodile feet and lamps shaped like lilies.

She had gone down to Kent that first spring and introduced her son to the glories of the Kentish countryside foaming with lilacs and roses. It was not so heart-wrenching as she had dreaded it would be, though the first days had been difficult. But when the days had lengthened to long, sun-drenched hours, drowsy with the hum of bees plundering hedges tangled with wild Canterbury bells and thrifts and meadowsweets, the ache of loss gradually eased and the happier memories revived. Each year after that it was to become easier as the past released its hold and the present grew more interesting.

She had finally relented and agreed to attend Mrs. Medvers-Platt's musical evening. Mrs. Medvers-Platt was Lady Stanier's bosom-bow from girlhood and had been especially pressing in her invitations to Jane. Having been in the habit of spending her winters away on the Continent when Jane was in residence at Payton House, she was exceedingly eager to meet this young woman who had married Sebastian.

"For say what you will, Shafto," she had confided to her husband in the privacy of her boudoir, "the boy was deformed. Why he never grew to be more than sixty inches tall if that!" Shafto, who had not said anything in the first place, made only his usual noncommittal grunt to this statement, but Mrs. Medvers-Platt took this as encouragement to proceed, as she had learned to do after twenty-five years of marriage to a man who rarely communicated anything not directly bearing on his own comfort. "You may mark my words on it that there is something wrong with the girl. Probably a knock-in-the-cradle whose parents were unable to make any other match for her!"

The girl who appeared beside Lady Stanier at the top of the stairs, however, was obviously in perfect command of her intellect and so beautiful it quite took Mrs. Medvers-Platt's breath away. She noted indulgently that her husband had come to life and was pulling in his stomach and brushing his mustaches back in anticipation.

Jane wore a smoke-gray satin tunic trimmed in silver-embroidered acorns and leaves over a deeper gray underskirt. Her black curls had been brushed high on the back of her head and she wore a tiara of diamonds and silver leaves mounted on thin silver wires so that they trembled and glittered with each movement of her head in a most enchanting way. It had been Sebastian's gift to her on their marriage. The gray was her concession to Lady Stanier's insistence that she put aside her mourning clothes. "A year would have been quite enough. Besides it doesn't become you and you are much too young to go about in such lugubrious garments for so long." Jane had felt conspicuous, almost naked, without the protection of her black and brown gowns at first, but the knowledge that one has never been in better looks had succeeded in alleviating that discomfort tonight. The high colour in her cheeks and lips was set off by the perfection of the soft, cloudly gray, and her eyes were sparkling with excitement to be among people in spite of her nerves.

Mrs. Medvers-Platt sailed forward to envelop Lady Stanier in a warm embrace and then turned to Jane. She was a large, stout lady with so imposing a manner that Jane was overcome with shyness, which charmed Mrs. Medvers-Platt so much she embraced Jane also before turning to present her to an eager Mr. Medvers-Platt, who clearly looked upon pretty girls as one of the creature comforts provided by a benevolent deity. He took her hand possessively in both his own and seemed disinclined to let it go, all the while complimenting her in a heavy-handed way and being enormously gratified by her blushes. Finally he pulled her hand through his arm proprietorily and bore her away without a word to the two older ladies. Mrs. Medvers-Platt turned to her friend with an apologetic smile.

"There, my dear, you will forgive Shafto for his rudeness, I know. He is so cast into the glooms by my parties until some pretty creature comes in for him to flirt with. It is just his habit, you know, he means nothing by it and would never take advantage of a young, inexperienced girl." Mrs. Medvers-Platt spoke with great earnestness, eyeing Lady Stanier anxiously. Lady Stanier's eyes were twinkling, but she replied soberly that she trusted dear Shafto completely.

After the first few uncomfortable moments, Jane realized that she also could trust Mr. Medvers-Platt and relaxed, actually enjoying having a flirt, even an elderly one, since it al lowed her to be less self-conscious among all these strangers. Her beau led her from group to group, introducing her, flattering her, and teasing her all at the same time until she quite lost her earlier apprehensions and began to look upon this mostly middle-aged gathering as benign and well-meaning.

It was, therefore, even more of a shock when she turned laughingly away from an ancient lady with a hearing trumpet who insisted, despite Jane's protestations, that she had been acquainted with Jane's mother, to come face-to-face with Lady Montmorency and her daughter, Lady Sarah!

Every nerve end in Jane's body leaped up jangling with alarm and for a moment she was so paralyzed she couldn't close her mouth, which had fallen open in shock. Then she felt her face grow warm and knew she was blushing furiously while Lady Montmorency stared with an icy indifference.

Mr. Medvers-Platt, in serene unawareness, pulled her forward and begged Lady Montmorency to allow him to present Lady Jane Payton to her. Jane managed a curtsy, though fully aware that had she not been holding Mr. Medvers-Platt's arm she could never have accomplished it without falling on her face.

Lady Montmorency acknowledged the introduction with a stiff little nod of her head that committed her to nothing. It was not her habit to accept anyone on faith. She was a stately, intimidating woman, with traces of Lady Sarah's beauty still discernible in her face. She was gowned in a purple-bloom satin and wore a turban of the same fabric, an astonishing concoction of gold fringe, pearls, and feathers, which added to her regal stature. She turned to present her daughter, who curtsied in her turn. Though Jane had been thoroughly grounded in social etiquette by the Dowager Lady Payton and was well aware that as a married lady of title she took precedence over Lady Sarah, it was still an astonishing sensation to have the haughty Lady Sarah dipping her knee to Jane Coombes! No, she reminded herself sharply, *not* to Jane Coombes, but to Lady Payton, mother of Lord Payton of Larkwoods, Seventh Baron Larkley, and as his representative she owed it to him to conduct herself befittingly. She raised her chin, said how do you do with a gracious smile and submitted without a flicker of an eyelid to Lady Sarah's raking scrutiny, which seemed to count the very silver-embroidered acorns on Jane's gown before it came to rest on her face. Jane, still smiling, raised one eyebrow ever so slightly, and Lady Sarah's glance flicked away. This small triumph enabled Jane to carry on a brief conversation quite creditably until Mr. Medvers-Platt tugged her away impatiently to meet an old crony of his in an astonishing blue brocade evening suit fashionable fifty years ago, complete with white powdered wig, a tiny black patch next to his mouth, and rouge filling out the cracks in his cheeks. He made her a most profound and elaborate bow involving a complicated flourishing of his scented, lace-edged handkerchief.

Though Jane smiled sweetly upon him and replied satisfactorily to his conversation, her mind was in a ferment, for it had just occurred to her to wonder if Lord Jaspar accompanied his mother and sister this evening! That Lady Montmorency had not recognized her was to be expected, for Jane doubted if the woman had even known Jane was in her employ, so far beneath her notice was a little backstairs maid. Nor was it surprising that Lady Sarah had failed to do so, for Jane was well aware of that young woman's preoccupation with herself to the exclusion of all else except for her effect on the male sex and whether another lady's gown was more beautiful than her own. But Lord Jaspar was another matter altogether. They had only met once, but he had taken a very good look (she felt her cheeks redden as she remembered) and could not be counted on to have forgotten her, though their encounter *had* taken place more than five years ago.

She swept an anxious glance about the room but did not see him, which perversely provided her with only a fleeting moment of relief followed swiftly by an even stronger feeling of disappointment which bewildered her. There was no time, however, to examine this unusual feeling, for the guests were all being requested to take their seats in the music room for the entertainment, and she found Lady Stanier at her side firmly leading her away over Mr. Medvers-Platt's protestations.

"I thought you wouldn't mind being rescued, my love. Shafto is the best-hearted creature in the world but a shade overwhelming, I sometimes find. Did you meet any interesting people? I vow, Fanny has managed to assemble as dull a crowd as I've seen anytime these past ten years. I wonder where she dug up that funny old court card, Alben Quint? I didn't know he even went into company anymore. Probably got wind that Fanny was entertaining a rich widow. He's been hanging out for a fortune since he first came up to London sixty years ago!''

Jane giggled and told her that she had found Mr. Quint enchanting and agreed that he might come to pay her a morning visit. Then, still somewhat hipped at her ability to carry off the meeting with the Montmorencys, she told Lady Stanier of it in a lighthearted way.

''No! Don't tell me they are here! Not, of course, that we need worry about their recognizing you. I doubt either of them could adequately describe her own dresser. Oh—yes, I see them now.'' She and Lady Montmorency saw each other at the same moment and exchanged stiff nods and tight little smirks that did duty for smiles between two women in a social situation who detest each other. ''Now what can Fanny mean by inviting her here when she knows I can't abide the woman! A colder creature I hope it is never my misfortune to meet, and so puffed up with her own conceit she can hardly bring herself to speak to anyone whose consequence is not so great as she thinks her own to be!''

This heated diatribe was most unusual for Lady Stanier, ordinarily the most sweet natured of women, but her natural dislike of people who behaved as did Lady Montmorency combined with her knowledge of that lady's treatment of Jane had hardened into active antipathy.

''Perhaps it was foolish—coming here, I mean. Somehow it never occurred to me that there was the possibility I might meet them.''

''Pooh, nonsense! I do not, in the ordinary way, ever come up with the Montmorencys. We frequent quite different circles, I assure you. Lady Montmorency enjoys dancing attendance on royalty and Lady Sarah the gaming tables, neither of which hold any interest for me. Not that it is of any consequence, for I should like to know why you may not go about as much as you please and simply ignore them, as I always have done when our paths happened to cross.''

Jane could not think of any effective argument to make to this suggestion that would not reveal her real fear concerning Lord Jaspar, for of course, though she had confided in Lady Stanier her responsibility in the situation that had led to her summary dismissal from the Montmorency household, she had not mentioned the part played by Lord Jaspar to anyone, not even Sebastian, she remembered suddenly.

She thought about this wonderingly. Now why had she

withheld that incident from dear Sebastian who had heard and understood everything else she had told him about her life, including her envy of Lady Sarah and the impulse to disrobe and put on the negligee, and the horrible scenes with Leach that had created her fear of men, a fear Sebastian had dealt with so masterfully that she never ceased to wonder that two acts so basically similar, could be accomplished with such different results as those she had experienced with Leach and Sebastian.

Sebastian had succeeded so well in introducing her to the pleasure her own body could give her that he had wiped out all her shuddering disgust at the memory of Leach. He had also, however, left her with a body that now troubled her with its demands, sometimes forcing her to pace the floor for many sleepless hours. She knew of no remedy for her condition, and was too ashamed of it to confide her problem to anyone. If Sebastian were here she could have confided in him without shame, but then, if he were here she wouldn't have the problem. Which brought her thoughts again to her strange reticence regarding her few moments with Lord Jaspar and she realized all at once why she had never told her husband of it: She had enjoyed it! It had been thrilling for the few moments that she had allowed it to go on, arousing the same pleasurable sensations in her body that Sebastian had so expertly induced.

The noise in the room suddenly ceased, causing her to come out of her introspection and look about. A thin, elderly man scuttled out to seat himself at the pianoforte, followed by a majestically bosomed lady with improbable red hair, who took her place squarely before the pianoforte with a condescending nod of acknowledgment for the thin spatter of applause which greeted her entrance. As she launched herself into an aria by Gluck, Jane allowed her mind to go back to that episode with Lord Jaspar that had been superseded by events so overwhelming, both good and bad, that she had not thought of it or of him for a very long time. She found she had no difficulty in recapturing every erotic moment of it, and even now the memory succeeded in arousing that only lightly dozing creature within her body to a tingling awareness. She felt the blood rush into her cheeks and glanced about guiltily, quite expecting to find herself the object of horrified glances.

All eyes, however, were fixed upon the soprano, though there was undoubtedly horror in some of them, or at least pain, for what the soprano was doing to the aria would have caused the composer to weep and tear his hair.

Jane fanned her hot cheeks and subsided gratefully back into her chair. Well, she thought, it is clear that I am a depraved creature who must confine herself to her own drawing room in the future or risk disgrace, for what might I not do if I happened to encounter Lord Jaspar again?

She raised her eyes and had her answer, for there, standing so far forward in the room he was almost facing her, was that gentleman staring straight at her with a bemused, disbelieving expression in his eyes. She gasped audibly in shock and all the blood rushed so precipitately out of her head to the aid of her violently agitated heart that she felt quite faint.

"My dear! What is it?" Jane heard Lady Stanier's alarmed whisper as from a distance. She bit down on her tongue sharply, determined not to call any more attention to herself by fainting away in the middle of Mrs. Medvers-Platt's musical evening. She opened her eyes and the room steadied and she turned to smile vaguely at Lady Stanier.

"Please ignore it if you love me," Jane whispered back. "I'll explain later."

Lady Stanier patted her hand anxiously but turned obediently back to the soprano. Jane sat with her eyes fixed resolutely on her white kid gloves, feeling the sword of Damocles to be not just hanging over her head but with its actual keen edge touching coldly against her neck, for she could not entertain the least hope that Lord Jaspar would wait beyond the ending of the entertainment before confronting her. After that it would be only a matter of moments before the story of Lady Payton's antecedents spread over the room. There was no point, either, in hoping that he would be merciful, not after the painful blow she had delivered to him on their first meeting and the insulting way she had flung his money back in his face—well, figuratively speaking, she amended—on their second and last meeting. No doubt he was standing there at this moment gloating over this heaven-sent opportunity to avenge himself and preparing to expose her in the most humiliating way possible as soon as the last notes had died away.

She dared not look up for fear of meeting his eyes again, and attempted to mentally visualize the room and the quickest escape route out of it. All would depend, really, on how quickly she could move after the program was over.

She was assisted in her resolve to escape by the other guests, who, after the most perfunctory applause rose eagerly to their feet and with great relief turned to their neighbours, no doubt to prevent the soprano from being encouraged to give them an encore. Jane leaped up, pulling Lady Stanier to her feet, and made what speed she could through the jumble of chairs and the milling crowd without actually elbowing people aside in too unseemly a way, dragging the bewildered Lady Stanier behind her. She had reached Mrs. Medvers-Platt who was waiting at the door, to direct her guests downstairs to a light supper, and was just opening her mouth to beg Mrs. Medvers-Platt's forgiveness, pleading that she felt a slight indisposition and must take her leave, when a voice cut in.

"My dear Mrs. Medvers-Platt, won't you present me to these charming guests?"

There he stood, smiling beatifically, and making a charming bow when Mrs. Medvers-Platt happily complied with his request. Lady Stanier graciously held out her hand to him, for Montmorency or not, he was excessively handsome and very prettily behaved and Lady Stanier had a weakness for handsome young men. After an exchange of compliments he turned to Jane who could *not* raise her eyes from the floor and who was blushing helplessly, to her fury. She could feel all of them staring at her expectantly and with her last bit of courage managed to say "How do you do?" in a strangled whisper.

"Immeasurably better than I had hoped when I set out this evening," he replied promptly with a smile. ".Perhaps you and Lady Stanier would do me the honour of allowing me to take you down to supper?"

Lady Stanier waited for Jane to reply and when she didn't, was in something of a quandary as to whether or not the invitation should be accepted. She hadn't understood Jane's headlong rush to the door and, of course, was not aware of the previous encounter between Jane and Lord Jaspar. At that moment she saw Lady Montmorency surging forward, doubtless to claim her son as her own escort, and turned with an impish smile to put her arm into Jaspar's.

"How delightful of you to ask, sir. We should be happy to have your company, should we not, Jane?"

He held his other arm out to Jane and after an instant she put her hand on it and was led mutely down the staircase she had climbed so unsuspectingly not two hours earlier, experiencing now all the joyful anticipation of Marie Antoinette in the tumbrel.

15

Jane eyed the lobster patty before her with distaste, then pushed it away slightly and took a sip of her iced champagne, which, though not a particularly favourite wine with her, served to relieve her parched throat. Refreshments had been gallantly procured for her and for Lady Stanier by Lord Jaspar, who had seated them at a tiny table for two in the supper room. When he returned with the refreshments he pulled up another chair between them, making the small table even more intimate.

Though made uncomfortable by this nearness, Jane felt it the lesser of two evils: at least they were spared any other company to be party to whatever revelations Lord Jaspar might have in mind. She had even more reason to be grateful when she saw Lady Montmorency and Lady Sarah enter with Mr. Quint. Lady Sarah looked eagerly in Jane's direction and seemed inclined to join them, but was led firmly away to the other side of the room by her mother and Mr. Quint.

Jane sighed with relief and turned back to her plate. Food, however, was the last thing she had any desire for at the moment, so agitated were her spirits—especially lobster patties. Why on earth hadn't the man the sensitivity to bring her something more soothing? A cream or jelly perhaps? She glanced up from the offending patty in irritation to find Lord Jaspar just pushing a quivering pink jelly before her.

"I fear the lobster has displeased you, Lady Payton. Won't you try this jelly instead?" he said with a smile.

She found this even more irritating, since she was convinced the man was only playing a cat-and-mouse game with her and when he thought he had soothed her fears he would pounce. It was distinctly unpleasant for her to be forced to sit here practically knee to knee with him, and affect an air of calm and indifference while he toyed with her. Her every instinct was to attack first. Jane Coombes would not have hesitated. But that girl had been brought up to behave so and would have been protecting only herself.

Lady Jane Payton, however, had the Payton position to protect, and more especially, her son's name. Therefore it behooved her to remain cool and wait to see what he would do. She gave him a brief smile, thanked him courteously, and taking up a spoon began to eat her jelly, wondering if the condemned, eating their last meal, had this same difficulty in swallowing. She concentrated on disguising the effort it cost her and thought darkly about evil young men who took pleasure in torturing their victims, an addiction from a boyhood spent, no doubt, in pulling wings from butterflies. She became aware of an expectant silence, the sort that always follows an inquiry, and looked up startled. What had he said? Had he—?

"I—I—b-beg your pardon, sir?" she stammered, her eyes caught and held for a long moment by his own. She saw again an amusement lurking there and threw up her chin defiantly. Let him say what he would! She would simply stare at him haughtily and deny everything he might say. Let him prove anything!

"I merely asked if you were from Kent, Lady Payton, as your late husband was?"

"Yes," she said firmly, but without enlarging upon the statement in anyway.

"Very lovely part of England. I'm sure you must miss it."

"Yes."

"Will you go down again after the Season?"

"Yes."

Lord Jaspar was apparently not the least discouraged by these monosyllabic replies, for he struggled gamely on through the weather, the Season, the various balls and parties, and possible mutual acquaintances. He received an unamplified "yes" or "no" whatever he said, or a small shrug of indifference when she could not make either of these answers, as though the subject were too boring for her to bother to discuss.

Lady Stanier had listened in some amusement to the beginning of this discourse before turning away to talk with an old friend seated behind her. She turned back in time to hear Lord Jaspar receive some reward for all his conversational efforts. He had just requested the honour of paying her a morning call.

Her cold indifference shattered, her eyes met his, wide with fear. "Why?" she gasped.

He studied her in puzzlement for a moment before answering. "Why, for my own pleasure, Lady Payton. But, of course, if you are not receiving visitors, I--" he paused with an inquiring smile for her answer.

"Of course she is receiving," Lady Stanier responded after an embarrassingly long silence, when it seemed Jane was not going to do so. Really, thought Lady Stanier with exasperation, what *is* the matter with the child? Here was this perfectly unexceptionable young man requesting that he might call, and no matter how unpleasant the females of the family might be, there was a definite cachet attached to social acceptance by the Montmorencys, aside from the fact that those women apparently presented no threat to Jane at all.

"Then I will do myself that honour," Lord Jaspar replied with a smile, turning politely to give Lady Stanier some of his attention. Jane scolded herself for behaving in such a cow-handed way and fanned her flushed cheeks briskly, grateful to Lady Stanier for drawing him off and giving her time to make a recover. She wished desperately that she had withstood Lady Stanier's urgings to come here, for it was clear Jane Coombes was *not* ready for the *ton* yet! How many times had dear Mother Payton said to her that a lady never reveals her feelings in company? Yet here she was blushing and stammering and nearly fainting her first time out. Surely if Lord Jaspar had not recognized her at sight, his suspicions would by now be thoroughly aroused by her eccentric behaviour. She forced herself to fan more slowly and take deep breaths.

But hardly had the hot colour receded from her cheeks than she saw an elegantly long white-gloved hand appear on Lord Jaspar's shoulder and a gay voice interrupted his conversation with Lady Stanier.

"Jaspar, do be a darling and give me your chair. I am near fainting with boredom from that Quint creature prosing on and on in his antediluvian way. I vow, I barely escaped with my sanity."

Lord Jaspar looked less than pleased but rose politely and gave place to his sister. Lady Sarah reached for his glass of iced champagne and surveyed Jane frankly over the rim with large blue eyes as she drank it all down greedily. Without speaking, or even looking at him, she held the glass over her shoulder to Jaspar, who, after an instant's hesitation took it resignedly and went away to fetch her another glass.

"I know you will forgive me, Lady Payton, for thrusting myself upon you in this rag-mannered way, but you are the only

interesting-looking person in this entire assemblage of bores!"
Lady Stanier raised an eyebrow at this wholesale condemnation
in which she was evidently included, but Lady Sarah prattled
on, unconscious of the insult. "As a matter of fact, the only
reason I came tonight was to see you. Mrs. Medvers-Platt happened to mention at the Tolley's rout last week that you were to
be her guest tonight and I immediately clamoured for an invitation. I had heard that you were quite beautiful, you see, and I
have been positively consumed with curiosity to see you ever
since I heard of the marriage, for of course no one ever expected Sebastian Payton to be able—"

A firm, tanned hand appeared before Jane's and Lady Stanier's horror-frozen eyes, grasped Lady Sarah by the arm and
lifted her precipitously from the chair. "Come dearest sister,
Mr. Quint is pining for your presence," said Lord Jaspar in a
voice tight with rage.

"Jaspar! What can you mean by jerking me about in this
rude way!" gasped Lady Sarah, her eyes flashing dangerously.
"And where is my champagne?"

"You've had quite enough, I think. Come along." Without
giving her time to speak he led her away.

Lady Stanier looked into Jane's shocked eyes and with a gay
little laugh said something about siblings, then that if Jane
would recommend it, she quite thought she *would* have the
other jelly, that is, if Jane was quite sure *she* would not like it.
Jane forced herself to smile back and disclaim any need for further refreshments. Several pairs of avid eyes lost interest as
Lady Stanier firmly led the way into a discussion of the quality
of the music provided by Mrs. Medvers-Platt and the bountiful-
ness of the refreshments. Jane dutifully followed this lead and
produced a very creditable imitation of a young woman with
nothing more important to discuss. She watched covertly as
Lady Montmorency, after a brief word from Lord Jaspar, rose
and sailed out of the room on her son's arm, an obviously angry
Lady Sarah pulled along on his other side.

Very soon after this, Lady Stanier signalled that they might
leave. When they were safely seated together in the carriage
Lady Stanier reached over to press Jane's hand warmly.

"That was very well done, child. I was proud of you."

"It was ghastly—every moment! I should never have agreed
to come with you! Everyone staring and Lord Jaspar teasing
and that dreadful creature making those insinuations about Sebastian. I cannot—"

124

"Pooh! What a to-do you are making. You must learn not to be so thin skinned, child! Naturally everyone stared. You are new to them and quite, quite beautiful That alone would make them stare, even aside from the fact of your intriguingly mysterious history. As for Lady Sarah, she was flown with wine and not accountable. Besides, she was only voicing what everyone was wondering about."

"But—but—how terrible of them—"

"Not at all—perfectly natural. If I didn't know the circumstances I should no doubt be speculating about it myself. We're a very parochial Society in London, after all. We all know each other and everything about each other. Believe me, it is a very rare skeleton that can stay decently hidden in the closet as far as we are concerned. The thing to do is just smile and be calm and by next week they will all have found something else to titilate them. Now—what was that you said about Lord Jaspar teasing you? I don't think I missed much of his conversation and I vow I noticed nothing out of the way. A very pretty-behaved young man, I thought, in spite of that mother."

Now Jane was in something of a quandary, for she could not think of anyway to explain the comment that had slipped out in her agitation. "I—oh—nothing really. I just felt nervous of him."

"But what did he say in particular to distress you?" Lady Stanier persisted.

Jane again replied vaguely, for in truth she could not really remember anything he had said besides asking if he could call. That request still clanged around in her brain as she tried to imagine how he intended to play the scene. Would he tease and hint at his knowledge or come right out and tell her he knew who she was? Would he say nothing to her but whisper it around the drawing rooms of London? Was he even now revealing to his mother and sister that they had just been formally introduced to their former backstairs maid? Indeed, that Lady Sarah had bent a knee to her?

Jane longed to pour this unresolvable problem into Lady Stanier's ear, but could even Lady Stanier's vast understanding and kindness extend to a tale of near seduction involving what could only be called complicity, for a few moments at least, on Jane's part? No! Better by far to bury her guilty secret, however much a burden it remained on her conscience. She would have to face Lord Jaspar and whatever he had in store for her alone.

Later, snuggled into her pillow and alone at last to vent her long-held-in-emotions, she found she had no tears to shed after all. Instead, she set herself to try to remember what he had said to her, but most of it remained elusive. She found his face continually materializing before her, however, and thought, "How blue his eyes are! As clear as the sky on a summer day. And as innocent of malice!" She looked again and it was true. She walked toward them, but they receded before her. Abruptly she was asleep.

Jaspar, meanwhile, bundled his mother and sister into the Montmorency carriage and sat grimly between them, staring straight ahead, his disapprobation apparent. Sarah on one side stared angrily, if rather blearily, out the window, demonstrating by her silence her anger with her brother for having dragged her away from the party just when it had become interesting. Lady Montmorency stared as resolutely and as silently out the other side. Her object was to prevent any altercation from breaking out between her children in the carriage when it might be overheard by the coachman.

When they reached Curzon Street, Sarah flounced out of the carriage and went straight up to her room without a word. Lady Montmorency turned to say goodnight to Jaspar before following her daughter, but he spoke first.

"If I could have a word with you in my study, Mama," he said and without waiting for a reply crossed to the door of his study and stood holding it for her. She shrugged and followed him. He closed the door on the interested gaze of Ornsby, the butler.

"Really, Jaspar, I wish you will not order me about in this way before the servants," said Lady Montmorency, sinking into a chair before the fire and shrugging off her ermine-lined velvet evening cloak. "Also I am very weary and not interested in a brangle tonight. If you have to ring a peal over someone, wait till morning and speak to your sister."

"When she is sober, do you mean?" he inquired with an awful irony.

"Jaspar! Of course I mean nothing of the kind! What a thing to imply—"

"Not implying, Mama, stating as fact. You had best look to your daughter, madam. She is becoming much too fond of drink and has no head for it. Worse still, when she's disguised her tongue wags at both ends."

"You exaggerate, my dear. She has always been volatile—"

"And another thing," he said, ignoring her protestations, "I don't know what sort of set you've been allowing her to go about with, but she has been indulging in some very deep play lately. Her pockets are always to let and she's already spent her next two quarter's allowance. I'll not advance her another penny and so I warn you! That's all I have to say and if you'll follow my advice you'll take her in hand at once before it's too late. I'll bid you goodnight now, Mama."

He crossed to the door and opened it and stood waiting politely for her to leave. She gathered up her cloak and came to stand before him, uncertainty in her cold, proud eyes. He kissed her hand, bowed, and she left with a murmured, "Goodnight, then, dear boy."

He went to throw himself into the chair before the fire, hands deep in his pockets, long legs stretched before him. He stared into the flames, and saw dancing there a pair of dark-fringed amber eyes gazing wide-eyed back at him. A memory stirred hazily deep in his mind, but was gone before he could capture it. He had experienced the same thing when he first caught sight of those eyes this evening as he stood leaning against the wall of Mrs. Medvers-Platt's music room, bored beyond expression, his ears assaulted by the execrable screechings of the soprano. Those startled eyes were familiar to him in some way. Somewhere he had seen eyes like them before. He cast about among his acquaintances but could not bring to mind their duplicates. It would come to him, no doubt, in time.

He allowed the problem to drift away as he sleepily called up the memory of Lady Payton in her entirety. There was no doubt she was the most adorably beautiful creature he had ever seen. How was it possible for such a woman to marry Payton, who by all accounts had been practically a dwarf? Perhaps it had all been a Banbury tale and the man perfectly normal, only sickly and unable to go about. For I'd stake my blunt that girl wouldn't marry for convenience or avarice alone, he thought. Not with that straightforward gaze. On the other hand, it is said that a good liar is one who can look you straight in the eye most innocently.

He dismissed the thought immediately as unworthy of his picture of her and again her wide-eyed gaze flew up to meet his as he asked if he might call. "Why?" she gasped. He leaned toward her to explain the absolute necessity of his seeing her again. She turned away. He followed—came slowly up behind her. His hands went around her—she was—

"M'lord! M'lord!"

127

"Wh-a-a-"

"Will you have your brandy now, m'lord?" inquired Ornsby.

Jaspar stared uncomprehendingly for a moment, then shook his head crossly and rose. Perhaps if he went straight to his bed he could recapture that dream.

16

At eleven the following morning Jaspar tapped peremtorily on his sister's door. His dream had eluded him completely the night before and his mood was not improved.

When he was told to enter he found Sarah in a wrapping gown of celestial-blue satin, extravagant with lace and satin ribands, seated on a small sofa. A stout gentleman was on his knees before her holding one of her small bare feet reverently. Wright, her dresser, stood to one side holding a tray with various implements arranged upon it. They all turned inquiringly at the interruption.

Jaspar stared in astonishment for a moment at this scene before he realized it was only the chiropodist attending to Lady Sarah's toenails.

"I would like to speak with you for a moment," Jaspar said shortly.

"Go away, Jaspar. I can't talk to you now," Sarah replied with a careless wave of her hand.

"Now! Dismiss your—er—attendants, madam."

She looked at him rebelliously for a moment, but saw something in his eyes that told her she'd best do as she was bid. She petulantly motioned to the chiropodist and Wright to withdraw.

As soon as the door had closed behind them she burst out in great irritation. "I wish you will not burst into my apartments in this boorish fashion, Jaspar. It is of all things what I dislike most in the mornings. What do you want?"

"Several things. First of all you exhibited such a lamentable want of conduct last night that you exceeded even my expectations of you. You came within an ace of saying something unforgivable to Lady Payton, though I don't suppose you can even remember it now.''

"Lady—oh—*her!* Nonsense, brother, we hit it off splendidly. Why should I say unforgivable things to her?''

"Why, indeed? My reading of the situation was that you were foxed again.''

"Er—what did I say?'' she asked guardedly. He told her and she had the grace to look flustered for a moment. But only for a moment.

"Pooh! I shouldn't refine too much upon that. I doubt she is such a dolt *she* would. After all, her sensibilities were not so nice they prevented her from marrying the man!''

"We are not speaking of her sensibilities, but yours. To refer to his affliction in that gossiping, rattle-headed way before all those people, not even bothering to lower your voice, was unspeakable. Think—if you are capable—think how she must have felt!''

"I shall have strong convulsions if you continue to shout at me in this way!'' she cried, clutching her temples. "I have the headache this morning.''

"That is the price one must pay for overindulgence in iced champagne,'' he said unsympathetically, "which is another subject I wish to discuss with you when we have settled the matter of Lady Payton.''

"I suppose you are making all this fuss because you have designs on the virtue of the Widow Payton,'' she said waspishly. His brows snapped down in a menacing frown. "Oh, all right, all right! I shall trot around and do the pretty to the dear little soul and we shall be bosom bows before the Season's over.''

"Now the second matter—''

"Jaspar, please go *away!*''

"—is your fondness for drink. If you cannot control yourself I will send you down to the country with a keeper. At least there you will not disgrace yourself before your family and friends.''

"You would not dare!''

"Try me,'' he invited calmly. "The third thing is that I would remind you you have been given your allowance for the next six months. Your fondness for deep play is your own business, of course, but you'll have no more from me.''

"Jaspar don't—you must—I must have—'' the words tumbled out in a frightened spate at this.

"Rolled up again, sister? And thinking I'll pay the dibs?

Well, I tell you I won't. If you think I'll beggar the estate just so you can indulge in a few seconds' excitement at the gaming tables, you are sadly mistaken.''

"I suppose *you* never play?" she was stung to reply.

"I have never been rolled up," he pointed out, "so it is not to the point. You, on the other hand, seem only to lose. I must suppose you experience some sort of thrill from it. Far be it from me to deprive you of any of your pleasures, but I won't continue to tow you out of the River Tick.''

"Just this one time, Jaspar, and I promise I'll never—" she said coaxingly.

"You've said *that* the last three times.''

"This time I—"

"No, Sarah.''

"But what shall I *do?*" she cried.

"I would suggest you begin throwing out lures for a rich husband. What about old Fitz-Clarence? Rich as Croesus and dangling at your shoestrings any time this last twelve months.''

"He's eighty years old!" she protested in horror.

"All the more likely to be dotty enough to pay your gaming debts, sister," he said consolingly as he trod across the room and exited.

She reached down for one of her satin slippers and threw it at him, but it only hit the closed door and fell uselessly to the floor. She burst into noisy tears. But ten minutes later she was chattering gaily with the chiropodist, urging him into scandalous indiscretions about his other clients.

That same morning, Jane came awake as her door burst open suddenly to admit Clinton and Wellington, who both clambered onto her bed with much laughing on the boy's part and barking on spaniel's, to give her equally damp good-morning kisses.

This morning romp had become a ritual, allowed by Nanny, hovering in the hallway, to last ten minutes before she entered clucking. Master Clinton's state of health was then discussed in minute detail, along with an account of all the scrapes he'd gotten into the day before. Clinton would burrow under the covers to cuddle against his mother's soft, sleep-warm body, while Wellington tried desperately to follow suit, until a scandalized Nurse would lift the dog bodily off the bed and threaten to put him out of the room did he not behave proper. He would then run from side to side of the bed yipping frantically, overcome with excitement at the tickling match now in progress on it.

This state of affairs lasted only a few minutes, for soon Dorrie came in with m'lady's hot chocolate and Nurse firmly carried her charge away, muttering dire predictions relating to young gentlemen who became hysterical before breakfast. The fact was, however, that anything that added to Clinton's happiness was sacred to her and she would have been shocked if it were suggested the morning romp be abandoned.

Jane sat up against her pillows to drink her chocolate and saw on the tray a tight little posy of pink rosebuds in a delicate ivory holder. Puzzled, she took up the accompanying card. It had only two initials on it: "J.M.," but they were enough to cause her heart to give a curious hard, little thump which in turn sent her leaping from the bed to stand indecisively in the middle of the floor.

"What is it, m'lady?"

"What?"

"I thought you was wantin' something, m'lady, jumped out o'yer bed like a startled rabbit you did, and now jest standin' there all starin' like."

"Oh—oh—well—you'd best brush my hair now—no—fetch hot water and I'll bathe first."

"Yes, m'lady. And will you wear your new gown today? Looks a treat on you, it does."

"Why, thank you, Dorrie. But no, I'll wear something else, I think." Dorrie's face fell, but she turned obediently to the door. "Dorrie—can you read?"

Dorrie flushed and looked away in embarrassment. Finally she whispered, "No, Lady Jane."

"Then you will learn. You would like that, wouldn't you?"

"Oh yes, m'lady!" Dorrie replied breathlessly.

"Then you shall. We'll start tomorrow—an hour a day. Only you won't have such a teacher as I had," she said, her eyes clouding, but then she shook it off and smiled. "But I will do just as he did and you will like it very well and so shall I."

Dorrie gave her an adoring smile and bobbed a shy curtsy before hurrying away for the hot water.

Some hours later, after consulting with Betty Crews and taking Nurse and Clinton along for her monthly visit with her old friend Mrs. Hawks, Lady Stanier's housekeeper, Jane was on her knees before a large trunk filled with books, all the ones she and Sebastian had used. She was glad they were now to be used to help another ignorant young girl better herself. In a way, by attempting to teach Dorrie, Jane felt she was in some part repaying a debt and she was grateful she'd had the sudden inspiration of doing so. She wished she had thought of it sooner.

She sat back on her heels to look at a diary of ideas and thoughts Sebastian had encouraged her to keep, and her eyes misted over as she read what he had written on the first page for her. It was a quotation from *Hamlet* that he had thought apropos for her book:

"There's rosemary, that's for remembrance—pray you love, remember—and there is pansies, that's for thoughts."

Before she could sink quite into melancholy by all the memories this called up, she was brought back to the present by Dorrie calling out to her urgently.

"M'lady, where you got yourself to now?"

Jane hastily wiped her eyes and went to the top of the stairs. "I'm here, Dorrie—looking out some books for our lessons. What is it?"

"A fine lady come to call, m'lady."

"What name did she give?"

"Montmorency, Lady Sarah Montmorency."

"Good heavens! And me in this old dress!"

"And all dusty too, m'lady," offered Dorrie helpfully.

"Quickly, Dorrie! Run ahead and pull out the new merino."

Dorrie turned and fled down the stairs, Jane hurrying after. Ten minutes later, face and hands washed and hastily buttoned into the new amber-coloured merino gown with its stiffened blond lace ruffle standing up around her face and coming to a graduated point at the bosom, she walked with a semblance of composure into her drawing room, where Lady Sarah sat turning over the pages of the latest copy of *La Belle Assemblée*.

"Lady Sarah! Forgive me for keeping you waiting."

Sarah tossed the magazine aside and rose. "The apology is mine, madam, for coming unannounced, but I shall allow you to feel a little guilty so that you will be more apt to forgive my stupidity last night. I speak too often without thinking, but I meant nothing by my words, I assure you, and I would not offend you for the world."

"My dear Lady Sarah—I—"

"*Say* you forgive me!"

Jane smiled, for she could not hold out after such a handsome apology. "Let us consider it forgotten."

"Then to prove it you will consent to come for a drive in the Park with me."

"Oh—well—I don't know that—"

"Please say that you will. I excessively dislike driving alone. One is continually being stopped to chatter. Whereas, if I have someone with me I shan't be obliged to. The carriage is waiting outside and it's such a fine day. Warm as June and not a whiff of cloud to be seen."

Jane allowed herself to be persuaded. She was not anxious to pursue an intimate acquaintance with the girl, who didn't seem at all the type of person she would respond to now that she knew her somewhat better than when she had hauled fuel to her bedroom fireplace. However, she felt it would be churlish to refuse, and she would quite like to go for a drive. But beyond these reasons was the more pressing one of the velvet pelisse made to go with her new dress, of the same shade of amber trimmed with sable at collar and cuffs, and an enchanting sable hat and an enormous sable muff to go with it.

After being complimented in a most gratifying way by Lady Sarah on this dashing costume, Jane took a seat in the carriage and was bowled along the streets to the Park. A great many other Londoners had taken advantage of the first fine day and swarmed into the Park in their carriages, on horseback or on foot. Sarah seemed to know everyone and bowed and waved all the while she kept up a steady stream of comment and anecdote on their histories and morals. She seemed unwilling to stop the carriage for closer encounters, however, declaring there was not one among them who was not a dead bore.

Jane was content to have it so. She was comfortable and amused and more at ease with Lady Sarah than she had thought to be when they set out. She found the girl not the cold, selfish creature she remembered at all. Not that she is probably any kinder to her backstairs maid now than she was to me though, Jane thought realistically. But I begin to see her behaviour has no real malice in it; it is just that she has been brought up by that dreadful mother to be too full of her own consequence to notice anyone so lowly as a backstairs maid, anymore than she "notices" the washstand or the fireplace tongs.

She had wit and beauty, but seemed to complain continuously of the boredom she experienced through nearly every waking moment. Jane pitied her in spite of herself. The girl had no character to sustain her, nor any inner life to fill the vacuum when she wasn't being entertained by outside events. She sought stimulation constantly and was wearied by the sameness of the avenues open to a well-brought-up girl. She was also bored with the sameness of the people she met day after day socially, always the same people. Which no doubt accounts for her interest in me, Jane thought wryly—I'm at least a new face.

It was close to midnight when Lady Sarah turned away from the baccarat table, the fizzing excitement she'd felt only a moment before suddenly gone flat, to be replaced by a feeling of nausea. She had lost a great deal of money and had only been able to give them her markers for it.

"Well, m'lady," said a harsh voice in her ear, at the same time her upper arm was grasped none too gently. "Been having your bit of fun, I see. I make it close to four thousand pounds, what with tonight's losses. Perhaps you'd like to join me in my private room for a glass of wine?"

She jerked her arm away. "No. I would not! Have my carriage brought around." She turned away coldly.

The man's eyes hardened. "Very well, Lady Sarah, if you will have it so. But I'm afraid I cannot extend you any more time. I'll have my money tomorrow. Do you understand me?"

She stood there, her back to him for a moment, but then her shoulders slumped and she turned back to him reluctantly. "I can't get it by tomorrow and you know it."

"Then I will go to your brother."

"No! I'll—I'll think of something. I'll—"

"There is one other way," he said with great deliberation. She looked up defiantly, daring him to say what she thought he was going to say. He smirked. "No. Not that. I saw you today in your carriage. In the Park. I've a fancy to meet your friend. Bring her here and I'll consider the debt cancelled."

Sarah felt such a gust of hope blow through her she was almost light-headed. She smiled. "Lady Payton! Well, I don't know if she plays, but I'll get her here one way or another."

She turned away with a careless little gesture of farewell. The man bowed and watched her walking away, his mouth twisting up on one side into a parody of a smile.

17

"I think, dear Lady Jane, that if you will but trust me in this I can assure you of an enjoyable evening. We shall go in domino, of course—I adore masques, do not you?—and be very merry. Very merry indeed!" Mr. Quint's gay smile cracked the surface of his painted face in a most disconcerting way. Jane watched in fascination for a moment before she could pull her eyes away from this interesting spectacle. "Yes?" he said, cocking his head to one side coquettishly.

"Oh—I thank you, Mr. Quint," replied Jane hastily, "but I fear Ranleigh Gardens will be just a little *too* gay for me."

"But, dear madam, *I* will protect you, though of course you need fear nothing, I assure you. I've gone many times and never encountered any rowdyism. Just all boys and girls together for an evening of pleasure. You must allow me to know best about these things, m'dear." He reached over to pat her hand, not at all in an avuncular manner. He allowed it to be a lingering, loverlike caress, clearly insinuating what he thought his position vis-à-vis herself to be.

Although Jane's eyes brimmed with suppressed laughter, she sternly repressed her merriment at the ridiculous situation in which she found herself. He had called upon her every morning since the Medvers-Platt evening party, and his manner had become progressively more possessive with each visit. He would assure her that she might safely attend various evening parties for which she received cards since he would be there to protect her from unwonted attentions. He would advise her against receiving the visits of certain gentlemen he assured her were established rakes. Jane attempted to dampen his ardours, but since he had not made a definite declaration as yet, it was difficult for her to disabuse him of his hopes. When she consulted Lady Stanier that lady only laughed.

"Dear Child, he is harmless, I assure you. Poor old Alben. I think it's more habit than anything else. He's been out for an

135

heiress since I was a girl myself. I think if he managed to capture one now it would frighten him out of his wits!''

''But it seems somehow dishonest to allow him to go on believing—'' Jane protested.

''Darling, you cannot control what he believes as long as he says nothing—and he's good value—accepted everywhere, you know, and if one needs a partner he's always available.''

Jane had continued to receive Mr. Quint, but was unable to erase the traces of guilt she felt at the falseness of her position. This combined with pity for the old gentleman caused her to treat his attentions more kindly.

She could not know that Mr. Quint took her kindness for encouragement of his suit, and in a burst of extravagance, feeling himself very near his goal, had proposed this present scheme to visit Ranleigh Gardens, where he felt the air of romance and mystery would lend the proper atmosphere for his proposal. For, contrary to Lady Stanier's opinion, he was determined to marry this wealthy widow. He was nearing seventy-five and weary of the genteel poverty to which generations of profligate Quints had reduced him. He knew that it was incumbent upon him to propose marriage in the very immediate future, before word got around of this unparalleled prize waiting to be captured. He was aware that once it had, he would have to fight his way to her door through hosts of suitors far more prepossessing and eligible than himself. He must be enterprising and awake in every suit if he was to snatch her from under their noses.

Now he bent upon her his most ardent gaze as he continued to caress her hand. Jane smiled gravely, and without a trace of maidenly confusion, removed her hand from beneath his and picked up her embroidery frame. She wished desperately for another caller to interrupt this uncomfortable, and boring, tête-à-tête. Even the dreaded appearance of Lord Jaspar Montmorency could almost be welcomed as a relief from the persistence of Mr. Quint!

Aside from this need, there was the need to know one way or another what Lord Jaspar intended. It was now five days since she had had the misfortune to come face-to-face with him at Mrs. Medvers-Platt's, and not a moment had passed since then when she was entirely free of anxiety. At this point she was ready to write him and beg him to call. She was exhausted from her dread of disclosure and her desire to have it settled one way or another. Apart from this there were the distressing memories revived by the sight of him. Memories that set her body clamouring for the physical release she'd thought she had finally conquered. She tried, with little success, to swamp these disgraceful urgings by whipping up her anger at the probability that he was planning to ruin her life by disclosing her past.

When this failed she tried, in vain, to remind herself of his cowardice all those years ago. Her more practical mind would reply that he'd been but a green lad and had not come into his sister's room that evening in pursuit of Jane Coombes, that she had most certainly put temptation in his way, and that she had without doubt repaid him in full for his temerity with her well-placed blow. Then, if that were not enough, she would remember that, dreadful as the sequence of events had been following their few erotic moments together, each step of it had led her to Sebastian, to those two years of joy, to her becoming Lady Jane Payton of Payton House and Larkwoods Manor, Kent, and mother of adorable Clinton.

The imagined scene of her trying to thank Lord Jaspar for attempting to seduce her brought an impish gleam of laughter into her eyes just as Crews appeared in the door of the drawing room, Lord Jaspar treading on his heels.

He distinctly saw the merriment in her eyes turn to apprehension at the sight of him. Crews had barely time to announce him before he was hurrying across the room to reassure her. She should not be frightened of me, he thought with dismay. Or perhaps she finds me physically repulsive and that look is disgust. He hoped he was not vain, but he had always been assured that he was a well-enough looking man, but then, he thought ruefully, there is no way to control the mysterious promptings that cause one to respond positively to one person and negatively to another regardless of physical aspect. But he could not bear for her to feel negatively toward himself.

She had jumped to her feet at his brisk entrance and instinctively held out her hand, not in greeting, but as though to ward him off. He took the hand into his own and bent to press his lips to her fingers. He straightened up and stood smiling warmly down into her eyes, still in possession of her hand.

"You said I might call. I have restrained myself as long as possible," he said with devastating frankness.

Jane blushed at his candour and the warmth of his tone. She glanced wildly about and caught the eye of Mr. Quint who was looking on at this interruption with an expression of outrage. He read entreaty into the look she sent him and gallantly leaped to his feet.

"Ah—er—I must say, Montmorency—I—"

Jaspar swung around in surprise at the sound of Mr. Quint's voice, then nodded good-naturedly.

"Well, well. Good-day to you, Mr. Quint. I hope you are keeping well."

"Why should you think otherwise, sir?" asked Mr. Quint testily, scenting the condescension of youth to age.

"Why, indeed I don't know why I should, Mr. Quint, when one has only to look at you to see that you keep very well consid—" Jaspar stopped abruptly as he realized the pit he was digging for himself. Mr. Quint pulled himself up stiffly, much affronted, but then prudently decided not to pursue this line of conversation.

"I believe Lady Jane would be much obliged to you if you would stop clutching her in that unseemly way," he said icily.

Jaspar looked down in pretended astonishment, as though unaware that he still held Jane's hand, or that she had been attempting to tug it free during his interchange with Mr. Quint. "Why—bless my soul—I had quite forgot." He raised the hand to his lips again and kissed the fingers provocatively before relinquishing it. Mr. Quint sniffed audibly in disapproval.

"Er—won't you sit down, sir?" Jane said faintly, sinking back into her place on the sofa. Jaspar promptly sat down beside her, to Mr. Quint's further outrage. He glared at Jaspar, who returned his look with one of bland innocence. Mr. Quint turned away from him deliberately and addressed Jane.

"My dear, it is settled between us then?" he said in a tone of what he hoped Lord Jaspar would take for great intimacy between himself and his intended bride.

A spirit of mischief got the better of Jane and she lowered her eyes coyly, "You must give me time to consider it, Mr. Quint. I fear it is all too sudden for me to give you my answer at once."

Jaspar raised a disbelieving eyebrow at her and she had all she could do to stifle a giggle. Mr. Quint smiled in a gratified way at her response, preened himself, and rose to his feet.

"I will await your answer with bated breath, my dear. Now, if you will forgive me, I will take my leave and hope that tomorrow we can have our little visit without any—er—interruption." He made her a bow, nodded coldly in Jaspar's direction, and strutted grandly out of the room.

Jane and Jaspar sat still as statues, not daring to look at one another until they heard the outer door closing after Mr. Quint.

138

Jane flicked a glance at Jaspar and found him grinning broadly at her, but then, perversely stifled her rising hilarity. She gave him a reproachful look and reached primly for her embroidery frame. A silence lasted through two carefully set stitches, while Jane became more and more aware of him sitting so near her.

"Well, sir—" she began, much louder than necessary in her nervousness. She halted and then began again in a more normal voice. "I must thank you for your flowers. Quite unnecessary, of course, but very kind."

"Dear lady, at the risk of contradicting you and being thought rude, I must protest that it is entirely necessary. Beauty must be acknowledged, even in so humble a way."

She lowered her eyes to her embroidery frame again, more confused than ever. His reply was complimentary to be sure, but was it a shade too glib for sincerity? Was there not a sardonic edge to it? Was he attempting to disarm her into a feeling of false security to make his revenge the sweeter?

She felt it becoming difficult to breathe and realized she was allowing herself to give way to panic in a most cowardly way and forced herself to take a deep breath and look him squarely in the eye.

"I have not seen your sister in many days, Lord Jaspar. I trust she is well?"

"She has an iron constitution, madam, and is never ill."

"How very fortunate. She was so very kind as to take me for a drive in her carriage some days ago."

"Must have been a dead bore for you. She has no conversation beyond the latest *on dits.*"

"On the contrary, sir, she behaved charmingly and I enjoyed it very much."

"I am happy to hear it. She can be a great trial to her family upon occasion, though I don't believe she does so purposefully. She's only bubble-headed and speaks without thought."

"She seems—er—somewhat discontented with her life. Perhaps she is exhausted from her continual round of gaity. Is there no one who could turn her thoughts in a more serious direction? Perhaps give her life more purpose?"

"Good Lord! Sarah? I doubt there is anyone could cause Sarah to have a serious thought. More hair than wit, that girl."

"I don't think you should speak so of your own sister to someone who is practically a stranger," Jane retorted, rushing to defend Sarah now, though while in her company she had found the girl as uninteresting as her brother seemed to. Nevertheless, she had pitied Sarah, and she thought Jaspar's remarks heart-less.

"Stranger? Are we strangers then?" he replied in a significant way, looking into her eyes.

She stared back, mesmerized, unable to look away, and experiencing again a rising panic at his words. Now, she thought. Now he will say it. With an abrupt movement she rose and walked away to the window. Aware that he had risen in surprise and was staring after her, she forced herself to turn about and face him.

"We m-m—were introduced," she hesitated only a fraction over the word, "last week at Mrs. Medvers-Platt's, sir."

"Indeed. A moment etched indelibly on my memory," he said fervently, but, to Jane's ear, with more insinuation than flattery. Drat the man, she fumed impotently! Well, I'll not give him best. I can be as enigmatic as he and he'll get no confession from me.

"And met for the second time today," she continued as calmly as possible, "which hardly forms the basis for a long-standing friendship. But we were speaking of your sister. She suffers, I believe, more than you care to acknowledge, from ennui. This can possibly lead her into reckless behaviour."

"Truer than you know, dear lady. But, if you will forgive me, I would much prefer to discuss other matters."

She felt as though an icy hand had clutched something in her mid-section and went absolutely still for a moment. Then managed to falter, "Other—matters?"

"Yes. For instance, that figure of fun, Alben Quint. Am I to understand that you are taking his proposal under consideration?"

She raised her eyebrows in a simulation of well-bred shock at the unmannerliness of such an intimate question. He acknowledged her response with a look of discomfiture, but did not retract it. After allowing him time to feel the full force of her displeasure, she answered coldly.

"You may understand what you like, sir."

"But surely you cannot be seriously considering—" he began eagerly, but was interrupted by a soft rap on the drawing room door, followed immediately by Crews to announce, "Lady Sarah Montmorency, m'lady," and that lady strolled in almost before the announcement was finished.

"Good morning, darling. I've come to see if you'll ride with me," she said, carelessly pulling off her black beaver trencher hat. Her long guinea-gold tresses, obviously turned up under the hat without pins, tumbled down her back below the waist of her pale fawn velvet riding dress.

Jane's mouth was slightly agape, not only in admiration of this studied gesture, but at the informality of her greeting.

"Lord, sister, you must have been practicing that all morning to have got it down so perfectly," said Jaspar irritably.

Sarah turned lazily toward him. "Oh—you're here," she replied without enthusiasm.

"I'm just off," he said resignedly, realizing the hopelessness of pursuing Jane with Sarah in the room.

"Good. Now, you will ride with me, dearest Jane. Say you will. How ravishing you look in that gray silk. I could never wear such a colour."

Jane, with an irrepressible feminine instinct, turned to the console mirror beside her. "Oh, do you like it really?" she queried, nervously pushing back a curling tendril that had escaped restraint and fluttered before her ear. Jaspar, in the act of moving to the door, came up behind her. Their eyes met in the mirror as he stood behind her shoulder. She gasped at this near-reproduction of their first meeting, and jerked aside to turn and face him.

She forced herself to extend a trembling hand, "Th-thank you for c-c-calling, Lord Jaspar," she said, her heart jumping around like a frightened rabbit in her chest.

He looked at her without replying for a moment, before taking her hand, bowing, and then turning away to the door. Jane watched him go, her hand pressed against her hammering heart. Well, she thought, that's well and truly done it for sure!

"Well, really," said Sarah, "he is beyond anything rude! To stalk out in that way without so much as a nod in my direction, not to speak of neglecting to say a word to you."

But Jane was grateful that he hadn't said a word, fearing she knew only too well what words he might say. After all, she found, she would rather *not* know the worst—not yet at any rate.

18

The days that followed became increasingly full for Jane. She would not allow anything to interfere with the hours she spent with her son, but now there were also Dorrie's lessons, morning callers (which included nearly every day both Mr. Quint and Jaspar), rides with Lady Sarah and calls or shopping expeditions with Lady Stanier. She would dine with Lady Stanier every evening, either in her own home, at Lady Stanier's, or with various friends of the older woman.

There were also occasional evening parties of the more staid variety, for despite all Lady Stanier's urgings, Jane was adamant in her refusal to attend balls or masques, feeling still too shy to embark on that sea of pleasure.

"Pooh! You are being much too nice, child. No one would find anything to criticise in a young widow of over three years' time going about again. Besides, dancing is very healthy exercise and hurts no one!" exclaimed Lady Stanier, waving away a pair of violently scarlet stockings with yellow clocks being held out for her inspection. She and Jane were seated in Mr. Pillotson's Emporium in Pall Mall, the first stop on an afternoon's shopping.

"But Aunt Stanier, I take a great deal of exercise and have never been healthier," Jane protested demurely.

"Provoking girl! Hmmm—I rather fancy that mauve sarcenet. Mr. Pillotson! Will you have your young man fetch it down?"

Mr. Pillotson snapped his fingers and his clerk leaped up the ladder to bring down the bolt of silk, which he reverently handed to Mr. Pillotson, who unfurled several yards with a dramatic flourish. He draped it enticingly over his arm and held it out in front of Lady Stanier, who raised her *face-à-main* with great deliberation and bent to examine the fabric minutely.

"Ah yes—well—what do you think, my dear? Do you like it?"

"No."

"What!" Lady Stanier straightened and turned to her. "You don't like it?"

"No. Not for you. The colour is difficult and—aging."

"Aging, eh? Yes, perhaps you're right. Take it away, Mr. Pillotson and bring—let me see—oh, bother! I don't really think I'm in the mood for this, after all. We'll come again another day, Mr. Pillotson. Come along, Jane."

Mr. Pillotson bowed profoundly and led the way out, escorting them across the pavement and respectfully handing them into Lady Stanier's smart landaulet. He stood smiling after them so long as the carriage was in sight, not at all dismayed at not having made a sale, for he knew to a penny the handsome profits that were his from Lady Stanier's custom, and now here was this well-dressed young woman, newly come to town, whose patronage would no doubt add even more to Mr. Pillotson's coffers.

Lady Stanier, meanwhile, was frankly eyeing Jane's walking dress of bright green velvet trimmed with chinchilla narrowly at neck and cuff, and in a broad band around the edges of the short double cape. "Would I be able to wear that colour, do you think? I mean, would it be 'aging' for an old lady?"

Jane laughed. "Now you are angling for a compliment. You know very well you don't think of yourself as an 'old lady,' nor does anyone else. You have as many suitors as any young girl of the Season. It's really quite disgraceful."

"Suitors? You call those maggoty old creatures suitors? I do not!"

"They certainly behave as suitors, in my view. Plying you with posies and proposing—ah, don't bother to deny it," Jane laughed, seeing Lady Stanier's mouth opening to protest, "if Lord Tremblay was not proposing to you last Tuesday, what was he doing on his knees when I came into your drawing room?"

Lady Stanier sniffed. "The old fool! He's been doing that regularly since I was sixteen. Claims he's never proposed to another woman since the day he first saw me. Actually, I expect it's true. He's always known I would never have him, so he's felt quite safe in proposing. He really has never had any intention of marrying—much too spinsterish in his ways—has been since he was a boy. But he likes bolstering his picture of himself as no end of a romantic fellow. Lord knows he needs some colour in his life if he bores himself as much as he does his long-suffering acquaintance.''

Jane had collapsed back against the squabs by the end of this tart speech. ''Oh, stop—please'' she gasped between gusts of laughter, ''it hurts to laugh so hard.''

''You would not find it so amusing if you had been subjected to the experience as many times as I have been. I vow I all but swoon with ennui just to hear his knees cracking when he gets down into that ridiculous posture and repeats those dog-eared words. I have always lived in dread of being discovered in that tiresome charade, and it finally happened. Thank heaven it was you and not one of those old tabbies with their tongues clacking at both ends who'd spread it all over town within hours. But that's neither here nor there. You still have not answered my question about the colour. I suppose that green is too bright for me really.''

''How you go on! Of course it is not. It would be most becoming to you.''

''But the mauve is aging?''

''I didn't mean it that way. I meant it is a colour I associate with elderly ladies and I see no reason for you to be wearing old lady colours.''

''Sweet child,'' murmured Lady Stanier, mollified. ''Oh, is that Sarah Montmorency waving to you from that carriage?''

Jane leaned forward and then smiled and nodded to Lady Sarah who was enthusiastically waving a large swansdown muff from the window of her carriage as she swept by in the other direction.

''It is the latest *on dit* that her brother has so far paid four morning calls upon you—speaking of suitors,'' Lady Stanier commented mildly.

Jane felt a quiver inside of something that she refused to identify. ''Mr. Quint has the lead on Lord Jaspar by several days—or is that of small consequence to the *ton*,'' she replied calmly.

''A source of amusement only. However, when Montmorency puts himself to the trouble of paying morning calls on a beautiful woman they sit up and take notice, I assure you."

Again Jane experienced the fluttering inside. It could be fear, she thought. But fearfulness could not suppress her curiosity. "I had thought so handsome a man would be much sought after," she said with a patently false air of disinterest.

"Oh, he is that! But much good has it done anyone till now. I can't remember him looking twice at a girl since he entered his first drawing room. He couldn't have been more than seventeen and one saw him everywhere for a time. Ah, *what* a good-looking boy, you wouldn't credit it. But after about a year he became more elusive. Frightened of being trapped into marriage, no doubt. For some years now, he's only gone into Society as an escort for his mama or Sarah. Probably he's found it wise to keep an eye on Sarah, who's been known to take more to drink than is proper for a young lady."

"She gets bored, she says," replied Jane in almost automatic defense.

"She confides in you?"

"Yes, I suppose she does," Jane admitted.

"It must be a bore for you."

"That's what her brother says, though I cannot think why everyone should assume such a thing," Jane said indignantly.

"Well, she seems a trifle caper-witted to me, but let's not come to points over it. No doubt she has a more intelligent side that I have not been privileged to see," said Lady Stanier equably.

"She has, I'm sure of it. She's just never been given the encouragement to be other than a—a—spoiled darling of Society. That overproud mother's only contribution has been to prepare her for the marriage market! I've read some poetry aloud to her and she was quite moved by it. She requested to borrow the book to read by herself. I'm encouraged to hope she'll discover there are other things worthwhile in the world besides gowns and balls and eligible *partis!*"

"And champagne and gambling, I think you should add," commented Lady Stanier drily. "However, I'm glad to hear she's attaching herself to someone with intelligence and taste. Shows she's got a spark of good sense at least."

Jane was too overcome by this compliment to reply, and dropped her eyes into her lap. Lady Stanier laughed softly and patted her hand. "Well, well, I won't tease you about it any more. I only hope she won't lead you into any uncomfortable situations with her foolishness."

"I doubt she would try to—oh—I had meant to ask you—she *has* been urging me to go with her to a place called The Golden Crocodile, or some such outlandish name. Do you know of it?"

"The newest gaming house," responded Lady Stanier promptly, always sure to know the latest in everything. "All the crack right now. Very deep play I'm told. Do you enjoy such things?"

"I was used to playing loo and whist with Sebastian and Mother Payton. Not for money, of course. I was very good at it, they would tell me," she added, somewhat wistfully.

"Well then, why don't you go? There can be no harm in a little play if one keeps one's head. I confess *I* could never do so—keep my head, I mean. Talked too much, I expect."

They drove along in companionable silence for a time, and then Lady Stanier returned to her previous thought. "About Montmorency. I hope you are not seriously discouraging his suit."

Jane flushed scarlet. "His 'suit'? After four visits it has become a suit?!"

Lady Stanier continued placidly, "For I must tell you, if you are worried about his recognising the little girl who had previously been in his mother's employ, I think you can forget all that. Obviously none of the family have done so, and I for one see no reason to suppose they ever will. You and Montmorency would suit very well, notwithstanding the dreadful prospect of Lady Montmorency for a mother-in-law."

"Mother-in—! But he hasn't—I can't—we aren't—"

"Dear heaven! *So* many negatives," laughed Lady Stanier.

"But how can you even think of such a thing? I have no thought to remarry!"

"You haven't? Then I think you had better take it into consideration. You are still a young girl, and I assume you are—er—as normal in your needs as the rest of us—"

"But *you* never remarried!" Jane protested, the blood pouring into her cheeks as the import of Lady Stanier's remark reached her mind.

"My dear child, I had thirty-two years of a very satisfying marriage—you had two. I was nearing fifty—you are twenty," Lady Stanier pointed out gently, "and if that carries no weight with you, I will add that my children were grown and married. Your son is still an infant, and in my estimation in need of a father. Sebastian would have made a wonderful father, but I don't think he would want the child to go without one just because he could not be here to fill the role, any more than I believe he would want you to mourn him for the rest of your life."

Jane felt a lump rise in her throat and she stared through blurred, unseeing eyes out the window. Unbidden, there rose in her mind the picture of Clinton leaning confidingly against Lord Jaspar's knee, explaining to him earnestly that though he had requested very politely that he be given a pony, Nurse and Mama would not heed him.

It had happened that several mornings previously the boy had escaped Nurse and come running into the drawing room in search of his mama. Jane was patiently enduring yet another visit from Mr. Quint, and at sight of the man Clinton had become rooted in apparent amazement. As Mr. Quint, stays creaking, leaned forward with a condescending smile, Clinton's eyes and mouth formed perfect circles and he became speechless. No amount of urging by his mama, or cajoling from Mr. Quint, dangling a watch chain literally clanking with fobs, served to stir the child to any other reaction than astonishment. When Nurse came panting to the drawing room door in search of her charge, she was able to lead him away unprotestingly, as he cast his round-eyed look over his shoulder.

The spectacle of Mr. Quint drew Clinton back on the following day, much to Jane's embarrassment and Mr. Quint's patent annoyance as the same scene was reenacted. On the third morning Clinton arrived to find Jaspar there instead of Mr. Quint, and with no urging at all walked up to him, bowed with all his four-year-old aplomb and held out his hand. When Jaspar had shaken the tiny hand gravely and reseated himself, Clinton came up to him, and propping his elbow casually on Jaspar's knee, proceded to make his complaint, man to man, about the unreasonableness of women who fussed over one unnecessarily, and refused to understand about ponies.

Jaspar was agreeing with him that women could be obtuse about the basic necessities of young gentlemen, when Alben Quint was announced. He tripped across to Jane and gave her one of his most elaborate, flourishing bows. When he straightened up he found both Jaspar and Clinton observing him with identical expressions of awe. Mr. Quint acknowledged them with a dignified nod of the head, sat down in his finicking way on a sofa and extracted his watch chain, evidently convinced that if he dangled his fobs long enough before Clinton's eyes, the child would eventually succumb to their blandishment. Jaspar reseated himself, but Clinton remained where he was, gazing at Mr. Quint with the same blank, almost imbecilic, look he reserved for Mr. Quint. Jane felt a strong desire to shake him.

"Clinton!" she said sharply. "Clinton! You will oblige me by making your bow to Mr. Quint and saying 'Good morning,' " she prompted very firmly. He seemed not to have heard her and remained standing at gaze, eyes never wavering, exactly like some clodpoll up from the country seeing Astley's Circus for the first time, Jane thought, torn between exasperation and giggles.

Jaspar leaned forward at that moment and spoke briefly, and very quietly, into the boy's ear. Clinton turned, regarded him silently for a moment and then nodded. Then, without hesitation, he marched across the carpet, held out his hand to Mr. Quint, and said, "Good morning, sir," very politely. He then came back to Jaspar and said in a whisper that carried clearly over the entire room, "Why don't *you* squeak in the middle when you bend?"

Nurse's timely arrival saved Jaspar the necessity of attempting an answer and Jane from the strong hysterics she felt were imminent. Clinton requested Lord Jaspar to please explain to his mama his problem regarding a pony and come again tomorrow to report on any progress, said "Good-bye, Mr. Quint" in a tone of unabashed finality and allowed himself to be led away.

In the silence following his exit Mr. Quint could be heard audibly grinding his teeth, while Jaspar stared with concentration at a portrait of a Payton ancestress that hung over the mantel, and Jane set several stitches into her embroidery in what turned out to be a random, and totally unsuitable way.

Remembering the scene now she could smile, but Lady Stanier's remarks stayed very much in her mind, being an aspect of the situation to which she had given no thought heretofore. She spent a great deal of time with her son, fierce in her determination to make him into a man his father would have been proud of. This was the first time it had entered her mind that her efforts might not be enough. Now she saw that the boy was smothered in feminine attention, the only male in his life being Crews. Of course Crews adored the boy, but a servant-master relationship was not a healthy one for a little boy who could get his own way by simply being in the dominant position despite his size and youth.

"Dearest, I hope I have not distressed you," said Lady Stanier, seeing Jane's brows drawn together in a frown.

"Of course you have not! It is only that I had not thought of things in that light before."

"Well, there is time still," replied Lady Stanier comfortably, "but it is something I felt you should open your mind to. You need to go about more—meet more people. The sorts of affairs I take you to are too—too—staid—too many elderly people. You need to be in the swim of things with people your own age."

"Prospective fathers, do you mean?" Jane asked with a grin.

"Well—you could put it that way. In line with that, and just to make the first step easier for you, I have decided to have a party. A dancing party. Not so grand as a real ball, for that would be too much work and less pleasure. Just something small—say twenty or so couples to stand up after dinner and a light collation at midnight. I'll ask only the most dashing and eligible young men and the liveliest girls and we shall go on delightfully! Of course, the Montmorencys will receive a card, and I'll even put myself out to be pleasant to the dragon mother. Now—is that not magnanimous of me?"

"I would not have you do so for my sake—I mean—if you think I look upon Lord Jaspar as—as—or he—" Jane floundered to a halt.

"I won't think anything at all, I promise you, unless you tell me I may do so. After all, he will be only one among many young men whom you may find far more attractive. Oh, I can see you now, going from one partner to the next! Truly, Jane, there is no woman in London to hold a candle to you!" Lady Stanier sighed happily in anticipation.

Jane sighed herself, but the picture she could see in her mind did not include any of those engaging young men who filled Lady Stanier's vision. There was only one man, a puzzling, enigmatic smile on his lips. The others were mere blurs in the background. Then she mentally shook herself to dispel the vision. Naturally, I would only see him, she scolded herself, since he's the only one I know! I shouldn't really go along with Aunt's plan in any case. I will be terrified and behave like a goose, and stumble all over my partner's feet and spill things. As she built up this nightmare it became very real to her and she resolved to tell Lady Stanier at once that she must not go ahead with any plans that included Jane, for she knew it would be unbearably tedious.

Then, irrationally, she began thinking of what she might wear to this tedious affair. Yellow, she thought, pale lemony yellow sarcenet and the heavenly topazes left to her by Mother Payton.

19

Jaspar arrived a quarter of an hour earlier than his usual visiting time the following morning.

"I've come to deliver my report to your son at his request," he said, turning from the fireplace and advancing to meet her as she entered the drawing room looking somewhat flustered. She had been hastily summoned from the back drawing room where she was conferring with Betty Crews on menus, and had had no time to prepare herself for the meeting.

"Your—report? But what have you to report? We've not discussed it at all!"

"Exactly why I've come along early—before that tiresome Quint or my equally tiresome sister could distract you. Now, my thoughts on the matter are as follows: one, the boy wants to ride, two, he should be allowed to do so."

"You surely cannot be serious about this?" she protested.

"On the contrary. I'm very serious. So is the lad."

"But—I—I don't want him to ride—ever!" she said flatly.

"If you'll forgive me, I think you're being most unwise."

"You don't understand!"

"I think I do," he said quietly, "it's because of what happened to his father. Yes?" Jane dropped her eyes and stood clasping her hands together so hard the knuckles showed white. He reached for them and held them enfolded in his own. "That was an accident, and accidents do happen. But you can't wrap the boy in cotton wool and try to protect him from life. I don't think his father would want that for him. Would he be proud of a lily-livered drawing-room dandy, afraid of draughts and dark streets? Would you?"

"He's too young—still a baby, really," she whispered one last protest, for she knew he was right.

"Not if he's held on by a groom and walked about on a very gentle, biddable sort of animal. I happen to know just such a one, and if you are agreeable, I thought we might ride over to see it. I'll take the boy up in front of me—just to give him a taste of the saddle and the height before we get there. I'll hold him very carefully, no fear, there won't be any danger."

She raised her eyes at last to find him regarding her with so much warmth and understanding it bewildered her. Surely a human being of so much sensitivity and sympathy could not also be capable of betraying her past to Society just to afford himself malicious amusement?"

"Why—why are you doing this?" she asked slowly.

"Because I like your son very much. He's just the sort of little boy I would want. And I want him to like me because it will be a point in my favour in his mother's eyes. It has become very necessary for me to get back into his mother's good graces," he added with that devastating candour that always took her by surprise.

"B-b-back?" she stuttered, fearful, in spite of all that had just passed, that he was referring subtly to their meeting before the mirror so many years ago.

"Well, perhaps that's the wrong word. I suspect that I was never in them—your good graces, I mean. But I want to be very much." He pressed the hands he still held, and she, remembering where they were, flushed and tried to draw them away, but he would not release them. He bent closer to her, his voice became soft and he spoke slowly. "I don't like that strange way you look at me sometimes, as though you disliked me or are frightened of me. I want to dispel that look. I want to see you happy—laughing—your eyes all lit up and sparkling like sherry wine." His voice trailed off to a whisper, and she, caught up in the slow rhythm, gazed up as though hypnotized, her body filled with a sort of languor.

What might have happened they were destined not to know, for at that moment Clinton, followed by a wildly excited Wellington, erupted into the room. Clinton ran straight to Jaspar and grasped him urgently by the knee.

"Did you explain it to her, sir? Did you tell her how important it is?" he demanded in his high, piping treble. Wellington seemed to be demanding an answer also as he dashed round and round them, yipping wildly.

Jaspar laughed and leaned down to lift Clinton into his arms. "Now, sir, we can speak face-to-face. What is your dog's name?"

"Wellington."

"Here, Wellington, down. Sit down I say, and be quiet!" Wellington miraculously collapsed, grinning up at them lopsidedly, his tongue hanging from one side of his mouth. Jane could only gape in astonishment. Not only to see the animal obey so instantly, but to see Clinton so far forget what he felt he owed to his dignity as to allow himself to be picked up by a stranger without demur. Only Nurse and his mama had been allowed this privilege for over a year now, and only when Clinton was extremely tired or feeling unwell. He was very resistant to coddling in the ordinary way, proclaiming that it was for babies.

"Now, young Clinton, here's how matters stand. I have discussed your problem with your mama and am even at this moment awaiting her decision."

Clinton nodded gravely, put his arm about Jaspar's neck in a comradely way, and they both turned questioning eyes upon Jane.

"Wretch," she murmured feelingly, but then could not help laughing. "Oh, very well. I'll go and change into a riding dress. Lord Jaspar knows of a pony, Clinton, and—"

She got no further. Even as she said the first conceding

words, Clinton was pushing imperatively against Jaspar's chest, clearly signaling his desire to be set down. Jaspar promptly did so and Clinton and Wellington began an ecstatic gallop around the room, to the accompaniment of triumphant whoops and barks. Nurse's scandalized face appeared at the drawing-room door, and Jane, after informing Nurse of what the celebration was for, fled up the stairs to change. When she emerged from her room thirty minutes later, she wore her new and very elegant riding costume, and wondered anxiously if Lord Jaspar would think it smart. It was a dark lavender blossom in fine broadcloth, the collar high and rolled in back and lapeled down the front. There was a deep cape, *à la pèlerine* and a broad belt with a steel clasp. At her throat was a high ruff of double-pleated muslin sloping to a point at the bosom. Her hat was of amber-coloured velvet with a band of velvet leaves and her York tan gloves were tied with amber bows.

She paused in the drawing room door in self-conscious shyness, but the scene before her erased all thoughts of her own splendour. There sat Lord Jaspar in a chair by the window and perched on his knee was Clinton. They were deep into a discussion of the best qualities to be looked for in horse flesh, Clinton attending very seriously. Jaspar, suddenly aware of her presence, looked around and smiled.

"Well, lad, here is your mama, looking excessively fine. I think you must jump down and go congratulate her upon her costume."

Clinton obediently climbed down. "My mama is always very fine," he said, as though it were a fact too irrefutable to need further comment.

"Indeed she is—but very special today," replied Jaspar with so compelling a look into Jane's eyes that she became quite breathless.

Nurse appeared and began buttoning Clinton into his coat, to the accompaniment of a steady stream of instructions as to his conduct while out of her charge, so that she would have no need to be ashamed of him. Clinton turned to Jaspar with a speaking look that said clearly what foolishly worrying creatures women were in his opinion. Jaspar snorted with laughter, which he covered with a cough, while Jane turned away to hide her smile and found Crews grinning openly in male sympathy.

Just as Clinton turned away from Nurse and took Jaspar's hand the door knocker was heard to thump and everyone stopped. Crews stepped forward to open the door, and there stood Mr. Quint, his hand still raised to the knocker. For a moment everyone stood suspended, staring at one another over the threshold. Then Mr. Quint's mouth opened and shut several times as though he wanted to speak, though no words issued forth. It was Clinton who broke the spell, having very important business on his mind.

"I think we should not keep the pony standing around waiting," he said firmly, the maturity of his words sounding absurd in his baby voice. Mr. Quint, however, was clearly not amused. To his mind, a very small taste of young children constituted a surfeit. He bent a quelling glare upon Clinton and then turned to Jane.

"Good morning, dear lady. As you see, I am here for our visit," he said with an intimate smile meant to convey the message that of course his arrival would cancel any other plans she may have made.

Jane had been a bit flustered by this rather embarrassing social situation, but his presumption caused her to retort sharply, "And as you see, Mr. Quint, I am on my way to an engagement with my son."

"But—but—my dear—we—I—" sputtered Mr. Quint.

"Mama!" Clinton reminded her impatiently.

"Yes, darling, I am coming. Good day, Mr. Quint."

The indoors party moved forward and down the steps to where the groom was holding their mounts. The sight of Mr. Quint's face, sagging with disappointment and confusion, caused Jane to turn back impulsively. "I'm sorry we must leave in this abrupt way, Mr. Quint, just as you arrive, but you do understand? One must not keep a pony waiting." She smiled charmingly. Mr. Quint's wrinkles pulled themselves up into a response and he gave her a theatrical bow.

"Till tomorrow, fair one. I shall count the moments."

Jane turned away to hide her distaste for this intimacy. Jaspar threw her up into her saddle and then mounted himself. Clinton was handed up to Jaspar by the groom, who then mounted and the party set off down the street. Clinton's short little legs stuck straight out on each side and he clutched the pommel and sat up very straight, staring straight ahead. His face seemed to be lit up from within, as one would imagine young Lohengrin looked when he set off to seek the Holy Grail.

* * *

When they returned, Clinton, who had remained ecstatically speechless throughout the excursion, could manage only to shake Jaspar's hand and grin. Jaspar grinned back, then turned to take Jane's hand, and kiss her fingers lightly.

"Well done, Jane! But I knew you were pluck to the back-bone," and without waiting for a response, sprang back into his saddle and rode away.

Once inside his own door again the dam broke and all Clinton's pentup emotion burst forth in a spate of excited chatter about the merits of the truly exceptional pony and how easy it was to ride him. Jane hugged and kissed him, a liberty he didn't even seem to notice as he continued re-counting every moment of his excursion. Laughing, Jane led him off to Nurse and then retired to her room to change into an afternoon dress.

While Dorrie was rearranging Jane's hair a note arrived from Lady Sarah:

> *Darling Jane,*
> *Please come with me to The Golden Crocodile tonight. It is so Important to me. I mean I shall go Mad if I must attend Another stupid Party with Mama! I don't trust my-self at the Gaming Tables alone, and I know your Presence will restrain me. Say yes—Please!*
>
> > *Sarah*
>
> *My man is waiting for your reply. If it is "Yes," may I dine with you first?*

Jane hesitated only a moment before impulsively dashing off an answer. She would go, she decided. Aunt Stanier had urged her to, and it would be amusing to play at cards again after so long. Fortunately Aunt Stanier was dining at Payton House this evening so she had only to instruct Crews to have another place laid. Possibly Aunt Stanier might like to accompany them to The Golden Crocodile.

Lady Stanier was agreeable to the plan. "Though of course I have no head for cards whatsoever. However, no doubt I will find any number of acquaintances there. Besides, I cannot ap-prove of two young women going to such a place alone, even though one of them is married."

So after dinner the three women arranged themselves in Sar-ah's carriage and were driven to the gambling house. Sarah kept up the same nervous chatter she had maintained throughout dinner, saying nothing of any consequence, but unable, apparently, to stop, thus confirming Lady Stanier's opinion that Sarah Montmorency was very little short of being a wantwit. Oh she was beautiful, of course, especially tonight in leaf-green that made her long, slanted eyes more green than usual. But not able to compare with Jane, thought Lady Stanier complacently, casting a proprietary glance at Jane. Jane's high-waisted gown of heavy amber satin was almost severe in its beautifully cut simplicity, the skirt falling in a sleek line from below the bosom to the floor without ornament. The low, round neckline of the bodice framed the double rope of Payton pearls. Her headdress was a turban of amber velvet with a pearl and diamond brooch holding a small white plume. Over her shoulders was a long sable cloak.

As the carriage pulled up before the door of a modest town house, Sarah became abruptly quiet, but Lady Stanier noted that she was now biting her lip. A liveried attendant stationed on the steps rapped sharply on the house door and hurried down to help the ladies out of the carriage.

"Good evening, m'lady," he said to Sarah, "we've been on the lookout for you."

They all crossed the pavement and mounted the steps as the front door opened before them, allowing a brilliant stream of light to spill down the steps. A very large doorman held the door open, an obsequious smile on his face. Lady Stanier nodded graciously as she went past him into a large entrance hall thronged with people, among whom she recognized some of the cream of the *ton*, all talking and laughing as they sipped champagne and strolled back and forth, passing from room to room opening off the central hall, where many games were in progress.

A footman came to take Lady Stanier's cloak as Sarah came through the door. At the same moment a tall gentleman pushed his way through the patrons.

"Ah—welcome, Lady Sarah. I've been waiting for your arrival. Did you bring—?"

Sarah did not answer his greeting. She simply stood aside to reveal Jane just stepping over the threshold. There were murmurs of admiration and interest from the spectators, whose attention had been drawn to the door by the man's loud greeting. He stopped as he saw Jane, as though he too was rapt with admiration. Indeed there was every reason for him to be, for Jane presented a breathtaking picture of regal loveliness, framed there in the doorway.

The small, anticipatory smile slowly faded from her lips and her eyes widened in shock, as every trace of her usual vivid colour faded from her face.

For there, directly before her, stood the one man she had hoped never to see again in her life. There was Leach!

She felt turned to ice in an instant and was aware of a faint sizzling sound in her ears. Leach recovered himself and advanced toward her, hand held out, smiling broadly.

"Well, well, this is an honour—er—Lady Payton," he said, emphasizing her title very slightly, and raising his eyebrow at her as though they shared a secret joke.

She drew back, staring in revulsion at the hand held out to her. Then suddenly she felt a flash of heat over her entire body, as though her very blood boiled. She had never experienced such rage in all her life. Two livid patches of red stained her cheeks and her sherry-coloured eyes turned nearly black. She raised her chin, stared at him with loathing, and then, without speaking, spun on her heel so quickly the sable cloak belled out around her, and walked back out the door.

Lady Stanier quickly removed her own cloak from the hands of the riveted footman. "Come, Sarah," she said and started for the door. Behind her she thought she heard the man utter something as Sarah moved to follow her. She turned back to see Sarah pulling her arm from the man's grasp.

"Oh—I—you go along, Lady Stanier. I'll join the Davanets for a short time. Just send my carriage back and tell Jane I will speak to her tomorrow," Sarah said with an attempt at lightness. But her eyes seemed to be pleading, and behind her, a dangerous glitter in his eyes, the man scowled ferociously. Lady Stanier merely nodded to Sarah and left.

In the carriage she found Jane huddled into her furs in the farthest corner, shaking uncontrollably.

"My dearest! What is it?" Lady Stanier pulled Jane into her arms. Jane made no answer, only burrowed close against her, shuddering. Lady Stanier ordered the coachman to take them to Payton House and they moved off. Lady Stanier held Jane tightly and wordlessly all the way home. Once there, she took her directly to the back drawing room, ordering a much concerned Crews to bring some brandy there. A fire still burned briskly in the fireplace, and Lady Stanier pressed Jane into the large chair before it.

When Crews brought the brandy, Lady Stanier poured out a generous portion and handed it to Jane. "Now, my love, I don't know what is wrong, but I can see you've had a shock, so you'll just get this down and sit quite quietly before you say a word," she ordered.

Jane obediently extended a white-gloved hand from beneath her fur cloak and took the glass. She sipped it slowly, staring into the flames, and gradually the livid red patches on her cheeks faded and a more normal colour returned to her white face. Finally she set the glass aside and sighed.

"That—was Leach," she said, "and it was not shock so much as rage. I felt quite—quite murderous. I think if I had held a weapon I might have killed him at that moment."

"Leach? But—but—I don't understand. I thought he was the Montmorency's butler."

"No longer, evidently," Jane replied drily. "No doubt he managed to put aside a great deal of money besides his wages during the years he worked for the Montmorencys. He was absolute ruler there, you know, even Lady Montmorency hardly dared to go against him in domestic matters. There's a lot to be made in such a position by a dishonest servant."

"But how *could* Sarah patronize such a man?"

"Oh, the Montmorencys thought very highly of him. And you know how restless Sarah is—always looking for something new."

"Hmmm—and she has been urging you to accompany her there?"

"Yes. I have been wondering about that also in the past few moments."

"I'm wondering if it was at his prompting."

"How could he have known we were friends?"

"Oh, that is easy enough. You are out around town with her quite often. He must have seen you with her and recognized you and suggested she bring you."

"But why should she want to oblige him?"

"Dear one, I *have* heard she plays rather deep. Perhaps her debt to him is great enough for him to make such a suggestion. Even to demand it."

"But what can be his motive?"

"With such a degenerate character it is impossible to guess his motive. Perhaps only the urge to strut his new status before you, or his sly way to let you know he had recognized you. I hope it is nothing more."

"More! What do you mean?" Jane asked in alarm.

"Well, it is possible he hopes to extort something from you based on his knowledge of your background."

"Money, do you mean?"

"Or perhaps your patronage as a wealthy titled woman who might draw others, give him more respectability."

"He will not have it! Never! Nor money either! I would never give him a penny of Payton money!"

"Darling, be calm. It is more than likely nothing will come of it. After all, it could not be to his advantage to expose you, and he doesn't strike me as a man who does anything that is not to his advantage."

Jane sat very still for a long time, staring unseeingly at Lady Stanier as she thought about it. Finally she sighed and slumped back into the chair.

"I hope you are right. Oh, I should never have taken this chance and come to London. Perhaps I should just go back. Take Clinton and go."

"Yes, I suppose running away would be one answer," replied Lady Stanier noncommittally.

"It would be for Clinton's sake. I'd *be* a coward for his sake if necessary!" Jane flung at her, hurt by the implication.

"My dear, forgive me. I should not have said that. Especially now when you are so distraught. We will work something out, I assure you. I think the first thing you must do is go to your bed. The whole thing will seem much less daunting in the morning. Then I think you should speak to Sarah and find out whether he *did* ask her to bring you there. It may very well be that he didn't do so. It *is* possible that he didn't recognize you at all. You have changed a great deal since he last saw you, don't forget."

It was a ray of hope, and feeble though it was, Jane grasped it gratefully. Yes, she thought, I must speak to Sarah.

20

Speaking to Sarah, however, proved, mysteriously, easier to decide upon than to accomplish.

As Lady Stanier had predicted, the morning light cast a clearer, less heated, view of the previous evening's events. Leach, after all, could not hurt her now. She need never see him or speak to him again in her life. If he dared to speak of her to anyone, surely Lady Stanier's credit with the world was great enough to disarm any stories he might put about. She could not dismiss her curiosity regarding the possible part played by Sarah, however. Nor could she dispel the slight oppression of spirits she still felt from the dreadful night she had just come through. She had slept little, and when she had finally managed to drift off, the old nightmare had pounced upon her: the huge, faceless form pressing down on her, her lungs bursting. She woke gasping and sobbing, leaping from the bed to stare wildly about in terror. The reality of her comfortable room, the fire still glowing behind its screen, finally chased away the stronger reality of the dream, but she could not bear to lie down again. She huddled the down quilt from her bed around her shoulders and spent the rest of the night in a chair before the fire. She only went back to her bed in the early morning when she heard Clinton running down the hall to her room for his morning romp.

This session with her ebullient little son did more to restore her spirits than anything else could have done. When he had been carried away by Nurse for his breakfast, Jane rose, dressed, and dashed off a note to Sarah, asking her, if it was convenient, to please call at the earliest opportunity. The footman was instructed to await her reply.

Mr. Quint called, as well as Lord Jaspar, but she sent down her apologies and word that she was slightly indisposed and not receiving this morning. Meantime, she paced about impatiently, waiting for Sarah's answer.

When the footman returned, however, he brought no reply. "She wasn't to home, m'lady. Leastways, that's what her abigail says. So I left the note and come away."

Jane dismissed him and resumed her pacing. How extraordinary, she thought, Sarah up and out of the house at this still very early hour of the morning! So unlike her. Where can she have gone? When no answer presented itself, Jane forced herself to go on with her day. She summoned Dorrie and gave her her daily lesson, afterward taking Clinton to Lady Stanier's for a visit with Mrs. Hawks, who, as usual, did her very best to spoil him beyond recall in the space of an hour. Jane quelled her need to rush home and see if she had received any communication from Sarah, and sat down to a light luncheon with Lady Stanier.

When she did reach home in the late afternoon, it was to find that a note had not arrived. She shrugged slightly, kissed Clinton, and sent him away with Nurse for a nap, and turned to the hall table where two posies were waiting. They proved to be from Mr. Quint and Lord Jaspar, each with a note expressing the hope that her indisposition was not of a serious or long-lasting nature, and they would both call to inquire on the following day. She smiled and told Crews to have the flowers taken to her room. She removed her bonnet and pelisse and was turning away to the back drawing room when the door knocker sounded faintly. Jane paused to look back just as Crews opened the door.

There stood Sarah, swaying slightly. "Jane!" she gasped when she saw Jane at the back of the hall. Jane rushed forward.

"Why, Sarah, you received my note at last! I wondered— Good God!" This last, shocked, exclamation escaped involuntarily as she came close enough to see Sarah's face clearly. It was grotesquely disfigured, the right eye swollen almost closed amid a large, purplish bruise which extended over most of that side of her face. Her golden hair, originally piled high on her head, was straggling down, and she still wore the leaf-green velvet evening cloak of last night, sadly crumpled now.

With an inarticulate cry of pity Jane swept Sarah into her arms, where Sarah gave way completely and began to cry. She sobbed just as a hurt child does, mouth open in a grimace of tragedy and emitting loud, racking cries. Crews hastily closed the front door. Jane, holding Sarah close, led her to the back drawing room, calling out to Crews to bring warm water and brandy to her there.

She pressed Sarah down onto the sofa and loosened her pelisse, all the while murmuring soft words of comfort. Her eyes widened as she noted the rusty spots liberally spattered down the front of the silk and gauze gown. That surely is blood, she thought, horrified. She said nothing, however, only continuing to soothe the distraught girl as best she could until Betty Crews came hurrying in with a basin of water, cloths, and various ointments on a tray, as well as the brandy bottle.

Nothing could have been more salutary than the brisk, unastonished way Betty set about administering the brandy, and, when it had served its purpose and Sarah's sobs had subsided, bathing her face gently and then expertly smoothing ointment onto the bruised eye.

"Though there's little good it will do. That eye will take over a week to be right again, to my way of thinking, though 'twont be painful that long," pronounced Betty, gathering up her things. "I'll just take these things away and have the maid air the bed in the Blue Room," she added, raising an interrogative eyebrow at Jane, who took her meaning and nodded affirmatively. For of course there could be no question of allowing Sarah to return home to her mama in this condition.

The door closed behind Betty and silence filled the room, broken only by an occasional hiccupping sob or a shuddering sigh. Jane sat on a footstool beside the sofa and held Sarah's hand warmly in both her own.

"Well, my dear," Jane said softly after a time, "will you tell me about it now?"

"It is so—sordid—so ugly—you will hate me forever!"

"Of course I shall not hate you, foolish girl."

"Yes, you will. But I had no one else to go to. You, at least, will not swoon away or become hysterical as my mama would, or any other of my acquaintances. I don't call them friends, you notice, for I realized when I was trying to decide where it would be best to go, that I could not turn to any one of them." She laughed shakily. "I suppose that may be counted as one lesson I have learned from all this. You are the only person I have any respect for besides Jaspar. Oh Jane, if only I had met you years ago!"

Jane's lips twitched at the irony of this statement in spite of herself and the dreadfulness of the situation. "Never mind, dear, just try to tell me what has happened so that we can decide what it will be best to do about it."

"Oh lord—where to begin? I suppose I must tell you that that man, that Leach, is holding my counters for—well—a great deal of money. He was—he was our butler, you see, and Mama always thought very highly of him. When he left us to set up his own business, we were all full of congratulations on his good fortune. When he sent around cards inviting us to patronize his gaming house, Mama said that I might go as it was sure to be respectable if Leach were in charge. Leach!" She spat out the name with loathing.

"He—he did this to you?" Sarah nodded, the tears starting in her eyes, but she blinked rapidly and took a deep breath, determined not to give way again. "But—no, I won't ask questions. You must tell me just in your own way."

"Well—I could not pay him. I had already spent *next* quarter's allowance and Jaspar said he would give me no more, and Mama had none to give me—"

"But surely your brother would relent if—"

"No! I—I couldn't! He would be very angry with me—I couldn't ask him. Anyway—Leach said he would cancel my debt if I—if I—"

"If you would bring *me* there?"

"Yes—but I swear to you I meant *you* no harm. Though I still don't understand what happened. Why did you look so strange and then walk out in that way?"

"He reminded me of something quite terrible in my own life—I had to go away." Jane said slowly, aware that she was dissembling, but unwilling to reveal more to this volatile girl, who was not always discreet in her speech.

Sarah was too involved with her own problem to give much attention to this excuse at the moment. She accepted Jane's explanation without question and plunged ahead.

"He was furious! I've never seen him in such a rage! He took it as a personal insult—hated having all those people see him being administered such a snub. He—he would not let me leave with you and made me come into his private apartment upstairs and—and—"

"Oh no, Sarah!" Jane gasped, "surely he didn't force you to submit to him? I shall never forgive myself if I caused you to be subjected to—"

"No, no—not that. Even *he* would not dare go that far. Jaspar would kill him—he might anyway if he ever finds out about this. Oh Jane—Jaspar *must not* hear of it,'' Sarah cried, clutching Jane's hand frantically.

"No, darling, no. We will think of something, don't worry. Now, he forced you upstairs and struck you?"

"Not right away. He raged and shouted a great deal first. Then he went away for a time and came back to begin all over again. All night long! I was so tired! And so frightened, because I couldn't imagine what he was going to do."

"Did he—speak of me?" Jane asked fearfully, even though it was clear to her that he could not have done so, or Sarah must surely have referred to it by now, or at the very least let it appear in her attitude.

"Oh—nothing I could make any sense of. Mostly of how high in the instep you'd become, but how he'd bring you to heel before he was done, and—oh, on and on about being insulted and everything. I stopped listening after a while. I was so tired and worried! I knew Mama would be frantic! Finally, I began demanding to leave and that's when he struck me. He just drew back his arm and slapped me so hard I thought my neck was broken and then he turned and left the room and locked the door."

"But the blood—that *is* blood on your gown?"

"That was from my nose. It began to bleed. God, it was so nightmarish. I kept thinking 'this *cannot* be happening to me.' And I cried and cried, and sometimes I'd fall asleep. Once he came in and made me write a note to my mama to say I was spending the night with you, then he just left me there alone for hours, not even bringing me anything to eat when morning came. In fact I've had nothing all day! Just a little while ago he came back finally. I think he was at a loss as to what to do about me. Then he said he would let me go, but that I was to tell no one anything or he would tell everyone I had spent the night alone with him, and he would go to Jaspar with my counters. Oh Lord, what *shall* I do? I daren't go home and let Mama see me like this."

"No—I have been thinking. I will take you down to Larkwoods with me. We'll stay there till you're quite recovered and we'll see no one. Will you come?"

"Oh, Jane!" and now the tears came and she could not blink them away. Jane silently held out her handkerchief.

"We'll send someone round with another note to your mama

and a request that Wright pack some things for you and send them here.''

"Oh Lord, she'll be in fits!"

"Your mama?"

"No, Wright. She'll want to come along."

"No!" Jane exclaimed forcefully. "We—we shan't need her at Larkwoods since we shall be quite quiet and Dorrie can take care of both of us. I think the fewer people who know of this the better. Since my servants are already aware of something wrong it is better to keep it this way. And my people would never dream of gossiping about me or my guests."

"You're fortunate. Well, Lord knows I don't want Wright along, I'll just be quite firm that she is not to accompany me."

"Then that's settled. One thing is not, however, There is still your debt. I think you must apply to your brother. I really cannot understand your reluctance in the matter. I have found him to be of an amenable disposition, always kind to my son, and exceedingly good-natured. I'm sure he would expect you to come to him with such trouble. He *is* your guardian, though he is younger, and stands in place of a father to you."

"He told me I must not gamble anymore and if I did he would not pay my debts."

"But I cannot believe—"

"Oh, he was right. I've thought about it a great deal in the past hours. And he cannot really be blamed, I think. He's paid so many times—and I always think I will never play deep again and then I do and he—well—he's paid his share, heaven knows. Besides, I can't apply to him now—after this. Nothing could stop him from going after Leach and—and—oh Lord, Jane, Leach is dangerous! He might kill Jaspar! He keeps a set of pistols in his office!"

"Yes. I see. Then I will send the money."

"I cannot allow—" Sarah protested hotly.

"Be sensible. There's no choice. You haven't the money, your mother doesn't, and your brother mustn't be applied to. You cannot simply leave London forever to escape him. Even if you did he might go to Jaspar, which must not happen. Therefore, I will pay the debt—unless you can think of someone you'd rather be indebted to?"

"No. There is no one in the world I would rather be indebted to," Sarah responded firmly.

"Thank you," said Jane, accepting the statement as the

compliment Sarah meant it to be. The offer had not been made easily, for she could still hear her own words to Lady Stanier that never would Leach have a penny of Payton money. But she knew Sebastian himself would want her to help Sarah, and it was not money spent on a few hours of pleasure for herself. "Now, I must know the amount."

After a long moment Sarah told her, her eyes closed in shame, "It's four thousand pounds."

"Good God," Jane said simply.

"I know. It is terrible. I hope I will never forget this moment, nor all the humiliation and pain my own stupidity has brought me to. I can only hope," she added bitterly.

"My dear," Jane exclaimed, taking her hands, her heart filled with pity for this brilliant, beautiful creature brought so low by her own careless need for excitement.

After a time she brought writing materials and persuaded Sarah to write the note to her mother, and sent it off with the coachman with orders to wait and bring Lady Sarah's box back with him.

"By the way," Jane said, suddenly remembering. "I sent your own carriage back for you last night. Surely he didn't allow it to sit all night in front of his house?"

"No, he sent it home. I came here in his carriage."

"*His* carriage?"

"Oh, indeed. There is no end to Mr. Leach's pretensions, or his ambitions," Sarah said.

Jane felt uncommonly depressed by Sarah's words, as though a stifling dark blanket had settled over her brain. There seemed something portentous to herself in the words. She stared into the flames, wondering what Leach's ambitions were regarding herself. Why had he been so insistent upon Sarah's bringing her there, to the point of being willing to cancel a four thousand pound debt!

Sarah reached out to touch her shoulder, as if to remind Jane of her presence, and Jane forced herself to throw off the dark thoughts and turn to Sarah with a smile.

"Yes, dear, here I am daydreaming and you patiently waiting to be put to bed. Poor darling, you must be exhausted. Well, up you come. Betty Crews has made all ready for you, I'm sure, and will no doubt ring a peal over me for keeping you down here talking for so long."

She took Sarah upstairs and turned her over to the patiently waiting Betty, then wearily made her way to her own room. She felt thoroughly exhausted and threw herself down upon her bed for a moment. It seemed a week since morning.

Tomorrow, she thought, I will go first thing to the solicitor's office and ask him to have the money delivered to Leach with only the spoken message that it is in payment of Lady Sarah's debt. That way Leach won't know it's from me. Then I must come straight back and get the party on the road to Kent. I will send Betty and Crews with Cook and Dorrie on ahead of us, and take Nurse and Clinton with Sarah and myself. The rest of the servants will stay here. Since Aunt Stanier dines here tonight I can tell her of the excursion then.

Oh dear, she remembered with a start, what of Sarah? She will not want to appear, of course, but I cannot pretend she is not here. And having told Aunt Stanier of that, what excuse can I make for Sarah's presence in my house—in bed!

She worried this problem about in her mind for a while, torn between betraying Sarah's confidence and being less than truthful with beloved Aunt Stanier. I will tell her, she finally decided, since it also involves me and Leach, and she is the only person I *can* share this fear with. But I will tell Sarah that I am going to do so. Surely she will see that I cannot tell lies to someone so close to me, and she can't really mind Aunt Stanier knowing.

Oh good heavens! Aunt Stanier's party! She sat up with a jolt, wondering if Aunt Stanier had already sent out the cards for this affair. She ran downstairs to the back drawing room and hastily scribbled a note to Lady Stanier, asking her, if she had not already done so, not to send out cards for her party yet, and that she would explain all this evening. She rang for Crews and had it taken round to Lady Stanier immediately, then sat back with a sigh. Before it had finished escaping her lips, she sat up again in dismay. She had still to inform the servants of tomorrow's exodus. Wearily, she pulled herself to her feet and went off to find Betty Crews.

21

With one exception, the entire party had been enjoying the removal to Larkwoods. The chilly spring rains of London had given way as they travelled south, to a warm, burgeoning awakening in Kent, with the trees covered already with a pale green fretwork of leaves and the fields dancing with the first wild flowers.

Jane and Sarah, each with a shock to recover from, spent long, healing days in the open air, in the saddle or afoot, roaming the Park without meeting anyone. The local gentry were, of course, aware that Lady Payton and her son were in residence, but since they were unaccustomed in the past to any intercourse with the family, they placed little importance on the event.

The Crewses, Nurse, and Dorrie enjoyed the more relaxed atmosphere of Larkwoods and the heady warmth of the Kent springtime. Even Cook allowed, grudgingly to be sure, that the stove drew better than the one in London.

The one exception was Clinton, who, once the excitement of the journey and the renewing of his acquaintance with forgotten toys had abated, remembered the pony. This happened at the end of the very first day. Nurse came to Jane in some agitation to say that the child had requested an immediate return to London and had refused his dinner upon being informed that it would not be possible to set off at once.

Jane went to him immediately. He explained to her that he needed to ride the pony every day or the pony would be disappointed. Jane said she could understand his feelings, but that poor, dear Lady Sarah was ill and needed a spell in the country to recover.

"Can not her own mama take care of her?" Clinton inquired reasonably.

Jane assured him that unfortunately she could not, but that she knew he would want to do everything possible to help Lady

Sarah make a good recovery. He stared at her, his black eyes, so like Sebastian's, sober and thoughtful. Finally he agreed, though he was clearly unhappy. Jane's heart ached for him and she was torn between her wish to give him so simple a thing and her pity for Sarah. She offered to have John, the coachman, go out tomorrow in search of another pony. Clinton thanked her politely but declined, saying he didn't think his pony would want him to ride another.

So the matter remained unsolvable for the next six days. Sarah recovered her spirits proportionally as her bruises faded, and professed that she might never return to London and be perfectly content, so well did she love Kent. The long days out-of-doors, quiet evenings of reading aloud and discussion with Jane, and the early bedtimes agreed with her. Jane speculated that Sarah's hectic quest of pleasure in London had led her to excesses of behaviour which must have caused her secret shame, and now, for the first time in years, she felt no guilt about herself, which must contribute to her sense of well-being and happiness. Eventually, of course, the quiet of the country would begin to pall, for she was a creature of eagerly adopted enthusiasms, as quickly burnt out. At the moment she was enthusiastic about country life and fresh air.

Just how short-lived were her enthusiasms was demonstrated on the sixth day when a note arrived for her from Lady Barclough, in residence at her magnificent country estate some twenty miles away. She had heard, she wrote, from Lady Montmorency, that Sarah was making a visit at Larkwoods and *begged*, underlined three times to emphasize her desperation, that Sarah and Lady Payton would pack their cases and come to make up a house party. Her female guests were all perfect antidotes and she had "the Beau himself!" coming down from London with a number of friends; all dashing blades who would find pressing engagements elsewhere when they surveyed the ladies, and here she'd sent out cards to hundreds of people for a ball!

"That Caroline Barclough is such a pea goose!" Sarah exclaimed after reading this urgent note aloud to Jane. "Absolutely incapable of planning a proper party. Oh well, what do you say? Shall we go and save her from disaster?"

"Not I, love, not even if the Prince Regent himself were going to be there!" Jane laughed. "Though I hope you will go if you want to."

"Oh *don't* say no so quickly!" Sarah begged eagerly, enthusiasm fanned by the promise of the Beau and a ball. "We shall only stay a few days, and my dear, you will set them all on their ears!"

But Jane would not be coaxed. "More like I'll set them on something else after climbing all over their shoes in a country dance! No, no, my dear, I much prefer to remain at home, but I think you should go. Your bruises barely show and we can easily disguise what's left, and I can see it will do you a world of good to go into Society again after all these stodgy days here."

"They were not stodgy! How can you say so, when you've seen how I gloried in every moment of them?" Sarah was indignant, and patently sincere. Jane was touched by her declaration, feeling that after all the sacrifice of Clinton's pony had not been wasted.

"Just the same, I think the party will do you good, and Lady Barclough will be in your debt forever, so you must go."

"Well—I should like to, if you're sure. Of course, Caroline Barclough will be devastated not to have captured you also, she—oh! good heavens! I've no ball gown!"

Jane thought for a moment. "I might have something that would do. You are taller, of course, but Dorrie could let down the hem. Come along to my room."

A reply was sent off to Lady Barclough to inform her that Sarah would happily join her the following day, though Lady Payton must regretfully decline, and the rest of the afternoon was spent on Sarah's wardrobe. A ball gown of Jane's was taken from its cover and tried on, and, as predicted, was several inches too short, though fitting very well otherwise.

"And most becoming too," observed Jane, "much more for you than for me. I have never been partial to that shade of pink, but it is ravishing on you. Aunt Stanier had it made up for me as a gift, hoping it would tempt me to go to the local Assembly last year. Naturally, I did not go, so the gown has never been worn. Now, I think if we remove that ruffle at the neckline and have Dorrie sew on this blond lace you'll be as fine as five pence. And Dorrie, of course, must go with you."

"But of course I could not allow you to—"

"You must—you cannot arrive at such a grand affair without a dresser, you'd cut no sort of figure at all."

Sarah was reluctant, but was finally persuaded. Dorrie was guiltily ecstatic: a dresser to such a fashionable figure as Lady

Sarah Montmorency! Why, her status in the servants' quarters would be dizzingly exalted.

The following morning they set forth in the grandest Payton carriage, as Jane waved them out of sight. Then she and Clinton collected a packet of bread and butter and fruit from Cook and set off on a long ramble through the Park.

When they returned in mid-afternoon, bedraggled, grass stained, and dazed by the long, sun-drenched hours, they approached the manor by the tree-lined front drive. As they came around the final curve, Clinton gasped and stopped. Jane followed his glance to see, standing at the front steps, a small pony being held by their own groom.

Clinton gave a resounding whoop and broke into a run, and Jane, her heart pounding in a most inexplicable way, followed more slowly. She found herself breathless, though she was not exerting herself in any way.

Clinton reached the pony and then stopped short. He was backing away when a familiar figure came out the front door and down the steps.

"Well, Clinton, I'm glad to see you've such a good eye for horse flesh. And you're right—this is not the London pony. It was not possible to bring him on such a long trip, you see. I found this one in Maidstone. I was sure you would like him."

Jane came up and Jaspar moved around the pony to take her hand. "I hope you will forgive me for thrusting my company on you unannounced, but I had business in the neighbourhood and could not resist the temptation to ride this way and pay my respects and inquire after Sarah. Then I saw the pony in Maidstone and wondered if the lad might be pining for his riding and—"

"Stop, stop—you've convinced me you had every excuse for coming," Jane laughed. They smiled into each other's eyes for a long moment, and might have continued to do so for a great deal longer, had not Clinton spoken. They turned to him hastily and somewhat guiltily.

"He is a very fine animal, sir," Clinton remarked judiciously.

"Indeed, I thought so. Would you like to have a ride now?"

Clinton looked longingly at the lovely beast, but then turned away resolutely. "Thank you very much, sir, but I don't think I can."

"But—why not?" Jaspar asked in astonishment.

171

"I don't think my pony in London would like it."

"I should explain, Lord Jaspar, that I had thought to get him a pony when he first came down," Jane interposed, "but he refused on the grounds that it would be disloyal."

"Bless my soul," exclaimed Jaspar, "well, now, young sir, I admire your feelings, but I think I can promise you that it would be all right with—er—by the way, have you decided on a name?"

"Brown Boy," replied Clinton promptly.

"Very good. Right, then—I think Brown Boy would appreciate it very much if you practiced as much as possible while you are here so that on your return you will be more at ease with him."

"You really think so, sir?"

"Indeed I do."

Clinton immediately requested to be put on the pony and the groom began to walk him up the drive. Jaspar turned back to Jane.

"What a lad it is!" he exclaimed enthusiastically.

"Yes, he is. And it was very kind of you to do this. He has been wonderfully manful about it, but very unhappy about leaving London and the beloved pony."

"Why *did* you leave so suddenly?"

"Oh—it was—just a sudden whim. Sarah and I were talking and—and—I was speaking of Larkwoods and—well—she professed a desire for rest so—we came away."

He did not allow his skepticism of this garbled explanation to show on his face, but she could tell he was aware that she was being less than forthcoming in her explanation.

"How very unlike her. Must really have been run off her legs to come into the country willingly. I suppose she is—er—resting now?"

Jane laughed. "No. Actually she went off this morning to a house party at Lady Barclough's, who's having a ball tomorrow night and was terribly pressing. I urged her to go."

"I see. Well then, I wonder if you could recommend lodgings hereabouts. I had thought to ask you to put me up for a night or so, but since my sister is not here—"

"I'm so sorry. I would happily have welcomed you."

"We won't fret about it. I'm sure Crews can find a place for me. I'll come over to take my dinner with you if I may?"

"Oh—but of course you must," she agreed warmly, then in a sort of mindless confusion caused by conflicting emotions, turned away and began walking after Clinton. Jaspar silently paced along beside her. After only a moment she turned back again.

"I—I—must speak to Crews about your lodging and then to Cook about dinner. If you would not mind staying with Clinton—?"

"Not in the least," he answered agreeably, clearly amused by her agitation.

"Thank you—so kind—I really can't express my gratitude— the pony—so thoughtful of you—" thus babbling incoherently, she made her escape into the house. She ran all the way to her room and throwing off her bonnet began splashing cold water onto her burning cheeks. Then she ran to the cupboards and began pulling out gowns and tossing them on the bed. In the middle of this operation she gasped and ran out of the room in search of Crews.

He assured her that a small inn existed not five miles away, which, while not used to catering to Quality, was a perfectly clean, respectable place, and a footman would be dispatched at once to secure the best room for m'lord. He gave her a look of approval at this request, for he had been more than a little perturbed by the arrival of Lord Montmorency. He liked the young man very well, but he and all the staff were agreed he was Lady Jane's suitor, and while they looked with favour on his suit, could not think it right that he sleep in the house when no other guest was present.

Jane smiled at his look, understanding its meaning very well, and went away to find Cook, after which she asked Betty to bring hot water for a bath to her room. While she waited for its appearance she threw herself down on her chaise longue, panting as though she'd run a race, her mind a jumble of emotions.

That leap of joy she'd felt through every vein at her first sight of Jaspar emerging from the house, only confirmed what she had known inside to be true but had refused to acknowledge. She had fallen in love with Jaspar Montmorency in spite of her fear of him. That fear had slowly dissipated under the influence of his presence. It had been replaced by a conviction that he had not recognized her after all. As Aunt Stanier had said, she had changed a great deal in the past six years. The fourteen-year-old serving girl had become an elegant young woman of twenty. He had no doubt forgotten all about the little maid in his sister's rose pink dressing gown—and nothing else, she thought, turning over to bury her burning face in her hands. And there, in the darkness, she remembered again, as she had more often than was good for her peace of mind, the day when he looked at her so meaningfully and spoke of "laughter lighting up her sherry-brown eyes."

She sat up quickly as Betty tapped and entered, followed by two red-cheeked village girls carrying a large oaken pail of steaming water between them. It was carried through into a room beyond which had been fitted out as a bathing room. Betty unbuttoned Jane's dress and helped her out of it.

"What a time we shall have getting those grass stains out," she scolded, "and I should like to know why them gowns is all tossed about on the bed in that harum-scarum way."

"Oh—I couldn't—which shall I wear for dinner, Betty?"

Betty didn't pretend to misunderstand her. "Why this one becomes you best, to my way of thinking, Lady Jane. And so warm as 'tis, would be fine for tonight."

She picked up a white spotted muslin of disarming simplicity. The sleeves were long and fitted, and the bodice, above the high waist, was so low cut as to be a mere scrap of fabric. Around the décolletage and the bottom of the skirt flounce were embroidered violets.

"Is it not too—too—" Jane asked, blushing slightly.

"No," pronounced Betty decidedly. "All right, girls, come away now."

The two girls came out of the bathing room and with shy glances at Jane hurried out of the room. Betty went in to check the bath water. "Shall I help you into your bath, M'lady?" she asked, coming out.

"No—that's all right, thank you, Betty."

When the door closed behind the housekeeper, Jane wandered over to the full-length glass that stood in the corner. She pulled open her dressing gown and stood gazing at herself in the mirror. She noted that she was not so slim as she remembered her fourteen-year-old self as being. Anxious examination revealed nothing sagging or unsightly however, in spite of the added fullness at breast and hip. The sound of Clinton's joyous laughter reached her through the open window and interrupted this rapt inspection. She pulled her robe around her and hurried into her bath.

She lowered herself into the warm, scented water and closed her eyes, surrendering blissfully to the singing rapture of being in love and knowing that the love was returned.

She knew she was not mistaken in this, for his eyes told her of a deeper regard than was required for simple friendship. Time was suspended while she enjoyed this sweet moment, when love is first acknowledged but still unspoken, and before even dreams of future fulfillment begin to build in anticipation. These happy projections, however, hover only moments behind. The first one that curled its way into Jane's consciousness brought with it a slowly growing chill that owed nothing to the cooling bath water. The picture of herself in his arms before an altar with all their friends crowding around to congratulate them brought with it the realization that such a scene must be preceded by a confession, a scene her mind stubbornly resisted.

She opened her eyes abruptly and began scrubbing herself vigorously. Now, she thought, I must think of all this sensibly and stop flopping about in this idiotish way. I am in love with him, and he shows a decided partiality for me, but what has that to say to anything? Is it possible for anything to come of prolonging our association? Now, what do I mean by that?

Come along, my girl, said her conscience sternly, stop havering and at least say what you mean to yourself!

Very well then, what I mean is, will marriage come of it?

Ah—then of course you propose to tell him?

Tell him! She dropped the soap in shock. Good God! I cannot. I *cannot!*

Her conscience pursued her remorselessly. Then you would marry him—if he asks you—under false pretenses.

No, no! He would be marrying *me,* as I am now, not what I was. Not to tell him would not be false. I daresay he would not care if he did know. In any case he will be much happier not knowing.

Havering again, my girl, replied her conscience coldly, and she knew it was true. She could still remember the day her mother found out Jane had not dusted the top of the wardrobe in m'lady's dressing room. "But, mam, she's not to know. She never even looks up there," the small Jane had protested. Her mother had simply looked straight into her eyes for a long, uncomfortable moment before saying, "But you will know," and turned away. Jane had trudged upstairs immediately and dusted the unseen top of the wardrobe.

And there, of course, was her answer. *She* would always know. Her secret would always lie between them, gathering dust might eventually choke off their love, for marriage meant sharing of everything if it was to work. And this was not a secret she felt she had the right to share because of her guardianship of her son's good name, as well as one she had no right to withhold from a man who proposed marriage.

That was it then, she decided, standing up quickly and reaching for the towel. I must forget this love, this churning need for the sweet fulfillment marriage brought. I've gotten along without it for nearly four years now and for Clinton's sake I will just go on without it.

When she entered the drawing room before dinner she had herself well in hand. She ignored the admiration she saw in his eyes and pulled her hand sharply away from the warm lips pressed against her fingers, turning away to lead him into Sebastian's study. She felt that there, with all its sustaining memories she would find strength to resist the desire he roused in her. She showed him the enormous collection of books, the globe, and the wondrous telescope.

"Your husband was a man of many interests," he said agreeably.

"He was a very learned man; everything interested him," she replied proudly.

"I can see that it must have."

"And he shared all of it with me."

"Good heavens, you quite frighten me," he said teasingly, "have I found a bluestocking hiding beneath that entrancing exterior?"

She had to turn away from the blandishment of those warmly smiling eyes before she found the strength to say coldly, "My husband taught me a great deal, my lord, but I've still a great deal to learn before I could be satisfied that I had conquered ignorance."

"That was a happy time for you, I think?"

"Very, my lord."

"You loved him very much," he went on, making it a statement, not a question.

"Yes. Very much."

"Hmm," was his only answer to this. He reached out a long slender finger to spin the globe and watched it revolve with no further comment.

She stiffened. "Do you doubt me, sir?"

"What? Oh—oh, no indeed. On the contrary. I am all too eager to believe you."

"Why should you be?"

"Because it has been my observation that people are always eager to repeat a happy experience. I had felt that you were one of those rare people who had experienced marital happiness."

"Do you imply that you have changed your mind?"

"Well, the last hour has seen a vast change somehow. There's a certain chill that was not between us before you went to change for dinner. Which seems very hard when I have worked so hard for your smiles since we've met, and to erase that fearful look from your eyes when you saw me. Though I thought I understood the reason for that."

"What—what reason?"

He studied her for a long moment, long enough for her to feel panic rising. She had been so confident that her fear of his remembering was groundless, but now—

"Why, only that you were nervous of gentlemen who made a push to engage your affection," he replied blandly.

At this cool avowal of his intentions she felt the heat of a blush rising from her breast and flooding uncheckably up her throat into her face. She wished desperately that she had not worn this revealing gown, and turned away, ashamed of being so exposed.

He came up behind her, and though he didn't touch her, he stood so close his breath stirred the tendril of hair fluttering before her ear.

"Now you know my feelings, my love, and I hope that beautiful blush tells me yours."

She jerked away from him and nearly ran across the room to the door. "We must go in to dinner, my lord."

"Jane—!"

"No, no—don't say any more! You must not speak of this again."

Without waiting for him she fled into the dining room.

22

Sleep did not come easily that night, though Jane pleaded her need for it as her excuse for bidding Jaspar good night immediately after dinner. The meal had been torture for her, though Jaspar seemed easy enough, maintaining throughout an easy, pleasant monologue, pretending not to notice her restraint and discomfort.

Jane's downcast eyes could not help being confronted with a great deal of bare skin, the firm, white mounds of her breasts seeming to be determined to expose more and more of themselves. She finally asked that her shawl be fetched and spent a great deal of time nervously arranging and rearranging its gauzy folds over her bosom. She caught Jaspar regarding this operation with a quizzical, amused interest at one point and felt the surge of hot blood rising as before to stain her cheeks. Very soon after that she pushed back her chair and begged him to forgive her early retirement, but the long ramble with her son that day had made her too sleepy to be a good hostess.

He had kissed her fingers and taken his leave without demur, promising to arrive early the next morning, with her permission, to assist Clinton with his riding lesson.

Now as she turned from side to side in her bed in a fruitless quest of sleep and escape, her mind was a jumble of images of him and stray scraps of his conversation. The most riveting image, the one that interposed itself into and upon everything else, was the picture of his hands: extended to spin the globe, cupped around his wine glass, firmly manipulating his knife and fork; long, bony, lightly tanned and devastingly masculine. Each image of them caused a small frisson of pleasure that became, finally, a torment. When sleep at last overcame her, the hands pursued her there, only now more intimately, caressing her into the most exquisite excitement.

This dream had disappeared into the innermost reaches of her consciousness by the time she woke the next morning, but later, when she went out to watch Clinton on his pony with Jas par in attendance, the first thing she saw was his brown hand run down the pony's back and her own back quivered responsively. Then the dream flooded back into her memory in its entirety. She turned abruptly back into the house, saying she found the morning air chill. She took herself silently, and severely, to task, and managed to regain her composure enough to return. She wished desperately that he would go back to London and leave her in peace, but could not bring herself to suggest it after his great kindness to Clinton.

They all ate an alfresco luncheon on the grass terrace, and afterward Clinton, Jaspar, and Wellington romped with a ball. She remembered another romp with this same dear, old Wellington and herself with Sebastian, and marveled at how very much her son resembled his father in spite of his rounded infant cheeks and the rosy little mouth.

After a time Clinton, red-cheeked and rumpled, flung himself into her lap. She pushed the damp curls from his forehead and watched as his eyes began to close, before calling Nurse to come and take him for a nap. Clinton went without too much protest. Jane, realizing she dare not allow herself to be alone with her guest, quickly rose and shook out her skirts, saying that she too would have a nap.

"I protest, madam. You cannot consign me to an afternoon alone on such a lovely day! That would be too cruel. Do come for a walk with me. I long to inspect some of the countryside, now I'm here. Do come," he said coaxingly, very like Sarah at her most persuasive.

Jane knew it was wrong to give in, but could not produce a single objection that didn't sound disobliging or patently false. Perhaps the part of her that wanted to go with him prevented her mind from working out a genteel-sounding refusal. At any rate, she found herself meekly pacing along beside him as they wandered away across the grass and into the speckled shade of the newly leaved trees. A breeze danced fitfully through the branches, bringing with it the scent of the joyfully awakened earth and its promise of barely leashed eagerness to set about the task of renewal. This sense of suspense in nature added to Jane's own feelings, creating a breathless dreaminess that stilled all the defensive alarms that should have been sounding. Her brain seemed to have withdrawn its function, leaving her body one great sensory, pulsing organ, able only to feel without analysis or criticism.

The soft warmth of the air with the intermittent, hectic little breeze, seemed to form a substance that she swam through effortlessly but slowly. The small copse of trees became an endless avenue that she could hope might go on forever. Jaspar also seemed caught up in the spell, for he didn't speak. From time to time their eyes met and they exchanged gentle smiles.

They crossed several fields in bright sunshine and came to a small forest, the trees older and thicker, the ground beneath spongy and damp. He took her hand so naturally that she had no thought of pulling away. Her hand curled around his and its warmth spread up her arm and pervaded her whole body. She was intensely aware of the source, that strong, masculine hand whose image had invaded her waking and sleeping dreams.

In the very center of the woods they emerged into a small, sunlit glade, tree-ringed in an almost perfect circle, carpeted in wild grass, already well-grown, with stately Queen Anne's lace bending graciously in waves as the breeze chased across the glade.

They advanced, still hand in hand, into the center and after a moment turned wordlessly to one another, eyes locked together in a long, searching look. Then without any conscious volition her arms came up around his neck as his own pulled her against him. Slowly, languorously, her lids fluttered closed and she raised her mouth hungrily to his as his bent to seek hers. That instant, as their lips touched, sent such piercing pleasure through her that tears started beneath her closed lids. His arms tightened, holding her ever more closely, but not enough, not nearly enough, her body protested, attempting to become even more one with his.

Without any sense of movement, she found they were lying together in the wild grass, his hard body pressing her into the earth, and she was looking up through the delicacy of Queen Anne's lace outlined against the tender blue of the spring sky, Jaspar's lips at her throat as he murmured her name over and over. She pressed his head closer and found herself breathing "Yes—yes—yes—yes."

Jaspar raised himself on an elbow, his need to see her overriding his need to kiss her. Her head on his arm was still bonneted. He pulled at the wide taffeta ribands and removed the bonnet and bent to kiss the dark curls and then her face and neck before pulling away to look at her again. His long, articulate fingers unbuttoned, one by one, the tiny buttons at the bodice of her gown and he pushed it down over her shoulders as she lay quiescent. Her breasts and shoulders were a satiny rose-pink in the sunshine and his fingers brushed over her flesh in wonder. She quivered at his touch, and then gasped as he cupped one breast in his hand and bent to kiss it, murmuring between kisses, "Ah God—I love you Jane—I've loved you so long—waited for this so long—since the moment I first saw you—"

Incapable of speech, she pulled him close urgently, arching her aching body against him demandingly. After that it was all movement and sensation, their feverish need demolishing all barriers so that even the constriction of clothing could not withstand it. She climaxed with a joyous cry almost as he entered her, and he followed almost instantly. They lay throbbingly together, drawing out the moment deliriously, before the hunger, unsatiated, moved them again and their bodies deliberately, sensuously began to explore the possibilities of more pleasure they could give one another.

He freed his arms to hold her full satiny breasts in each hand, burying his face between their softness, touching his lips to her nipples and biting them gently, teasingly, until she moaned ecstatically, frantic for more and more—and then more. He pushed deeply into her, deliberately slow, again and again, before pausing, for a moment of torture for both of them, to hold the final fulfillment at bay for a few more exquisite moments. At last, with a moan that admitted defeat, he drove against her frantically and felt her body respond, seeming to rise from the ground to clasp him as he exploded within her. Consciousness receded for a moment leaving only the wild beating matched by that inside her.

His senses gradually returned and he found himself cushioned still on her body, his face buried in the warm, sweet hollow of her neck. He remained there, happily breathing in the scent of her skin and the tangy smell of the crushed wild grasses on which they lay, too overcome by the complete torpor of his body to want ever to move. Presently Jane turned her head slightly until her mouth rested against his damp forehead. They stayed there, in such perfect peace and understanding they had no realization of how much time passed, whether only a few moments, an hour, or several. Presently, in unspoken agreement they stirred, rose and, without any show of false modesty, adjusted their clothing. Jaspar picked up her bonnet and placing it on her head with great delicacy, tied the ribands in a precise bow beneath her chin. Then, still without speaking, they wandered slowly back the way they had come, arms about one another. Occasionally they halted to kiss as a reminder of their spent passion, a reassurance that they were still one.

When they reached the house she led him around to the French windows of Sebastian's study to avoid any encounter with servants and showed him into the dressing room attached to what was once Sebastian's bedroom.

"I'll have some hot water sent in before I go to my room to change for dinner," she said shyly.

He tilted up her chin with a long finger and kissed her. "You are a wonderful woman and I love you. Keep that in your mind as you change. Keep saying, 'Jaspar loves me' over and over until you come down, so you won't forget me."

Her little gurgling laugh was her only answer as she left him. In her room she stripped off the grass-stained muslin gown and wrapped a dressing robe around her before ringing for Betty Crews.

"Oh, Lady Jane, I'm so glad you've come!" Betty cried out as she entered the room. "A rider came galloping up with a message for Lord Montmorency an hour ago and I was that worrit, not knowing even which direction you took for your walk. I told him he would just have to wait. He's below in the kitchen now, since I thought it likely his lordship would stay here for dinner, but I can send him on to the inn if—"

"No—er—you are right. Lord Montmorency decided to remain so I showed him to Lord Sebastian's dressing room to wash before dinner. Please have Crews attend him there—and send the messenger to him, of course." She raised her chin slightly as she spoke, anticipating some sign of disapproval, but Betty's budget of news was not empty, and the remainder was too worrisome for her to be bothered about the nicities of where a guest washed his hands.

"Yes, m'lady, but—" she hesitated nervously.

Jane, thinking she was going to object to the arrangement, raised an eyebrow in what she hoped was a cool way, though her pulses were pounding. "Yes?"

"Well, it's—now, you're not to get all upset, Nurse says, but his little lordship was some feverish this afternoon and wouldn't take his supper. Nurse has put him to—"

But Jane was already out of the room, running down the corridor to the nursery, her heart pounding frantically. She burst into the room, eyes starting wildly in her paper-white face. Nurse turned calmly from the bed, but came hurrying forward at the sight of Jane's fear.

"There now! And I told Betty she was to say it was nothing to worry you," she protested, leading Jane to a chair and pressing her into it, "just sit down for a spell, m'lady, and calm yourself. 'Tis nothing serious, for goodness sakes. Children have these turns when they are young—"

"But what—what—?"

"Over-excited about that pony is what it was. He got himself all worked up and brought on a little fever. But he'll be right as a trivet by morning, mark my words."

"You are sure?"

"Positive, m'lady." Nurse fetched a glass of water. "Now, you drink this and calm yourself." She pressed the glass into Jane's hand and guided it to her mouth, coaxing her to take a sip and then another, clucking soothingly all the while just as she would have to Clinton.

Jane handed her the glass with a sigh, closing her eyes as her head sank against the back of the chair, her jerking pulses gradually slowing as Nurse moved quietly around the room, putting it to rights. After a time she came and put her hand on Jane's shoulder. "Why don't you go and lie down on your bed, m'lady. You look done up, and that's the truth. You could do with some sleep before dinner."

Jane sat up abruptly. "No, no. You go along to your supper, Nurse. I'll just sit with him until you return."

Nurse Watkyn attempted to protest, but Jane was adamant. "But what of Lord Montmorency, m'lady? He'll be waiting for you to come down to dinner."

Jane looked up startled, for impossible as it seemed, she had forgotten him completely. As memory returned, however, she was unable to prevent a deep tide of colour flushing up her neck and over her face. "Good heavens, how silly of me!" She laughed nervously, "I am a bad hostess, I fear. When you go to your supper, just ask Betty to go and extend my apologies for

the delay and tell him I—I will come—that dinner will be somewhat delayed—"

"Now, there is no need for that, m'lady, I'll—"

"No, no, Nurse. I will sit here until you have had your supper. Go along now."

There was that in her tone which Nurse Watkyn knew better
than to argue with. She went away to her supper.

Jane pulled her chair closer to the bedside and reached out to
touch Clinton's round pink cheek. Warm still, but not in an
alarming way. She sighed with relief, and sat for some time,
content just to watch him sleep.

The door opened softly and Betty tiptoed in. "Are you all
right, m'lady?"

"Of course, Betty. Nurse says it is nothing to worry about."

"I know. She didn't half ring a peal over me for scarin'
the wits out of you. I am that sorry, m'lady, I never
meant—"

"Never mind, Betty, it is all right now. Did you speak to
Lord Montmorency?"

"Oh—there now, I was near forgettin'—he give Crews this
to give you before he left," Betty said, pulling a folded paper
from her apron pocket.

"Left?"

"Yes, m'lady. He had this message from Lunnon, you
see, and Crews said he read it and swore somethin' fierce
and then ordered his carriage and wrote the note and went
away."

Jane opened the note and read,

*My dear, Crews tells me the child is unwell, so I won't
allow them to disturb you. I have had word that my
mother has broken her hip in a carriage accident and I
must return immediately. I will stop at the Barclough's
and take up Sarah. Will write. Love, J.*

Jane folded the note again and turned away to the bedside.
Keeping her face averted she said, "My lord has been called
back to London. His mother has been injured in a carriage accident, poor soul."

"Dreadful dangerous things, them carriages can be," Betty
said encouragingly.

184

"Yes. I—I will just sit here until Nurse comes back and then I will have a bath and a tray in my room. Thank you, Betty."

It was a dismissal and Betty, who would have liked to hear more about Lady Montmorency's accident, had nothing to do but go away. Jane sat down again, her eyes on her sleeping son, trying to shut out all else. She pushed away the damp curls clinging to Clinton's forehead and laid her lips to it and then to his cheek in the age-old mother's test for fever. Nurse was right. It had been only a slight thing and was now over.

How soundly he sleeps, she thought, admiring the small red mouth, pouting slightly open, and his dark lashes making stiff little fans against his cheeks. One chubby fist was curled into the side of his neck, and she remembered that Sebastian had used to sleep with his hand held so. She felt a distant, remembered ache at the thought. She recalled that same small fist grasping Sebastian's finger. Thank God he lived long enough to see his son, she thought, at least I gave him that!

With that silent protest there came flooding back to her the memory of the afternoon and she realized why she had needed to remind herself of her one accomplishment for Sebastian. She knew it was by way of a justification before she could charge herself, as she knew she must. Yes, here it came and she could no more stop it than she could stop breathing. She, Lady Payton, mother of the heir to the Payton name, had disported herself today like any witless village girl behind the hedges with her swain, while her son, Sebastian's son, had been ill.

Oh God! She rose abruptly and paced about the room, twisting her hands together in anguish and guilt. What have I done? Is this the way I carry out the responsibility handed on to me? Is this the way Clinton's mother should conduct herself? What would the Paytons think of me now? What would Aunt Stanier think?

And what must *he* be thinking of me now? No doubt the same way the village swain thinks of the hedge-girl—and with good reason! I led him out into that field and lay down with him. I practically seduced him!

He was no doubt happy to make his escape so easily. He is probably congratulating himself now on how lucky he is to have a mother who so obligingly extricates him from the sticky aftermath of an afternoon's romp. If that fortuitous message had not arrived he would soon have found another reason to go to avoid the possibility of becoming entangled. Oh, he will come back, she thought bitterly, when he believes I have understood just what sort of love affair we are having. After all, why shouldn't he do so? Why should he not take advantage of what is being so freely offered?

On and on her mind ground out a monotonous litany of self-recrimination, not allowing the smallest break for less condemning thoughts to enter. She did not want hope or consolation to soften what she now saw as the truth. She wanted total self-reproach to lash her as punishment for what she conceived as her sin against the Payton name.

When Nurse Watkyn returned to relieve her vigil she dragged herself off to her room. The night wore itself away finally, after fitful sleep, and the dawn brought another brilliant spring day to remind her cf the one before. If only it had rained, she thought drearily.

She informed the servants to make ready to return to London as soon as Dorrie arrived back with the carriage. Larkwoods, whose happy memories had held her after Sebastian's death, now seemed a place she had despoiled. A place she must get away from as soon as possible.

23

The rain to match her mood greeted her on her arrival back in London with a dank chill made all the more depressing by the fortnight spent in the warmth of Kent. Exhausted by the long journey and the strain of hiding her wretchedness from her son, she stepped down from the carriage at her own doorstep in the gloomy twilight and went straight to her room. Dorrie assisted her out of her travelling costume and into a bed gown, Jane sent down word for the groom to accompany Clinton to the stables

for his ride the following morning and retired to her bed, grateful for a weariness that promised sleep. And sleep she did, so
deeply that the morning was well advanced before she surfaced
again to find Nurse drawing the curtains to admit a pallid sunlight.

"Well, m'lady, such a long sleep you've had. I could see
last night you was wore to the bone, so I wouldn't let young
master come in this morning and wake you. He was too excited
about seeing that Brown Boy of his to grumble. Just sit up
there, now, against your pillows. Dorrie's coming with your
chocolate."

Jane did as she was told. "Has he gone off already?"

"Why, bless you, he went hours ago—it's near midday. I'm
expecting him back any minute. At least he'd better be or I'll
have that William's ears for watch fobs!"

The chocolate was brought in by Dorrie, still full of the tale
of the Barclough's ball and all the Quality who'd been there,
and how fetchin' Lady Sarah had been in m'lady's pink silk.
"Suited her a treat, it did, and she were—was—the belle of the
evening. The Beau himself stood up with her twice. And I was
given me—my—dinner in the housekeeper's room," Dorrie
concluded triumphantly, "and was taken in by Lord Barclough's valet!"

Jane remembered with a pang almost of grief for her own innocence, a time when Dorrie's triumph at the Barclough's had
encompassed the heights of her own ambitions.

"Now, m'lady, what gown will you have?"

"Oh—the dark blue silk. I will take Clinton to see Lady Stanier when he returns from his ride. I am not at home today,"
she added, just in case Jaspar should come around before she
could leave the house or, God forbid, Mr. Quint!

She dashed off a note to Lady Stanier to inform her of their
early return and that she would, with Lady Stanier's permission, call later in the day, then dressed, and went down to
breakfast. She sorted through her post, which had accumulated
during her absence and seemed to consist mostly of cards of invitation to social events she would not attend, having already
made up her mind to make no further ventures into Society. In
another month she would close up this house and retire perma-
nently to Larkwoods. By then the place would surely be exor-
cised of its unhappy memories.

Crews came in with a note from Lady Stanier saying how
happy she was that Jane had returned and how much she had

been missed. She said that she hoped Jane would dine with her, as she was sure that by then she would be recovered from the headache which was keeping her from rushing around at once to hug her darling Clinton.

Jane started. Clinton! Where on earth was the child? The door opened as she had the thought, to reveal Nurse's anxious face.

"Madam, I'm that worrit! What can have happened to them to be so long?"

Jane felt a sharp stab of fear, but firmly suppressed it for Nurse's sake. "No doubt William could not persuade him to come away. The child is possessed by that pony! I'll go and fetch him myself. Have Dorrie bring down my pelisse and bonnet and tell Crews to have the carriage brought round."

Ten minutes later she was bowling down the street, biting her lip to keep her panic in check, telling herself she was being foolish to fly into the boughs when the child was only a bit late.

When she arrived at the stables, however, she found no Clinton there, riding his pony around and around the stable yard. The owner, a bluff, red-faced man, explained that the young master had had his ride and finally, after much coaxing, been persuaded to quit and was taken off home by the groom. "He's a game 'un, he is, your ladyship, and would be ridin' still if 'twas left to him. But off they went, more nor an hour since."

An hour! Jane thanked the man and hurried away, telling herself it was possible they had dawdled on the way and were no doubt there waiting for her now. Why they must have passed each other unknowingly going in different directions. Of course he was there—he *must* be there!

But he was not. Only the servants, huddled together fearfully in the front hall, waited for her, Nurse in the forefront, her white-knuckled hands wringing together painfully. She emitted a choked cry when she saw Jane enter alone, and threw her apron over her head and burst into tears. Dorrie began to sniff ominously, and Jane knew in another moment she would have a hall full of wailing servants.

"Nurse! Stop that at once! I'm surprised at you giving way like this. I made sure I could count on you to be sensible. After all, we don't know of anything dreadful having happened, and you know how persuasive Clinton can be when he wants something. I imagine he wanted to stop for a street show or something and William was unable to bring him away.''

''I shall ring a peal over his head that he'll be long recovering from if so,'' Nurse ground out darkly. ''Dorrie! Stop that snivelling! Now, m'lady, what shall we do first? Send for Lady Stanier, is what I say.''

''No. She's in her bed with the headache and I would not alarm her unnecessarily. It is now half past one. They are no more than an hour late. I think we should wait another—half hour—then organize the footmen and stablemen to search the routes they may have taken home. Then—well—we shall see. After all—it's perfectly possible they will arrive in the next moment.''

The doorknocker punctuated her words with a sharp rap, and the whole group started forward eagerly, anxiety replaced by hopefulness, for surely this would be young master at last.

Crews stepped forward to open the door. A liveried footman was revealed, mouth just opening to make his speech, hand extended with a white envelope. His mouth dropped and he fell back a step at the sight of a large group of people looming forward at him.

''Uh—uh—uh—'' he stuttered.

The group fell back, their expressions turning grim once more. The man found this even less reassuring, for he interpreted their expressions as disapproval of himself. He straightened his hat and his face assumed the injured look of one unjustly accused.

''A message for my Lady Payton,'' he said, a whine edging into his voice. He lifted his hat, handed over the message, and scurried away as quickly as possible.

Crews handed the message to Jane, who glanced at it indifferently, not recognizing the handwriting. ''An untimely moment to receive an invitation,'' she said, forcing herself to smile. ''Now, we have twenty-five minutes to wait. Let us all be patient and cheerful. I will be in the drawing room.''

She left them and thankfully closed the door on their worried faces, unable to any longer support the combined weight of all their anxieties. She sank down upon the sofa, rigid with fear, her mind a chaos of tumbling images involving Clinton in various accidents, one so ghastly she cried aloud and clapped her hand to her mouth. It was then she became aware that she still held the message, as the sharp edge of the folded paper stabbed into her lips.

She stared at it blankly for a moment and then impatiently broke the seal and opened it. The words made no sense to her at the first reading as her brain refused to acknowledge the possibility that they could be true. She read it again:

Dear Janey

By this time, I make no doubt, you will be anxious about your young gentleman, so I send this along to let you know he's safe with me. You'll want to fetch him home, I'm sure, so I'll expect you, alone of course, within the hour. Naturally, you will inform no one, since it will be best for the lad if we keep this just between you and your ardent well-wisher

Jeremiah Leach

As the full import of this message sank into her mind, with its implied threat, she felt again that tide of red rising with such heat that her body shook with rage and the room turned crimson in her vision.

That—that *animal* dared to touch her son! Sebastian's son! A Payton! Threatened to harm him if—the room began to spin. She fell back against the sofa and waited until the dizziness passed. She must not allow herself to faint now, she told herself grimly. I must think very calmly about this.

She sat unmoving, fighting down the panic that surged up, until her heart slowed its dreadful hammering and she began to think. Should she consult Aunt Stanier? No. Desperately as she needed her support at this moment, she dared not do anything that would endanger Clinton. It was perfectly possible Leach had set someone to watch the house, so there was no way a message could be sent to anyone for help, nor could she allow anyone to leave the house for any reason. Very well, then. She would have to go alone.

After another moment's thought she turned abruptly and marched out of the room. The servants, still clustered together at the back of the hall, watched in silence as she trod across and entered the library, closing the door firmly behind her. Then she stopped as a thought struck her and opened the door again.

"Dorrie, bring me my swansdown muff at once," she ordered. The girl stared at her blankly for an instant, then gave a little jump and hurried up the stairs. Jane waited silently in the doorway until Dorrie returned and handed over the very large, feathery muff. Jane thanked her and closed the door again.

A few minutes later she emerged. "I must go out. I—have thought of where they have gone and will return with them within the hour. In the meantime, no one is to leave this house. Is that understood? No one for any reason. Not even as far as the pavement."

She turned away from their frightened, pleading eyes, knowing they would follow her instructions, however little was their understanding of the reason. Crews opened the door and she went out to her carriage, still standing before the steps. She gave the coachman the direction of The Golden Crocodile and was driven away.

Crews closed the door when the carriage had disappeared from sight. "Now then, I think we should all go about our business. If Lady Jane says she will return with Lord Clinton within the hour, then I'm sure she will and we can all put our minds to rest."

They looked at him, they looked at one another, and then slowly began to move. Betty, Cook, and the maids disappeared through the door to the servants' quarters, Nurse and Dorrie upstairs. Crews sighed and sat down wearily on the bench beside the door, where he remained unmoving for quite two minutes before the sharp sound of the knocker brought him leaping upright in shock. Running footsteps were heard, and before he had even reached for the doorknob, all the servants reappeared and stood breathlessly waiting. He opened his mouth to remonstrate, but shrugged and turned to open the door.

"Hellow, Crews, I've come to—" Sarah stopped at the sight of all the servants peering past Crews at her. "Good heavens! What is this?"

Crews flicked a dismissive hand behind his back and the staff obediently melted away. "Nothing at all, m'lady. A domestic difficulty," he replied smoothly.

"Oh—well—I've come to see Lady Payton. Will you tell her I'm here or shall I just step up and—"

"I'm sorry, your ladyship, but m'lady is not at home at present."

"Do you mean she's not receiving or that she is actually out of the house?"

"She—had an errand, m'lady."

"When is she expected to return?"

"She said within the hour, m'lady."

"Ah! Then I will wait since I've nothing better to do. I'll just go into the drawing room and make myself comfortable. Could I have a cup of chocolate there, and perhaps a biscuit?"

"Certainly, m'lady," replied Crews, going before her to open the door. She went to the camisole mirror to remove her bonnet and smooth her hair, then took up a copy of *La Belle Assemblée* and settled herself on the sofa before the fire. Her eye was caught by a crumpled paper at the other end and reached for it and smoothed it out on her knee.

As she read her eyes widened in horror. She sprang to her feet shouting, "Crews, Crews!" as she rushed out into the hall.

"Yes, m'lady?"

"Where has she gone!?"

"I—I—she—sh—"

"Stop spluttering, Crews, and answer me!"

"I—truly, m'lady, I don't know."

"Lord Clinton is missing?"

"Y-y-yes, m'lady."

"How long?"

"About two hours now."

"A message came and Lady Payton left immediately?"

"Why—why, yes—she did—well, she went into the study for a few moments after she asked for her swansdown muff."

Sarah's brows contracted as she tried to imagine Jane stopping at such a moment to think about her costume. She turned slowly and went across to the study to see if it could offer any clues to the strangeness of such behaviour. Glancing about, the only thing to strike the eye was that the bottom drawer of a desk stood slightly open. She pulled it out and saw that it contained only a large, flat inlaid rosewood box. She opened it to find one gleaming pistol lying inside. The outline in the velvet was all that remained of its twin. She dropped the box and hurried out.

"M'lady, please—what—?" Crews gasped as she rushed past him, bonnetless, to the door.

"I can't stop now. I must find my brother," Sarah cried, rushing out the door and into her waiting carriage.

A quarter of an hour later she tumbled out without giving her men time to assist her, and ran into the Montmorency mansion, praying as she had never prayed in her life that her brother would be at home.

She stumbled up the stairs calling his name.

"Good lord, Sarah, what is all this? Mama is resting, and you must—"

His voice came from below her and she turned to find him standing in the library door, gazing sternly up at her. She turned and flew back down the stairs.

"Oh, Jaspar! Thank God you're here! It's Jane—she's—Leach has taken the child and—she has a revolver in her muff and—"

He grasped her shoulders with an iron grip and shook her sharply. "What are you saying? Start at the beginning and tell me everything—and slowly, please."

She took a deep, sobbing breath and gave him, to the best of her ability, an account of all she knew and suspected. "—and you must go there— *now* Jaspar—before—before—"

He literally flung her aside, returned to the library for a moment, then strode past her, tucking his own pistol into his pocket, and out the door without a word, his expression so grim she burst into tears as the door slammed behind him.

24

The carriage drew up before The Golden Crocodile, and Jane stepped down without taking the coachman's hand so that he would not feel her own trembling.

"John, in a few moments I hope Lord Clinton will come out with William to wait for me in the carriage. If anyone—*anyone*—comes out and tries to take him back, you are to lash the horses and drive away. Don't stop until you reach the house."

John looked indignant. "I cannot leave you here, m'lady!"

"You will do it, John," she replied in a voice that brooked no argument.

"Very well, m'lady, but I cannot approve," he agreed stiffly.

She turned away and mounted the steps to the door, every faculty concentrated on her object: to safely remove her son from this house. She rapped smartly, and the door was opened immediately, by the same large butler, still displaying the same large obsequious smile. "My Lady Payton! Good day. If you will just step this way, Mr. Leach is expecting you."

He led her across the hall she had last seen lit by hundreds of candles in the sconces and thronged with elegantly dressed people. Now, as such places do that are used for evening entertainment only, displaying a strangely desolate coldness. She walked past him into the room, but advanced only a few steps beyond the door. It closed behind her as Leach rose up from a large, winged chair before the fire. He grinned at her jovially.

"Come along up to the fire, Janey, and warm yourself."

"Where is my son?" she said shortly.

"Now, now, girl, just be easy. We're old friends, aren't we? You know your son is safe with me. Fine little fellow."

"Bring him to me at once."

"In a moment—in a moment. I thought we could have a little talk together first, about old times, eh?" he grinned and winked insinuatingly.

She felt the heat of her suppressed rage rising from the very pit of her stomach and her fingers clinched convulsively around the heavy cold metal inside the swansdown muff. She took a deep breath. Not yet, she promised herself, not before you get Clinton out of here.

"I cannot be easy until I have seen the child. Surely you can understand that?"

"I hardly think you are wise to dictate to me in that hoity-toity way, my girl," he warned.

Careful, she thought, don't anger him. She forced her lips to curve up in what she hoped would resemble a smile. "I had not realized I was giving offense. You must put it down to a mother's anxiety."

"Ah, to be sure," he replied, all smiles again, "you are all the same. I'll have the lad brought in to make you easy and then we'll have our talk." He crossed to the door and Jane heard a low-voiced order given and footsteps going away. In a moment that seemed endless she heard them returning, accompanied by lighter steps. Her heart leaped as the door opened, and there, *oh, thank you, dear God!*, stood Clinton. His dark brows were drawn together rebelliously, but when he saw her the frown disappeared. "Mama!" he cried, the joy and relief in his voice bringing tears to her eyes. She knelt and held out her arms and he ran into them unhesitatingly, flinging his arms about her neck in a stranglehold and burrowing his face into her neck. She held the sturdy little body as close as possible for a long, blessed moment and swallowed the large lump in her throat. She blinked back the tears, however, unwilling to allow Leach to see her cry.

"There, darling, there. It's all right now. Help me to be brave before this man," she breathed into his ear. Clinton pulled away immediately, and she rose, his hand securely in her own.

"Now, if you will tell me where my groom is—" she suggested.

"Ho —you want him too! Well, you may have him for all of me." Leach motioned to the butler who still waited at the door and the man went away again, to return in another moment with William, a large clotted gash on his left temple. When he saw Leach he lunged at him with clenched fists, but was jerked back by the butler.

"Oh, you'd like another round, would you?" laughed Leach, "you'd best be careful, me lad, or I'll give you a clout over the other eye."

"William, take Lord Payton to my carriage and wait there for me," Jane said authoritatively. William turned in shock at the sound of her voice.

"Here now —" began Leach, but she held up her hand with a little, artificial laugh.

"Good heavens, surely you cannot want to have our talk before all this company?" she asked, investing the question with as much suggestiveness as she could command.

He smirked. "Ah—of course—well, ladies must have their way, bless 'em, and we men must indulge 'em. Very well, I suppose there's no harm in it now we understand one another. You—William—take the boy out to the carriage and wait for her ladyship there," he ordered grandly.

William gave her a frightened look as he came forward to take Clinton's hand, but Clinton moved away from him.

"You go along, William. I will wait with my mama," he said firmly, putting back his shoulders.

"Clinton, you will please wait for me in the carriage," Jane ordered firmly, looking him straight in the eye. His brows contracted into a scowl and he stared back defiantly. Then, seeing no relenting in her look, he let go of her hand, took William's and went away without more protest.

When the door closed behind them, Leach rubbed his hands together in satisfaction and went to the side table. "Now, my girl, just you go up to the fire and be comfortable, and I'll bring you a glass of the best claret to be had. I ordered it especially for your visit."

She went to the fireplace and turned to face him, as he came up to her with the glass of wine. She took it gratefully and sipped, for fear had dried her mouth.

"Lay aside that muff and take off your bonnet, Janey, and we shall make ourselves comfortable. No need to stand on ceremony with an old friend." He sat down on a sofa and patted the place beside him invitingly.

"Why did you take my child?" she said, her voice tight with rage.

"Ah! Because I knew that would fetch you around smartly. Also, I didn't care for the way you behaved to me that night the Montmorency girl brought you here and thought you could do with something in the way of punishment."

"What is it you want with me?" she asked coldly.

"Why, to see your pretty face again, Janey, my girl. You've grown a treat, you have," he added, his eyes sliding over her body lasciviously. "I saw you in the Park one day in your grand carriage and made inquiries. Why, look at what our Jane's made of herself, I says, now that's a clever girl, if ever I saw one. I watched out for you after that. Surprised myself, I did, acting like a green lad gawping at a grand lady, hungering for a grown woman. You know my taste has always been for the young ones," he added, leaning forward confidentially. "But you were always the prettiest little thing, and stap me if those fancy duds don't make you better."

Jane felt a wave of nausea and set the glass down on the mantle. "I mustn't keep my son waiting in this chill—"

"Whoa there, girl! Not so fast then. We're to have a cosy talk—remember?" he protested, giving her an injured look.

"You have more to say?"

"Well o' course! You think I went to all this trouble just to pay you a compliment on your clothes? I've a proposition to make to you, my girl, that I fancy you'll like. You're as smart as you can stare, Janey, and I admire brains in a woman."

"You are mistaken. I am not in the least clever."

"Ah, don't try to cozen me, girl. Anyone who can parlay a pretty face and a good figure into a title and a fortune to go with it is clever as a roomful of monkeys for my money! I says to myself, there's a woman could help a man. I've got a successful business going here, and you swanning around the rooms all classylike—why there's no end to the money could be made!"

"You—you want to engage me as—as a hostess?" she said incredulously.

"Engage you?" He goggled at her for a moment and then burst into a great roar of laughter, slapping his knee gleefully. "Oh—oh -that's a good one, that is. Here I'm proposing and she thinks I'm trying to engage her services."

She felt a chill of horror at his words. "You—are—are proposing—to me," she whispered, her voice expressing all the loathing she could no longer suppress.

He sat up, all traces of amusement wiped off his face in an instant. "And why not, I'd like to know? You're no better nor me for all your airs and graces and your title. Underneath it all you're still the little backstairs maid, the bastard child of another backstairs maid. Oh, smart enough to throw out lures to a crippled dwarf no one else would have and trap him into marriage, I'll admit, but servant class for all that when all's said. Why, I've only to drop a hint in the right place and you won't be able to put a foot in any drawing room in town. So don't you go turning up your nose at an honest proposal of marriage from me, my girl." He stared at her with hard eyes, daring her to refute his words.

She stared back silently for a moment, then said flatly, "I'd sooner be dead."

She walked rapidly across the room, but he moved even quicker. He grasped her upper arm and swung her around.

"Here, not so fast, my girl. You'll find it don't pay to insult Jeremiah Leach." He pushed her so hard she staggered back onto the sofa. He crossed and flung open the door. "Get that brat back in here," he ordered, and turned back to her, a dangerous glitter in his eyes. "We'll see how proud you are after he watches you raise your skirts for me right here—or perhaps you'd like a demonstration of how easy it will be to make him a cripple like his pa."

Jane held her breath and sat very still. She heard the front door open, and then, almost immediately, she heard her coachman give a cry, and the crack of the whip, and then, blessedly, the sound of the wheels jolting rapidly away over the cobblestones. She let her breath go in a whoosh of relief.

The butler evidently returned, for Leach called out impatiently, "Well?"

"He drove off! I couldn't stop him!"

"Idiot! Well, don't just stand there! Close the door and get back to your own quarters and stay there. I don't want to be disturbed, d'you hear? If anyone calls just ignore it, and no matter what you hear you just stay in your chair back there and mind your business." He slammed the door and turned upon Jane. "So—you'd play little tricks on me, eh?"

She rose and whipped around behind the sofa. "Don't come near me, Leach! I warn you!"

"Ha! Games is it? I know what it is—you'd like a little rough stuff first, like last time. Gets you all excited, don't it? Been hankerin' for it ever since, eh? Been wantin' some more of the same? Couldn't get it from the dwarf, could you?"

He leered at her, all the time advancing upon her, as she backed away around the sofa, her heart pounding, her breath coming in gasps.

"I—I warn you again, Leach. If you touch me I'll—I'll kill you," she panted, her hand inside the muff clinching into place around the cold metal.

His hand shot out and clutched one of her breasts, his fingers digging in brutally. "Ha!" he cried triumphantly.

It was the last sound he made, for at the shock and excruciating pain of his cruel gesture, her fingers pressed the trigger of Sebastian's pistol and the room was filled with an explosive roar that stunned all her senses momentarily. She and Leach stared at one another, his mouth still open from his last cry, the air between them filled with a snow of floating white feathers. Then, slowly, his hand fell away from her breast as his face sagged. He looked down in amazement. She followed his glance to see a large red blossom on his shirt front.

His knees began to sag and she watched him blankly as he fell, unaware of the loud voices in the hallway. As Leach hit the floor the door burst open violently and Jaspar stood there, pistol at the ready, the butler's scared face peering over his shoulder. Jaspar took in the scene before him in a quick raking glance, reached back to jerk the butler into the room, and closed the door.

"Where's the boy?" he rapped out.

"He—he got away, sir. She—"

"Who's in the house?"

"A—a—a—"

"Quick, man," Jaspar raised the pistol.

"Only me now, sir," the butler replied with a gulp, his eyes riveted on the gun. "Staff only comes in evenings."

Jaspar went to Jane and put his arm around her. She didn't react, hardly seeming aware of his presence. Her eyes had never left Leach, who lay sprawled grotesquely at her feet, an obscene pool of blood forming on the floor beside him. Jaspar led her to the door. "Jane—Jane! You must go outside, get into my carriage, and tell my driver to take you home. Do you understand?" She did not respond. He shook her by the shoulders, then tilted her face up to his. "Listen, my love, you must hear me. Go out to the carriage and tell him to drive you home. Nod if you understand me."

The blank, wide-open eyes staring up at him had regained some small spark of comprehension as he spoke and finally she managed to nod her head.

"Good girl. Here you go now." He removed the tattered muff from her hand, carefully pried the gun from her fingers, and opened the door to push her gently from the room. "Go now, my dear. Straight across the hall and out the door. My man will drive you home."

He watched her move dazedly across the hall, pull open the heavy front door, and step out. He then turned back to the room and closed the door. Crossing rapidly to the body, he knelt and folded Leach's hand around the gun, finger over the trigger, then stood up to confront the frightened butler, who watched him silently, his face blanced and greasy with perspiration.

"Where are some writing materials?" Jaspar snapped authoritatively. The man scuttled across the room and scrabbled about at the desk in the corner.

"Here sir. Here they are—paper—pen—ink—"

"Right! Sit down and write as I tell you."

"I—I—don't write, sir."

"Can you sign your name?"

"A course I can sign me name!" the man protested.

Jaspar sat down and wrote swiftly, stopping only once. "You brought the boy here?" The man nodded. "Did you have a weapon?"

"Me knife," the man confessed, "but I never hurt 'em. It was Leach hit the man after we got here. I—"

"Very well, that's enough." Jaspar finished and handed the pen to the man. "Sign there—at the bottom."

"What's this then?"

"It's a confession, admitting that you forced Lord Clinton and his groom to come to this house at knife point, and assisted in their unlawful retention here against their will. I will keep this paper. If I ever hear Lady Payton or her son mentioned in connection with the death of this man I shall know it came from you, at which time I will take the confession to the authorities and lay charges against you."

"Here now!! No cause to be that way, yer lordship. I'll sign and all, and no fear I'll ever open me mouth. But what'll we do about—him?"

"As soon as I leave, you will take that glass on the mantle to the kitchen and wash it and burn this feather muff in the fire. Then you'll run to the nearest authorities and tell them, in great distress, that you were in your own quarters and heard a shot. You came in here and found your master had killed himself. Beyond that you know nothing at all. Do you understand? Nothing."

"They'll think I done it," the man protested.

"They'll have no reason to think anything of the kind if they don't find any of his possessions on you or among your effects, so see you don't steal anything. You'll look completely innocent, and it will never occur to them to think anything other than that, for some unknown reason, the man killed himself. That's all anyone will be able to say. Now sign this and I'll go. Follow my instructions exactly."

The man bent and laboriously traced out the letters of his name. Jaspar made a great show of folding the paper and stowing it away in his pocket before striding out of the room without a backward glance.

25

The trip back to Payton House was a jolting nightmare as Jane relived, over and over, that deafening moment of the gun's explosion, followed by the vivid crimson splotch appearing on Leach's chest. She watched helplessly as those few seconds repeated themselves tirelessly before her eyes, horror-fresh each time.

When the carriage stopped, however, the image was wiped away on the instant by the sight of Clinton standing in the open doorway of her house between Crews and William, peering anxiously. All logical reasoning, which had been blasted into tiny fragments to the outmost edges of her consciousness, suddenly clicked back together at the sight of that small body in the doorway. He was the only thing that mattered. His person was secure, and now she must forget everything except putting this whole thing into proper perspective for him. She could not allow him to become a victim of unnatural fears because of this.

As it happened, however, Clinton's four-year-old mind, uncluttered by adult reasoning, had already grasped the essentials of right and wrong in the matter.

Jane flew up the steps and lifted him into her arms for a long, wordless embrace. He hugged her close and kissed her cheek, a concession which vividly demonstrated the depth of his worry for her. She carried him into the house within a circle of hovering, tearful servants.

"You should not have sent me and William away, Mama," Clinton chided her, "you are only a woman and I should have stayed to protect you."

"I know you are very brave, darling," she said, kneeling before him, "but they were so much bigger than you and I was afraid they might do you an injury if you tried to protect me. I know you were not afraid of them."

"I—I *was* afraid when that man hit William and made him bleed," Clinton confessed reluctantly.

"So would I have been. But it's good to be afraid, otherwise how can one be called brave? And you were very brave."

"Oh, he was that, m'lady," William offered with a grin. "When that Leach hit me, young master went for him like a tiger."

"Good God!" Jane was horrified at what Leach might have done to such a small source of annoyance. "Did he—?"

"He only pushed him off and told his man to lock him in another room," said William.

"But if I had had my papa's pistol I would have killed those bad people," said Clinton firmly.

"Oh darling, you mustn't—" Jane protested faintly.

"Yes, I would too. My papa would have killed them for treating me so and hitting William! When I am bigger I will take my papa's pistol and kill those bad people. My papa would expect me to."

Jane's eyes filled with tears and she hugged him convulsively, too overcome with the irrefutability of this statement to comment on it. He allowed the embrace for a moment before wriggling free. "Why are you crying *now*, Mama?" he asked, bewildered by such an excess of emotion now danger was over. He looked at Crews. "I expect it's because she's a woman. I think they cry quite a lot."

Jane, feeling hysteria close to engulfing her at this condescension, rose to her feet, bidding Clinton go along with Nurse now while Mama went up to change, and dispersed the servants. She just managed to reach her room and privacy before giving way. She wept wholeheartedly for a short time and felt very much better for it. After washing her face and rearranging her hair, she changed to a house gown and sat down to compose herself.

I, Jane Coombes Payton, have killed another human being and must somehow learn to accept the fact. True, the man was evil, and treated me in a bestial way once, apart from the way he treated Sarah and then threatening to cripple Clinton or force him to watch his mother being raped before his eyes. Oh, I would not have allowed that! I would have shot him first, and felt no compunction. And if I had not remembered Sebastian's pistols, he might very well have been able to carry out his threats and I would have been helpless.

Well then, should I have stayed my hand when he attacked

me? Would not any woman with a weapon in her hand at such a moment have done the same and find nothing to blame herself for? No, and I will not condemn myself. No doubt the thing will haunt me for the rest of my life, but that is small enough price to pay for—

She suddenly shot straight up out of the chair, every nerve end jangling with fear. It was not until that moment that she realized her act, however justifiable in her own eyes, was a crime in the eyes of the rest of Society and as such, punishable by hanging!

She saw again that dreadful moment, and heard the reverberating sound of the shot, and then—then? What exactly had she done then? She tried to recapture the events immediately following the shot, but her mind remained stubbornly blank. The next thing after that was the sight of Clinton standing at the top of the steps of Payton House. Great heavens! How had she gotten there? A carriage, of course, she remembered that much, but where had it come from? She must have walked out of the house and found a carriage for hire. Had she paid the man? Crews must have done so.

But wait, what of that grinning butler? Was it possible his master's orders had been followed so carefully the man had not dared show his face even when a pistol shot rang out? No doubt he had crept up after she had gone and found Leach. Had he then run for help and even now the authorities were on their way to arrest her?

She clutched her temples distractedly and rushed downstairs to find Crews. He could provide her with at least an answer about the carriage. She had not far to go to find him, for he was just admitting Lady Stanier, her face sheet-white.

"Jane!" she gasped and promptly fainted away. Crews caught her expertly and carried her toward the back drawing room, Jane running ahead to open the door for him and find the vinaigrette she kept in her workbox there.

In only a moment, Lady Stanier's eyelids fluttered open. "That was a helpful thing to do now, wasn't it?" she commented wryly. Jane smiled and bent to kiss her cheek. "Oh, Jane," sighed Lady Stanier, "what a dreadful ordeal for you. He said you and Clinton were safe, but all the way here I was so fearful. The sight of you sent me reeling."

Jane nodded dismissively to Crews, who withdrew discreetly. "Er—he? Who told you I was safe?"

"Montmorency, of course."

"But—but how—?"

"Poor darling, you're all about in your head, and no wonder. He sent you away at once, and you may be perfectly easy now, he has taken care of everything beautifully."

"He has?"

"Yes, thank God, and very well, too, to my way of thinking. He says that after he shot the man and got you out of the house he put the gun in Leach's hand so—"

"Wait! Wait!" Jane's mind was spinning chaotically. "He was there? I don't understand—he says that *he*—" Jane's voice rose hysterically on the last word.

Lady Stanier rose from the sofa and took charge, all faintness gone. She pushed Jane onto the sofa and applied the vinaigrette, before crossing to pull the bell rope vigorously. Crews entered immediately.

"Bring some brandy," ordered Lady Stanier crisply.

"Wait—Crews—what carriage was I in when I arrived home?"

"Why, Lord Montmorency's, m'lady."

"Oh Lord," Jane sighed, falling back onto the sofa resignedly. She was, without doubt, losing her mind. The anxiety and fear had finally driven her over the edge into madness.

"Please bring the brandy, Crews," requested Lady Stanier, and when the door closed behind him said to Jane, "now, my love, just be quite quiet and don't worry. Clinton and you are safe forever from that monster and I shall bless Montmorency every day of my life for dispatching the brute from the world. And due to his quick thinking it will never be linked with you or him. It's all arranged to look like suicide and he has the butler's confession in writing as to his part in the business so there's no fear we'll ever hear from him again. Oh, it has all been attended to very tidily, believe me."

Jane closed her eyes wearily. Tidiness seemed to her the least appropriate adjective for the confusion in her mind, but she felt unequal to the task of sorting it out. Jaspar had fired the shot and Clinton was safe upstairs with Nurse and she would not be arrested and—and—She felt the sharp sting of the vinaigrette in her nostrils and opened her eyes to find Aunt Stanier bending anxiously over her, a worried Crews, tray of brandy in hand, beside her.

"Gracious—did I faint? I never faint," Jane said in surprise.

"Just let me raise your head, dearest, and you'll take a few sips of this nice brandy and be fine as five pence in a moment.

It's all right, Crews, only reaction to all the excitement. She'll be all right now."

Crews left, somewhat reluctantly, and Jane sat up, against Lady Stanier's protests. "Please, Aunt Stanier, I'm truly all right. Just let me sit here and I'll drink the brandy and I want you to tell me, word for word, exactly what Jas—Lord Jaspar said to you from the moment he appeared."

Lady Stanier obliged her. His story was that he had forced his way into the house, found Leach on the point of attacking Jane, and had shot him. He had then sent Jane away, made his arrangements with the butler and come to fetch Lady Stanier to Jane's side.

"But how did he know about Clinton and Leach and everything?"

"From Sarah."

"Sarah?"

"Yes. She came here and was waiting for you to return and found a note to you from Leach that you must have dropped. She questioned Crews and then discovered about the gun—really, the girl has more brains than I've given her credit for!—and went straight to Montmorency and sent him after you."

"Good heavens!" Jane exclaimed faintly.

"Yes, the girl kept her head admirably. Here I've always thought she was a complete ninnyhammer. Why, she saved your life!"

"Yes, I must send for her and thank her. Where—why did not he come here with you?"

"He said you would not want him at a time like this, you would want to rest and that I could be more help to you there than he could be. Besides, he knew Sarah would be wild with worry and he felt he should go and reassure her at once. Then there's his mother, you know. She was thrown from her carriage in an accident and her hip was broken."

"Yes, I know. That's why he—why Sarah and I cut short our visit to Larkwoods," Jane answered, turning away so her unhappiness would not show. For though she was still wildly confused about the nightmarish episode at The Golden Crocodile, one thing stood out clearly—blindingly so. For all his willingness to come to the rescue in time of danger, Jaspar was not eager to expose himself to the danger of an emotionally distraught woman making some sort of claim on him before a female relative. Not if sufficient reasons were at hand to justify his staying away.

All the heart-stopping anxiety of Clinton's disappearance and rescue had blotted out for a time her previous despair, but now it came rushing back to engulf her, and she sank into it helplessly, her overburdened emotions no longer capable of withstanding against it. The tears poured silently down her cheeks. She allowed Lady Stanier to take her to her bed, where she pretended to go to sleep immediately so that she could be alone with her misery, though she was sure she would only toss for hours tormenting herself with recriminations over her behaviour at Larkwoods, or, if she managed to fall asleep, be tortured by nightmares. Nature took charge, however, and she dropped without any awareness into a sleep fathoms deep that held her unmoving for twelve hours.

Her eyelids were only pried apart by the first, tentative fingers of the rising sun the next morning and she stirred stiffly, for a few seconds completely at peace before memory sprang at her. However, body and mind refreshed by her long sleep, she was able to face it without the cringing despair of yesterday and the days before.

There is no point crying about it any more. I gave myself to him without his needing to ask, and I cannot deny my pleasure was at least as great as his. If I am going to behave like a man, taking my pleasure as it pleases me, not only must I be cavalier about it, as men are in like circumstances, but I must expect him to behave just as he has. His declaration of love in the heat of the moment was not meant to be taken seriously. Men quite often, I imagine, say such things at such times to have their way with us. My life, however, will not end because of a disappointment in love. I'm much too healthy to pine away like a lady in a novel. Besides I have my son's future to think of, and the administration of his estate until he is of an age to take care of it himself. So I will put this behind me. I'll remove to Larkwoods in a week or so and stay there.

This decision made, she turned her mind to unravelling yesterday's mystery. In spite of Jaspar's story to Lady Stanier, Jane *knew* now, in the clear light of a new day with hours of sleep between herself and the event, that *she* had fired the shot that killed Leach. Since she was standing within inches of Leach at the time and the red flower of blood had appeared instantaneously, there was no possible way Jaspar could claim to have shot Leach. Therefore, he was trying to shield her, even from Lady Stanier. It was an unnecessary act of gallantry on his part, for which she would thank him from the bottom of her heart in an unemotional little note, and hold her tongue about the matter to Lady Stanier. Since there was no possibility of either of them having to face charges, there was no point in burdening Aunt Stanier with the truth and perhaps destroying her peace of mind.

These matters settled as far as possible, Jane rang her bell rope, sat up against her propped pillows, and waited for Clinton and Nurse. After breakfast she would take him herself for his ride on Brown Boy. The best thing for him was to behave as though yesterday's events were only an unpleasant break in his normal routine. She could hope it would all soon fade completely from his memory. After all, in spite of his precociousness, he was still only a very young child.

That he was so, and that the events of yesterday held little importance today in his mind, was demonstrated as he entered her room with a rousing cry of joy, accompanied, as usual, by a yelping Wellington. They both scrambled onto her bed and attempted to kiss her—and the romp was on!

Later she took him to visit Brown Boy and when they returned, sat down to write her heartfelt gratitude to Jaspar, as unemotionally as possible, ending it with the hope that his mother was mending and instructing him to ask Sarah to call when she could.

The last turned out to be unnecessary, for five minutes after the note had been dispatched, Sarah appeared, resplendent in claret velvet and sables.

"Isn't it odd to need furs after the warmth of Kent?" she sang out from the doorway, throwing the furs carelessly across a chair and advancing, arms held out, upon Jane. "Darling! You are brave as a Cossack! Who would dream you capable of taking a gun and going after the villain alone? I've never been so terrified in my life! Are you all right?"

Jane laughed at her extravagance. "Perfectly. And don't try to make a heroine of me, my dear, when you know perfectly well it is you who deserve a medal. Aunt Stanier is full of your praises—and so am I. And so very grateful, dear Sarah, for your cleverness and quick action."

"Ah well," Sarah said, brushing this away in embarrassment, "how is the child?"

"I honestly believe he's practically forgotten it already. I wish it were so with me," she added wistfully.

"By next week it will only be a vaguely remembered bad

dream," Sarah assured her, "but I die of curiosity! What did he want? Leach, I mean. Why did he do it?"

"To pay me back for snubbing him the night you took me there," Jane said, wishing to be as truthful as possible, but unwilling to confide the *entire* truth.

"How did you get Clinton out of the house?" Sarah persisted. Jane explained her ruse and its effectiveness as briefly as possible. "But then what happened? What did he want to talk *about?* You're being most unforthcoming, Jane."

"He—he wanted my help in his business, a sort of—of lure to draw customers. I refused and he sent for Clinton to be brought back. Then when he discovered my trick he became very angry and came after me and—and—"

"Jaspar burst in and shot him! Hurrah!" Sarah broke in irrepressibly, "oh, dear Jane, if you could have seen him go galloping off to rescue his fair damsel from the dragon! I have always hoped that you and Jaspar—"

"Please—no—" Jane held up both hands in a vain effort to stem what she knew was coming, her face showing her great distress.

"Oh, no blushes now. Surely we are such bosom-bows by now we can be open in all things?"

"But there's nothing—"

"Ho! I'm not such a paperskull I can be fobbed off with maidenly protests! Have I not eyes? I've seen the way he looks at you when he thinks no one is noticing."

"Sarah, I beg you not—" Jane began desperately, but Sarah, the bit well between her teeth now, rushed forward headlong.

"And nothing—*nothing*—will please me more than to be able to call you sister!"

Jane knew she could not bear another moment of this conversation. She said quite sternly, "No more, Sarah! Now tell me all about the Barcloughs. Who was there?"

Sarah unexpectedly blushed. "Oh, you know, the Beau and some of his friends, and some rather insipid women, Caroline was right there! There was only one really interesting man— Tom Gately. Do you know of him?"

"The one who spent several years with savages someplace in a desert?"

"Yes, that's the one. Bedouins, in Egypt. We had a long talk and he told me some wildly fascinating stories of his adventures. I should so love to go to such a place!"

"No parties, no gowns, no plays or operas, no—" Jane said teasingly.

"Pooh! As if I cared for that! I've been bored to death with all that anytime these past three years, as you well know. Oh, Jane! I do believe I've found something that I want to do!"

"With or without Mr. Gately?"

Sarah dimpled demurely. "With, if things fall out as I plan."

"Good Lord! You are serious!"

"Never more so in my life," Sarah replied fervently, "but I shall go on my own if necessary!" She lifted her chin proudly, as though to face an anticipated rejection by Mr. Gately. She followed this extraordinary declaration by a long passionate monologue featuring burning sands, tents, solitude and silence, and the brilliance of the stars at night over the desert. She then stated that when she returned she would write a book about her travels and adventures.

"Ha! First you will have to learn to spell!" said a voice from the doorway. They spun about to find Jaspar regarding them quizzically, one eyebrow raised in sardonic amusement.

26

"Jaspar!" Sarah protested indignantly, "I wish you will not creep about like that! We might have been having a very *private* conversation!"

"If you mean about Gately, I've already been informed about him from several sources, and so has Mama and I warn you she is prepared to have palpitations. 'Gately?' she says, 'I've never heard of any Gatelys!' However, *I've* no objections at all. I've met the fellow, and if you can bring him up to scratch send him along to me for my blessings."

"*What* a vulgar expression," Sarah replied loftily.

"There was posy and a note delivered after you left. I assume it was from him."

"What? Oh—oh dear—well, I think, Jane darling, if you will

209

forgive me, I'd best be getting home to Mama now. I don't like leaving her alone too long," she added virtuously.

"Right, you run along," urged Jaspar encouraged, holding the door open invitingly, and barely concealing his impatience as she resumed her furs and took her leave of Jane.

Jane, completely tongue-tied by his unexpected appearance, picked up her workbox, and stared uncomprehendingly at her embroidery frame.

Jaspar closed the door after his sister and crossed the room to stand before her. After a long silence, while she sat mute, her eyes firmly lowered, he said, "I received your note."

"Ah."

"I was somewhat disconcerted by the tone of it."

"The tone?"

"Somewhat—missish."

"*I?* I am never missish!" she flared up indignantly.

"Well—formal then. However, I didn't come here to quibble about that."

"You came to quibble about something else?" she inquired politely.

"No, I came to boot old Quint out on his ear if I found him cluttering up your drawing room."

"I don't think he has heard that I've returned," Jane admitted candidly before catching herself and adding starchily, "though I hardly think you have reason to feel yourself free to dispose of my visitors so cavalierly."

"Only those dangling at your shoe strings."

She drew herself up proudly. "Lord Montmorency, I realize that after what—what happened, you have reason to feel that I—I will naturally be willing to—to—but I will not be any man's—"

"Wife?" he suggested helpfully.

"Wife?" she repeated in bewilderment. "No—I meant—"

"I know perfectly well what you meant, and if I were not in such a happy frame of mind I would probably be very insulted that you could entertain such a notion of me, even for a moment."

"I apologize if I have mistaken your meaning. Since we seem to be talking at cross-purposes, perhaps you would be good enough to enlighten me as to the purpose of this visit."

"There you go again," he complained, "why do you keep taking that toplofty tone with me? I won't stand for it any more!" And with that he pulled her abruptly out of the chair and into his arms. "Now—you *are* going to marry me aren't you?"

She pulled back to search his eyes, unsure if she had heard aright. He held her look, completely serious now. Finally she pushed away his arms and walked over to the table against the wall, staring with great concentration into the glass, pretending to be very busy rearranging a stray curl.

"I cannot marry you, Jaspar," she said simply, trying to keep any suggestion of emotion at bay, "though I am honoured that you have asked me."

"Why not?" he asked bluntly.

She dropped her eyes to the bowl of roses on the table and ran her fingers over the cool, velvety petals. "I am not at liberty to discuss my reasons."

"Is it because of this?" he asked softly, his breath fluttering the loose curl by her ear. She looked up, startled, to find him just behind her, his arms coming around in the remembered embrace, a hand over each breast. She whirled about to face him.

"You *did* know—all along!" she gasped accusingly.

"Not all along," he said, "not until I came to call the first time."

"But why didn't you ever say? I hoped—well, I convinced myself that you hadn't recognized me."

"How could I forget you after meeting you in such an enchanting and memorable way?" he teased.

"Even though I—uh—hurt you?"

"Even then—at least, after the pain subsided," he grinned at her, "and by then you'd disappeared. Can you forgive a green, callow boy who hadn't the courage to admit his part in the business?"

"It wouldn't have made any difference. I was your mother's maid, Jaspar. You could not have done anything honourable, your mother would not have allowed it. And after all, what could you have done? *I* would not have allowed it in any case."

"Yes—I remember the coin flung back in my—face." She giggled, then blushed, remembering the moment. "Good God!" he exclaimed, "Leach! That's where he—"

"Yes, he—" she hesitated, and then decided she was not capable of reciting the revolting tale of Leach's treatment of her all those years ago. Maybe someday she could face it, but now she could not bear to spoil this happy moment with such ugliness. "—he recognized me and wanted me to help attract customers to his establishment." Never, she thought, never would she admit to anyone that he had made a proposal of marriage to her. It was too humiliating.

"Good Lord! What damned cheek! I beg your pardon, love, but one must curse when one speaks of such a bounder. I wish I *had* shot him!"

"After frightening Clinton in such a way, I'm afraid I must confess that I'm glad *I* did."

"I still cannot understand his reason for abducting the child."

"He knew I would come there and that he could persuade me to talk with him that way. Also, I had publicly insulted him the night I went there with Sarah and he wanted to punish me for it."

"That is another matter I want to take up with you, my dear. Sarah has confessed everything, and I have visited your man of business and paid the four thousand pounds back into your account. We Montmorencys seem continually to be in your debt."

"There was no need—and you exaggerate. What other debt was there but that one?"

"Ah, my generous love, have you forgotten I cost you your position the first time we met? All the times you have really needed me, I was not there—"

"How can you say so?" she cried. "Why, I might even now be in prison if you had not arrived and taken charge yesterday!"

"Nevertheless, I intend to make it my life's work to make up to you for all that I haven't done till now. I've loved you to distraction before, but since the afternoon in the field it is verging on madness! The only cure is marriage, so that I can have you forever. Do you love me?"

"How can you doubt it? Unless you think I am in the habit of pulling gentlemen down into the grass at every encounter," she laughed.

"You still haven't said it," he insisted, pulling her breathlessly close.

"Jaspar! Yes, darling—yes, yes, I do love you so," she cried, flinging her arms around his neck to pull his head down to her own. When their lips met she felt as though a flame was ignited, sending fire through every vein in her body.

They drew apart dazedly as the door was flung open to admit Clinton astride his hobby horse. "Mama! I—" He halted abruptly, owl-eyed at the unusual scene before him. After a moment he asked Jaspar, in a man-to-man tone of voice, "is she crying again, sir? She cries a lot because she is a woman."

Jane laughed shakily, "I'm not crying, darling."

"Then why are your eyes all shiny?"

"I think it is because I'm so happy. You see I—we—Jas—Lord Mont—oh dear—" she stopped in confusion.

"What she's trying to say," Jaspar explained, "is that, with your approval, of course, your mama has agreed to be my wife."

Clinton considered this statement solemnly for a moment, and then went right to the crucial heart of the matter. "Will you be my papa now?"

"Yes," Jaspar replied simply.

Clinton jumped straight up into the air and then turned and galloped away on the hobby horse, shouting at the top of his lungs, "Hurrah! Hurrah! I'm to have a papa! Nurse, where are you? I'm to have a papa!"

Jane began to giggle, while Jaspar strode over to close the door. "I take it he approves. Now," he pulled her back into his arms, "there was something I wanted to discuss with you—"

"Jaspar—darling—please wait a moment We haven't really thought of this enough. I mean—what of your mother? She will hardly welcome her former maid as a daughter-in-law."

"I have no intentions of telling her before we are safely married. She's been trying to get me married for years, and will welcome a young, wealthy widow, socially acceptable, with the cachet of the Payton name, and a proven breeder of sons. She'll be ecstatic. Now—"

"But someone else may tell her—Wright, for instance."

"Who the devil is Wright?"

"Your sister's dresser, for goodness sake, she's been there for years. How can you not—"

He brushed this aside "Wright will do as Sarah tells her. Besides, Sarah will probably marry that young explorer fellow and go off to the wilds of Africa. She won't need a dresser there."

"It seems dishonest—" she protested doubtfully.

"Nonsense. You're obsessed about honesty. You and I are the only people concerned and your past is fine with both of us. Now let's forget all that and discuss the future. There's something—BLAST!!"

This explosion was caused by the door opening again to admit Lady Stanier.

"Oh! Oh—I do beg your pardon—I just had to—well, Clinton is rushing about madly shouting the *most* incredible—"

"It is—incredibly—true," Jaspar answered, not loosing his hold on Jane.

"Bless you, darlings—bless you," Lady Stanier beamed at them and then disappeared, closing the door softly behind her.

Jaspar crossed, turned the key decisively, and came back. *"Now!"* he said in a no-nonsense voice, pulling her roughly into his arms.

"Yes, my darling, what *is* it you so urgently need to discuss with me?" she laughed, pressing as close to him as was humanly possible.

"It's about a rose-pink negligee I want you to get for our wedding night—" he began.